Agent Provocateur is back with a selection of some of today's finest erotic writing.

Soixante Neuf, a wonderful concept: something for everyone and a thrill at every turn. So too with this book, there is a story for every mood, whether you feel like a sex kitten or a naughtier vixen, complete with stunning images from David Bray that will stimulate your own fantasies.

So, run yourself a hot bath with plenty of perfumed oils and sink back into these stories that will tease and tantalise…

Happy reading

Love Miss A.P. x

Agent Provocateur

Soixante Neuf

PAVILION

First published in Great Britain in 2009 by
PAVILION
An imprint of Anova Books Company Ltd

Design and layout © Anova Books Company Ltd, 2009
Illustrations © David Bray, 2009
Text © Anova Books Company Ltd, 2009, except:
Text © Agent Provocateur for *Lady of the Manor*, *L'Appartement* and
Inside My Knicker Drawer
Text © Ashbourne Welles for *Julia at the Glory Hole*, *Sixty Nine*
and *Esther's Hands*

Commissioning editor: Emily Preece-Morrison
Project editor: Kate Oldfield
A.P. editor: Jess Morris
Copyeditor: Ian Allen
Authors: Neo, Angelina, Ashbourne Welles, Susanna Forrest, Annie Blinkhorn,
Vita Rosen, Saffron Mayhew, Sareeta Domingo, Sarah Griffin, Bassma Fattal
Illustrator: David Bray
Jacket and page design: Georgina Hewitt
Typesetting: SX
Production: Rebekah Cheyne

The moral rights of the authors have been asserted.

A CIP catalogue record for this book is available from the British Library.

ISBN 978–1–862058–38–5

Printed and bound by Mondadori, Italy

10 9 8 7 6 5 4 3 2 1

This book can be ordered direct from the publisher.
Contact the marketing department, but try your bookshop first.

The Pink Side Contents

En Pointe

E sme stood at the window of her hotel room, looking down at the street. Rain spattered hard, glossing the pavements. Low afternoon light reflected at strange angles.

She thought of rain she had seen falling in other cities, on other pavements. As a professional ballet dancer she had enjoyed ecstatic receptions to her leads in *Swan Lake*, in *Le Corsaire*, in *Don Quixote*. She had visited Rome, Paris, Seville, Sydney; always travelling, dancing, applause ringing in her ears.

Performing is always performing, but some audiences are more appreciative than others.

At fifteen, trapped in her southern American home town but knowing a bigger life awaited, it had been easy to ignore the gaze of local boys and men. She felt their stares, but they meant little to her then. The studio, the theatre: these were the places where Esme lived out her life, intensely and exclusively, and the only looks she drew there were of envy and admiration. She worked her body every day, as she had done since she was four years old. She no more had to think about her dancing than she had to think about breathing: Esme moved fluidly, gorgeously, telling expansive physical stories with arabesques and pirouettes. Ballet was everything.

Now, at nineteen, things were more complicated. Her passion for

dance was undimmed; she was giving the performances of her life at the Operaház in Budapest. The opera house itself was beautiful: the building's opulence, its outrageous frescoed ceiling and glimmering gold spaces, enthralled her. Esme was playing the part of Clara in *The Nutcracker*, but this was no children's Christmas experience. In a new interpretation, the choreographer highlighted the darker, transitional parts of the story: the young girl moving into womanhood, her repressed fears about the unknown and the forbidden playing out in her nightmares.

It was the most exhilarating professional challenge, emotionally and physically exhausting. But away from the theatre, away from the stage, Esme was distracted. In the solitude of the afternoon, before the thunderous applause of the evening, some other passion called to her.

✳ ✳ ✳

That night, on the wrong side of Esme's dressing room door, stood a young man, his face tense with nerves. He raised his hand, paused, and then knocked. Esme prepared to receive the usual bunch of flowers from a fourteen-year-old girl or an older queen. Instead, there stood a beautiful local boy of twenty-four, resplendent in grubby overalls.

'I just wanted to say I thought you were wonderful,' he told Esme in his slow, difficult drawl, his eyes shining. 'You looked very lovely. I work up there,' he added helpfully, pointing to the lights in the roof of the stage. 'Normally I work on operas, serious pieces . . .' he trailed off, looking awkward. 'I have not worked on a ballet before.'

Esme wasn't listening properly. She was distracted by sharp blue eyes and prominent cheekbones, and a melting accent. 'Thank you,' she said. 'Thank you. That's really very kind.' Platitudes came easily; she barely knew what she was saying when she thanked her fans nowadays. this was no different but for other, more complicated reasons. And she barely knew what she was saying now, but for other, more complicated reasons.

✳ ✳ ✳

She woke in the night with her heart pounding. She felt the pillow next to her, and was shocked to find there was no one there. Her dream had felt so real that it was painful to wake and see it had not been. But she was relieved. In the dream, she had opened the door to the gorgeous Hungarian boy again, and instead of chatting politely in the doorway, this time she had let him in, and shut the door behind him.

'That's really very kind,' she was saying, but he reached for her and kissed her on the mouth, pulling her more closely to him, and Esme began to feel a small fire stoke and burn within her. The dream moved quickly and, with a young man's eagerness, so did he. Seamlessly he pulled her astride him on the small stool at her mirrored table and tugged at her leotard, slipping the strap off one of her shoulders and licking and nibbling and pinching her exposed nipple. It was unbearably exciting. He moaned and shuddered and Esme sat stock-still, did not utter a sound, even when he tore at her tights to make his way between her legs, pushing aside the shimmery fabric and sliding his fingers into her surprisingly wet pussy.

Esme was crushed to wake at this exact point. She parted her thighs now in the still darkness of the bedroom: she was slippery wet, horny from the dream. She thought about her admirer in his overalls, his serious, lovely face, and began to touch herself, slowly at first and then greedily, imagining and willing the scene onwards. She pictured his hands between her legs now, instead of her own; his fingers deep inside her and a thumb rolling lazily over her clit, over and over again, and she tried unsuccessfully to slow herself down. Esme imagined him bending to her, pressing his face into her pussy, licking up her wet juice and lapping at her; she yearned for hard, pinching fingers on her soft nipples. Struggling silently with herself, she thought unbidden of the boy moving up, bending her over her dressing table and watching her face in the mirror, the shock as he roughly pushed past the stiff taffeta and net of her skirt, fumbled with himself and eased his cock deep inside her.

She savoured every moment. The size and feel of him, and every crashing magical thrust, shoving her rhythmically across the mess of tubes and jars, make-ups and creams on her dressing table. The sensation of his cool hands on her breasts was amazing. In the darkness, Esme gasped and came, her legs taut, wishing to God she was really being fucked.

After that night, things were both clearer and more complex for Esme. She could not shake off the memory, not just of the appearance of the man at her door, his innocent compliments and their impact on her, but of the fantasies he awoke in her. She felt truly embarrassed when she saw him working on her return to the theatre the next day: it was as though he had actually bent her over her dressing table that night and shown her a part of her mind and body she had never used before.

At night now, the evening's performance behind her, Esme was no longer in charge. Her dreams and fantasies merged, and sometimes crept over into her daydreams too. Always the same theme: the promise and power of her performances melting away, and Esme at the mercy of her own desires, and the men that stoked them.

After the show one evening, Esme lay in the bath, soaping herself and stroking her aching muscles. She wished hard for a man that would enter the room, snap the light off, climb in and help himself to her body. She thought instinctively of her Eastern European boy. She imagined dancing for him, and for other men. Not ballet; a different kind of performance. Just her – or perhaps someone on stage with her? As soon as she dared think one thing, her mind leaped ahead to another. Her nipples ached at the sudden, vivid thought of being fingered, fucked, in front of a sea of men. Oh, yes . . . her tutu still in place, her breasts free . . . bent over the lap of a man from the audience as he rolled her tights down in front of everyone . . . rolled her knickers down . . . and began to spank her, hard, with his palm, no, with a newspaper, for they often had newspapers on their laps.

Now she began to touch herself as she thought more about the idea of being touched on stage. She would be helpless: perhaps he would tie her hands behind her back, like a vaudeville damsel in distress. Her tormenter would be excited: she would feel his hard-on pressing into her stomach as she lay across his lap, and he would forget himself and slide two fingers into her welcoming cunt. The majority of the male audience would not be able to see, and they might grow restless and cry out – in the bath Esme stroked and soaped her breasts – and he might have to move her so the other men could see her properly. He could sit her on his lap, make her open her legs: the crowd would be able to see everything. How deliciously, horribly rude. Esme was wet with excitement, even through the bathwater, and slipped her hand down, over her flat stomach, down between her thighs, and groaned with relief and pleasure.

Perhaps he would fuck her there and then, or perhaps he would invite someone else to! Maybe he would hold her there, on his lap, facing out, and someone would come up the few stairs to the stage, take out his cock without a word. He would stand in front of her and she would swirl her tongue around the shaft and begin to move and suck up and down, and forget anyone could see any of this except the men would be whooping, they love to see a blow job, or maybe they would be silent and tense. Maybe they would be wondering if they could form a queue . . . The man standing in front of her would paw at her and grope her and he would come, his eyes tight shut, and then he would turn and leave her exposed again, and the audience would know that she was disgusting and horny and they would all be desperate to fuck her. They would see how slick and hungry her pussy was, and the guy who was holding her would be all over her, his hands squeezing her breasts from behind, reaching down and grazing her cunt with his thumb, making her buck in pleasure, growing more and more desperate, and he would not be able to resist and would shift her weight momentarily, lifting her whole body and fumbling with himself and then dropping her gently back down onto his lap, but this time onto his stiff cock, and she so wet she would slide down it, the men watching would see the cock get swallowed up and then as he moved her up and down on himself, up and down, gradually faster and faster, with her legs spread for her audience's pleasure, they would see her cunt swallow that cock over and over again, and how her body was almost limp, her face rosy with desire and heat and her body entirely given up to the thrall of the man who slid her up and down over his eager prick until she was forced to reach down and touch her clit herself, only for a couple of seconds and then she was groaning, her noisy coming echoing round the silent room, and she could not hold back or slow down and the man exploded into her, fucking her and making her fuck him hard and her body was there for all to see, groped and squeezed and sweaty and objectified and adored.

The early evening sun was as hot as day as Esme walked to the Teatro Verdi for opening night that autumn. She was principal dancer in a beautiful interpretation of *La Bella Addormentata* and she moved unseeing through Florence's lovely squares and streets, full of anticipation and excitement, thinking only of the performance before her. Turning happily into the dark of the theatre entrance, she swung past rows of red plush seats and down the corridor to her dressing room, opened the door, and stopped. There he sat.

'Hello,' he said, with that little shrug, a side smile, nervous himself. 'So, I saw on the posters that it is you, that you are in this ballet, and I thought, she will not mind, maybe, if I come to say hello once more, she will remember me, maybe.'

His words tumbled out, but Esme could not speak. Her heart thudded in her chest, emotion rising despite her best efforts to stay calm.

'I didn't know when you would come today, just that you would, so the man, I know the lighting man, he said I could just be waiting, in your waiting room, your dressing room. Is this OK?'

Esme moved towards the boy, and he opened his arms and they were kissing, hard and desperate kissing, woven with softer, melting kisses, and smiles, and his hands were in her hair and she was alive with sensation, in her heart, her hair, her skin. Finally, finally, she peeled herself away. After so many months, an eternity of nights, of fantasising, she could not squander the moment, despite the intensity of her desire.

'Wait until tonight. Wait for me,' she asked him, her hands on his chest, 'until after the show. Will you be here?' and she smiled with relief when he nodded.

✳ ✳ ✳

That evening, she danced as never before. Her performance was full of emotion: she shone, vibrated with intensity. The audience gasped during her final grand jeté, watching in amazement as she appeared to float momentarily before them, graceful and otherworldly. But when the ballet was over and she bowed to them, her heart fluttering, smiling widely at the standing ovation, she was thinking only of her other prince, waiting somewhere in the wings.

And then the crowds were gone, the audience meandering happily home through dark streets, while inside the theatre peace gradually returned. Esme shook with nerves as she waited in her dressing room, the chatter of the other dancers dying out as they left backstage with armfuls of flowers, heading for first-night celebrations.

Finally he came. He knocked on the door, and Esme opened it smiling with happiness and relief to see his face again. He lifted her to him and crushed her, showered her with kisses, and she felt his hardness against the rough tulle of her skirts. 'Dance for me,' he whispered in her ear. 'Show me again how you dance.' Nodding, wanting to express how she felt but wanting to feel him more, Esme nonetheless let him lead her by the hand from her room and they skittered down the empty corridors into the dark wide space of the theatre.

The long months peeled away. Esme remembered the precise fragrance, the echo of the Hungarian opera house. The emptiness in her stomach every night, every night after the show, the disappointment his absence from her dressing room had roused in her. Every night since, throughout the spring and summer – long after she'd left Budapest – he had remained in her mind, his strange, gentle accent and his long gaze potent in her memory. She had taken different men into her bed after that night, growing into a woman, a lover, but in these experiences she had not felt a fraction of the emotion and lust that welled in her now.

Taking to the stage in near darkness, in the still of the night, Esme began to dance. Dust span in the dim light before her. She felt alive with desire, and her initial shyness at the overwhelming intimacy of what was usually a public performance soon gave way to her intuitive need to express herself physically. At first she danced without taking her eyes off the boy, and then began to lose herself, showing her feelings and her swelling heart in her movements instead of her gaze.

He watched her without moving, spellbound by her graceful energy, as she pirouetted three, four, five times across the stage. Her movements were clean and sharp, and looked effortless but for the sheen on her skin. She looked back at him and smiled, enjoying his attention. She turned from him and moved quickly across the stage before leaping, her strong thighs tense, a perfect split in the air, then leaping again seemingly in slow motion, a half-turn towards him. He had watched the performance with the rest of the audience earlier that evening and his heart had swelled at the sight, but now this was just for him, and all it made him want to do was sweep her down from the stage, peel off her costume and fuck her.

Slowing to a halt, Esme met his eyes once more, and rising slowly onto her toes she lifted her leg high into an inviting arc. She paused before spinning, and this time as she came to a halt en pointe she smiled coquettishly. Turning her back on her lover, Esme reached behind her and unpinned her neat bun, a dark cascade of hair falling immediately about her shoulders.

Then she pulled slowly, painfully slowly, at the first bow at the top of her stiffly boned corset. The ribbon rustled as she began to unthread it with a hesitant hand. She could feel the man's gaze on her back and finally she turned again to meet it, hugging the pale pink satin to the front of her body. 'Go on,' he said, in a low voice.

Slowly Esme flexed her legs and she moved once more onto her toes, her thighs tight and her whole body – her stomach tense and flattened, her back straight – sharing the effort. Esme held the pose before launching into a series of dainty pirouettes, flinging the corset from her with the last turn.

She stood there, still tense on the very tips of her toes, her breasts pale and bare, the nipples stiff with excitement. Her shining hair lay about her shoulders, her tutu emphasised her tiny waist, and she watched the boy's breath come shallower. He made her feel like a goddess merely by the way her looked at her, and she felt compelled to fulfil his wish.

Slowly, she moved her hand to the back of her tutu and began to unzip it, before slipping the layers of net down over her narrow hips. The boy began to move from where he had stood looking up at her to the edge of the stage, and then climbed up onto it, impatient now, crazed with lust for Esme's pleased, naughty smile and her pliable, wide-open body. He moved towards her and caressed her breasts, nuzzling into her collarbone. Dizzy with desire, Esme found the strength to push him gently away. 'Wait,' she said. 'Let me finish.' He took a deep breath, and nodded. 'But hurry', he said, and it was a command, not a request.

In tiny pink silk knickers and her beloved satin ballet shoes, Esme moved away from him and began to dance once more. En pointe she moved across the stage and executed beautiful leaps and spins while all her admirer could concentrate on was the subtle bounce and sway of her naked breasts, the dark indentation of her inside thigh when she spread her legs in a leap. He stared at the flat planes of her belly and could bear it no more when she pirouetted towards him, five perfect turns coming to a stop not a metre from him. She stared at him with an indefinable look before turning and, taut as she stood on her toes, she bent to touch them. The flimsy pink silk covering her arse showed up every intimate crease and then she reached up to hook her thumbs over the sides of her panties. Wordlessly Esme slid them down, down over her long legs, pushing her naked cunt into prominent and irresistible view. Then she stood and, breathing hard, turned to face the man.

He said nothing and did not smile, but scooped Esme into his strong arms and carried her across the stage. In the shadows of the wings he set her down on a table before pulling at his jeans. Aroused by his impatience, the strength of his desire for her, after the tension that had grown between them, Esme was desperate now to have him inside her. Standing up, he looked deep into her eyes, and she opened her legs wide in answer as he moved between them and eased himself inside her. Crying out with pleasure, taking him in and feeling a flood of relief and joy as he began to move inside her, to kiss her, his warm hands moving over her cool skin, she wrapped her legs tightly around her lover's waist and began a slow blissful slide towards orgasm as the boy from Budapest fucked her hungrily and hard, a perfect pas de deux in the silent empty theatre, without fantasy or audience, and for once Esme was thinking of nothing as she came.

Silver Service

It was the most pedestrian of requests that started the whole thing off. Mrs Sullivan had asked me to reach up to the top cupboard and fetch the large green teapot, the one that holds ten cups. There was an extended family tea in the rookery and she didn't fancy getting up on the chair like she used to, not with her knees the way they are.

I was happy to oblige but the teapot was at the very back of the shelf and I had to stretch a fair way into the cupboard, which lengthened my muscles, which pulled up my formal black uniform, which revealed my stocking tops (and possibly the lace trim of my underwear) to the gentleman seated at table twelve. He wasn't in my designated area; I serve the garden and tables one to ten, so I might not have otherwise noticed him, but as I turned around our eyes locked and he knew he'd been caught looking. Instead of averting his gaze and looking embarrassed, however, he leaned back in his chair, allowing a smile to lighten his handsome features.

He was mid-fifties, I guess, and he had about him the grace of someone at ease with life. I didn't have time to be cross, as my attention had instantly been diverted. On the table in front of him was an art directory open at a page displaying the work of the symbolist artist, Félicien Rops. I had only recently discovered Rops. My Cambridge degree syllabus eschewed genre painters of the *fin de siècle*, as they weren't considered weighty enough in the canon of art history, but I'd happened upon him via an Aubrey Beardsley website where a link took me to the wonderful *Pornocrates*, Rops' watercolour of 1878. It's an arresting image: a blindfolded woman naked but for black stockings, a hat and leather opera gloves is walking a pig on a leash. The work has never been available as a postcard or print in the capital's galleries and museums, which I think is a terrible shame, as it's a curious and highly stylised painting that cannot fail to exercise the imagination.

So I immediately forgot, or subconsciously ignored, the fact this man had been exercising his own inappropriate curiosity when I seized upon the catalogue with an enthusiast's verve.

'Do you know Rops' work? I've never met anyone who's even heard of him.'

'Oh yes, very well,' he replied. 'He doesn't have the technical skill of Moreau, but he teases a sublime sensuality from his subjects no one else has achieved.' He flicked through the pages. 'Look at the woman in *The Temptation of St Anthony*. Is she not the absolute embodiment of the rapture of female sexuality?'

Wow. I hadn't expected to hear that in the tearooms. Usually the conversation was of gardening, second-hand bookshops, post office closures. It was crushingly dull there most days, but as a way of earning extra money in the holidays waiting tables was gentle and easier than the trendy bars in town – and the American tourists tipped very well.

I looked at the picture to which he had referred. An athletic, gleeful woman assumed the image of Christ on the cross while a kneeling monk beneath her clutched his head in torment.

'Ah, the tortures of unrealised, forbidden desires,' he said. 'Not something I've suffered from since, oh, must be about thirty-five years ago now.'

I smiled. Despite the huge gap in ages between us, I have to confess I found him instantly attractive. His bohemian vibe appealed to me. He looked after himself, his expression communicated a healthy *joie de vivre* and, although his thick, grey, swept-back hair was all too redolent of a dastardly charming 'silver fox', I felt compelled to find out more about him. His statement was an obvious invitation to ask questions that would unleash his libertine history but, just as I was about to enter into a dialogue, Mrs Sullivan came bustling up to me, apron a-flap.

'You found the teapot, then,' she clipped, removing the spherical vessel from my grasp. 'If you have a moment, tables seven and ten would like some service today.'

It was slightly irritating being patronised by this busybody with her snarky tone, but it didn't bother me all that much. I contented myself with the knowledge that I have something she's never had – a mixture of erotic allure and subversive intelligence that draws a certain type of man like moths to a flame. Thing is, those men are all too rare.

There aren't many obvious signs that I'm anything other than a middle-class art student. My hair is longish, my appearance bookish, and I suppose I could be accused of being a little dreamy. If you were harsh you might call me feckless, indulgent, a female dilettante; if you were generous you might say I was a butterfly, an enthusiast, flighty. And if you look closer you may notice one or two things about me that hint at mischief: a playful sparkle in my eyes; an ease with my own body, and the faint outline of suspender clips, stocking tops and half-cup bras concealed beneath the most conservative of clothes. A plain skirt and grey wool jumper are transformed into something tantalisingly incongruous when you know there's a hundred pounds' worth of silk underneath.

I've got a thing for tight-lacing, too. I love mini-corsets and waist cinchers. I sometimes wear them with cropped tops and low-slung jeans to add a surprise factor to my outfits. All in all, there are a few clues to my nature, if you care to look. And the silver fox most definitely liked to look. His knowing eyes roamed freely over my body, devouring me, exciting me, communicating desire. Right there and then I wanted to pose for him in provocative outfits; clothes I wouldn't dare wear in the street. It amused me to imagine myself squeezed into such garments whilst serving teas. Maybe I'll try that out on the last day of my summer job . . .

After a brief, arty conversation, I extricated myself from his company and shook off my idle whims. A pastel-clad family of seven wanted a cream tea in the garden and a high-chair brought to their table without delay. By the time I'd taken their order the fox had departed, but he'd left something on his bill plate and I hurried across the restaurant to retrieve it before Mrs Sullivan got to it. Folded inside the bill was his card – 'Charlie Critchley' it said, in a beautiful copperplate script sporting one of those addresses you know is grander than anywhere you've been in your life. You know, like The Boltons, The Ridings, that sort of thing. I flipped it over and he'd written a message: 'Am enchanted. Having private garden party on the 14th. Looking for someone to serve drinks and canapés. You would be well looked-after and handsomely paid. Call me.'

The fourteenth. That was two weeks away; plenty of time to swap shifts. I could get to know Charlie better and get paid. It sounded like a win-win situation. Charlie Critchley was exactly the kind of person I'd been fantasising about recently – older, wealthy and liberated – someone who knows what he's doing; the sort of man who can make a very naughty girl feel special.

And it isn't every day I meet someone who shares my artistic interests. Most of my fellow students think my tastes eccentric, old-fashioned. And sexually it's tricky to find someone on my wavelength. How I've longed for the opportunity to experiment, but boyfriends of my own age seem too embarrassed or gauche to initiate anything more transgressive than doing it outdoors. The times are many when I thought I'd made it obvious that I'd like to be put over someone's knee and have my knickers pulled down for a spanking, but the signal has never been strong enough. When I did manage to once get a boyfriend in the proper position, he kept asking me if I was OK, which was infuriating and rather defeated the object.

But Charlie . . . well, it seemed he might just be the answer to my saucy girl wishes without me having to explain the power dynamics. And being occupied by serving drinks at his party means I wouldn't be standing around a posh gathering looking nervous and not knowing anyone. I could be supercilious or charming, as I see fit. But maybe my imagination was running away with me. Maybe the attendees would be a bunch of fusty old art collectors. Whatever, I was going to make sure I looked irresistible.

It was Friday the 13th, lucky for some, as Charlie had sent me the most outrageously tempting outfit to wear the next day. I tried it on several times and whichever way you looked at it, it was designed to be arousing – for the guests and the wearer. It was a classic French maid shape, with a flared skirt and low-cut top and a darling white hair-band to match the white half-apron that cinched in my waist. He handwrote a letter to accompany the uniform, saying he was aware that it was on the revealing side, but it was a very special party and the guests always looked forward to being served by pretty young women in cheeky costumes. I had every chance to decline the offer, but £500 for an afternoon refilling champagne flutes and handing round *vol-au-vents* seemed too good an opportunity to turn down.

We'd talked on the phone a few times now, as he wanted to know my every measurement in order to send me the correct size of uniform. Those calls went on for longer than I expected, and Charlie managed to tease rather a lot of personal information from me. It was when he told me to speak very slowly and describe how I liked lacing myself into constricting garments that it tipped over into being phone sex, but I didn't mind at all. In fact I enjoyed being made to confess private stuff to this flirtatious stranger, and the best thing was I trusted him to keep my secrets.

It's a subtle art, affecting the pretence of innocence, and it requires a delicate balance of explicitness and reserve – 'I shouldn't really be telling you this, but you're so persuasive . . .' – that I found myself divulging the most intimate details. I knew instinctively he would not appreciate coarse language, although there was to be no stinting of specifics – of just how wet it made me to pull on my four-inch-high ankle-strap shoes; of the exact nature of the excitement that coursed through me when I imagined an older, attractive man peeling my satin knickers over my peachy bottom. And could I guess what he was doing? Could I imagine how hard it was in his trousers? Did I know what was very likely to happen all over my face if I sat with my legs apart in front of him once my knickers had been taken off?

Oh, yes, I did. I answered each question breathlessly, perfectly, aching for something to fill me and take away the longing I knew so

keenly. No one had ever asked me these things with such authority – and to speak so frankly in reply was both electrifying and liberating. The rewards would need to be earned, he told me. I was obviously a very demanding young lady who knew what she wanted but it was high time I was taken in hand. I'd done things to him, he said, which needed to be acknowledged. And I had an impatience that needed to be – and then he said it, someone had finally said it – *spanked out of me.*

I was so excited I could barely sleep the night beforehand. It was as if Charlie had switched something on inside me – a dazzling sense of joy and frivolity wrapped up in a pretend veneer of the utmost seriousness. My bad behaviour was no laughing matter, he'd told me, when we'd had our final telephone conversation prior to the party. I'd made him very, very hard and he couldn't concentrate on organising things until he'd attended to his pressing need. He made me tell him how I pleasure myself, sparing no details of the sex toys I bring to my bed when my young friends have disappointed me.

Once I got used to the novelty of speaking explicitly he commanded me to touch myself while he was on the line. The rule was that I had to reach orgasm first. He also asked me to call him 'Daddy' as I came – he was certainly old enough to be so – but instead of his request shocking me it sent a powerful bolt of illicit pleasure through me that was so strong it felt as if I were being penetrated there and then. I writhed on the floor of my bedroom with my exquisite pink and black panties stretched between my legs as my cunt pulsed for him and I longed to take him in my mouth.

❋   ❋   ❋

And now I'm standing in Charlie Critchley's locked drawing room, my eyes covered with a velvet mask and my hands folded neatly in front of me, my wishes about to be realised. I must have worked all of three hours before being relieved of duties and led by the hand, by Charlie, to a quieter part of the house. There's dancing in the marquee on the lawn this evening, and male staff have replaced the five young women who served canapés and drinks this afternoon. The other four have been dispatched to various rooms in the house with instructions for their evening roles. They are all very pretty and talkative and of a certain type that I suppose you might call 'game girls'. Two of them have the 1950s retro thing going on, with dyed red and black hair and amazingly curvy bodies. If it weren't for their colourful tattoos, you'd think they'd stepped out of a Vargas print from the 1940s. We had a good laugh earlier when we were serving drinks. There was already some playing around and pretend spanking going on, and the whole atmosphere has been very friendly. Two of them went off giggling with a wealthy artist friend of Charlie's who likes busty women to wield the whip hand.

And what about me? Well, despite the vulnerability of my situation – and the fact my parents would have a fit if they could see me – I feel strangely at ease; it's as if I was always meant to be here, like this, waiting for a master to take all the guilty responsibility away from me. Of course I've read about such games but this is my first time and it's so exciting I can barely breathe properly.

Charlie is over by the window, dressed in an expensive white suit, gently issuing me with orders. He's already asked me to raise my skirt very slowly and show myself to him. You see, he made me take my panties off an hour ago. I entrusted my favourite pair of oyster-grey satin French knickers to him so he could get used to my scent – a neglected sense in this age, he said.

The blindfold is my training mask – it's to prevent me getting too embarrassed by not knowing where to look when he asks me to do and say things few people would regard as decent. He's considerate like that. There'll be lots of opportunities later on for eye contact. Right now he's asking me questions. Would I like to tell him how wet I am? Am I aroused by the thought of him doing whatever he likes to me? How much do I deserve to be put over his knee and striped? Am I Daddy's naughty little girl?

I think I've answered correctly because he is walking around me now and he's taking all kinds of liberties. He smells divine – wearing some expensive perfume made specially for him by a gentleman's shop in Jermyn Street. I've been asked to stand with my feet apart and he has very slowly begun caressing my bare buttocks. I'm squirming, which he thinks is so sweet, as I'm not trying to escape but to move his hand closer to the source of my intimate pleasure. I've never felt so painfully turned on. It's worse than having an itch you cannot scratch. I am almost at the point of blindly feeling my way around the room and rubbing myself on one of the sofas. I'm not used to being denied – and Charlie knows it. I want to come by his hand, but being an expert tormentor of female desire he is feeding off my heat, dragging out my delayed gratification for as long as he can.

I am damp and longing for him to touch me between my legs. I want his total attention for ever and the thought this may be routine for him, or that I am one of a number of playmates, inflames me with a jealous fury. Clearly, my emotions are in turmoil. All I know is that I'll do anything to please my 'Daddy'. I want him to quench my need, make my life exciting, fill me with his magnificent cock. He lightly touches me, barely a butterfly's wing-beat on my clit, and it's too little, too longed-for, and I fold to the floor, trapping his arm between my legs.

'Please, please, do something to me,' I implore him. 'I can't stand it any more.'

The blindfold is lifted and his kindly face regards me with a smile.

'Oh, my poor little wanton creature,' he teases. 'Does she want to come?'

'Yes, yes, please,' I beg frantically, batting my eyelashes, desperate to perform or suck him or do anything that will involve contact.

'Then so you shall, but only when you've learned to behave!'

With a deft movement he grasps me by the wrists and pulls me to the sofa. I'm breathless and perspiring and I know instinctively that I cannot be seen to be too desperate for what I know is coming. I know he wants a struggle, as much as I want to feel his strong, clothed body exercising power over me. But after some wriggling and feigned protest I'm soon upended over his lap.

He can see everything, and takes full advantage. One hand circles the globes of my cheeks while the other settles at the nape of my neck, holding me in position. My skirt is lifted methodically, tantalisingly slowly, as he shushes my cowardly bleating for him to be gentle.

Then he goes into old-fashioned disciplinarian mode: 'You've been too long without a firm hand, my girl,' he admonishes. 'Too long driving men to the brink of madness flaunting your sexy little underwear and your wet little cunt.'

I giggle and squeal simultaneously as I anticipate the stinging blows. But even now he's making me wait, while I beg him to teach me a lesson and repeat his words five times: 'I'll be a good girl and not tease my daddy.'

Then his palm beats down on my fleshy backside in rapid strokes. It's a keen, hot pain and I shout out obscenities, which only adds to the duration of the spanking.

'Dirty girls must learn how to behave,' he says sternly, as I feel my cheeks getting warmer until a wonderful, calming sensation spreads through me and I find I'm not struggling so much. Instead I'm begging for him to touch me. And finally not even he can resist and I am rewarded with his fingers sliding into the slippery molten core of my sex. And as I lie there face down and allow him to explore me, I silently pray he will continue and take me to my depraved conclusion.

The cheeky role-play has mutated into something deep and delicious. I'm giving myself over to him and he's not disappointing me by asking if it's OK, or if he's being too rough. We're communicating solely through intuition and touch, and it's bringing me to a body-shattering climax. Turned on my front being done like this is all I ever wanted. I feel magnificently looked after. And when I'm about to erupt I let him know so he can fully enjoy the moment. My breath is rapid and shallow and I can feel the liquid gold gathering between my legs. And then it happens. It happens while I'm on his lap, recovering from my first proper spanking. I cry out his name and tell him he's making me come and that I want to do it forever.

And before I'm too far gone in an altered state, we're tumbling onto the carpet and he's undone himself to reveal his magnificence. There's no doubt in my mind that I want him to enjoy exactly what I have just enjoyed, however he wants to get there. He's fully prepared for safe sex and, although it doesn't last long, the intensity is greater than anything

I've ever known. In a way, it's like having my virginity taken all over again. If this is what it's like with older men, then the future of my sex life has been revealed. No more timid boys. No more fumbling, nervous questions. Just make me beg, flip me over, warm my bottom and make me call you Daddy.

❋ ❋ ❋

Mrs Sullivan scowled at me as Charlie held my hand and explained very politely that I wouldn't be coming back to the tearooms, as I was a very badly behaved girl and he was looking after me now. I tried not to giggle as I stood there wearing a very short see-through dress and tarty slingback shoes.

He couldn't bear the thought of me working long hours for what he called a pittance and, anyway, serving champagne at country parties is much more fun. I'm getting to know his friends, who are utterly charming and pay me lots of attention. And I'm learning loads more about art than I did in the whole of my first year. Strangely enough, next term we have a module on the femme fatale in the Western tradition. Charlie says I know enough about that already – but I'm persuading him to let me stage my own Félicien Rops tableau on his lawn for an autumn party. I've got the boots, the leather opera gloves and the leash. The only thing is, where on earth can we obtain a live pig?

Song of Solomon

Who can resist the *Song of Solomon* with its heady unguent double entendres and tender entreaties of erotic hope between two lovers? Also known as the *Song of Songs*, or *Canticles* this, the 22nd book of the Bible, can be read on many levels – but of course we know to which level we aspire . . .

Ripe with allegory and bursting with suggestions of courtship and consummation, the *Song of Solomon* has fuelled the desires and the imagination of writers and readers for centuries, from Geoffrey Chaucer in the *Miller's Tale* whose Absolon uses it to woo Alisoun, to Kate Bush who alludes to it so sensuously, bathed as it is languidly in the delicious voices of the Bulgarian choir, in her eponymous song from the album *The Red Shoes*.

So powerful is its erotic vocabulary that Jewish boys were forbidden to read it until they had reached the age of thirteen years.

The heady perfumes and ripe-fruit laden imagery is enough to make any lover swoon – make sure you whisper sweet excerpts in their ear as you prepare to 'feed among the lilies'.

Love Miss A.P. x

Chapter 1

The song of songs, which is Solomon's.

Let him kiss me with the kisses of his mouth: for thy love is better than wine.

Because of the savour of thy good ointments thy name is as ointment poured forth, therefore do the virgins love thee.

Draw me, we will run after thee: the king hath brought me into his chambers: we will be glad and rejoice in thee, we will remember thy love more than wine: the upright love thee.

I am black, but comely, O ye daughters of Jerusalem, as the tents of Kedar, as the curtains of Solomon.

Look not upon me, because I am black, because the sun hath looked upon me: my mother's children were angry with me; they made me the keeper of the vineyards; but mine own vineyard have I not kept.

Tell me, O thou whom my soul loveth, where thou feedest, where thou makest thy flock to rest at noon: for why should I be as one that turneth aside by the flocks of thy companions?

If thou know not, O thou fairest among women, go thy way forth by the footsteps of the flock, and feed thy kids beside the shepherds' tents.

I have compared thee, O my love, to a company of horses in Pharaoh's chariots.

Thy cheeks are comely with rows of jewels, thy neck with chains of gold.

We will make thee borders of gold with studs of silver.

While the king sitteth at his table, my spikenard sendeth forth the smell thereof.

A bundle of myrrh is my well-beloved unto me; he shall lie all night betwixt my breasts.

My beloved is unto me as a cluster of camphire in the vineyards of Engedi.

Behold, thou art fair, my love; behold, thou art fair; thou hast doves' eyes.

Behold, thou art fair, my beloved, yea, pleasant: also our bed is green.

The beams of our house are cedar, and our rafters of fir.

Chapter 2

I am the rose of Sharon, and the lily of the valleys.

As the lily among thorns, so is my love among the daughters.

As the apple tree among the trees of the wood, so is my beloved among the sons. I sat down under his shadow with great delight, and his fruit was sweet to my taste.

He brought me to the banqueting house, and his banner over me was love.

Stay me with flagons, comfort me with apples: for I am sick of love.

His left hand is under my head, and his right hand doth embrace me.

I charge you, O ye daughters of Jerusalem, by the roes, and by the hinds of the field, that ye stir not up, nor awake my love, till he please.

The voice of my beloved! behold, he cometh leaping upon the mountains, skipping upon the hills.

My beloved is like a roe or a young hart: behold, he standeth behind our wall, he looketh forth at the windows, shewing himself through the lattice.

My beloved spake, and said unto me, Rise up, my love, my fair one, and come away.

For, lo, the winter is past, the rain is over and gone;

The flowers appear on the earth; the time of the singing of birds is come, and the voice of the turtle is heard in our land;

The fig tree putteth forth her green figs, and the vines with the

tender grape give a good smell. Arise, my love, my fair one, and come away.

O my dove, that art in the clefts of the rock, in the secret places of the stairs, let me see thy countenance, let me hear thy voice; for sweet is thy voice, and thy countenance is comely.

Take us the foxes, the little foxes, that spoil the vines: for our vines have tender grapes.

My beloved is mine, and I am his: he feedeth among the lilies.

Until the day break, and the shadows flee away, turn, my beloved, and be thou like a roe or a young hart upon the mountains of Bether.

Chapter 3

By night on my bed I sought him whom my soul loveth: I sought him, but I found him not.

I will rise now, and go about the city in the streets, and in the broad ways I will seek him whom my soul loveth: I sought him, but I found him not.

The watchmen that go about the city found me: to whom I said, Saw ye him whom my soul loveth?

It was but a little that I passed from them, but I found him whom my soul loveth: I held him, and would not let him go, until I had brought him into my mother's house, and into the chamber of her that conceived me.

I charge you, O ye daughters of Jerusalem, by the roes, and by the hinds of the field, that ye stir not up, nor awake my love, till he please.

Who is this that cometh out of the wilderness like pillars of smoke, perfumed with myrrh and frankincense, with all powders of the merchant?

Behold his bed, which is Solomon's; threescore valiant men are about it, of the valiant of Israel.

They all hold swords, being expert in war: every man hath his sword upon his thigh because of fear in the night.

King Solomon made himself a chariot of the wood of Lebanon.

He made the pillars thereof of silver, the bottom thereof of gold, the covering of it of purple, the midst thereof being paved with love, for the daughters of Jerusalem.

Go forth, O ye daughters of Zion, and behold king Solomon with the crown wherewith his mother crowned him in the day of his espousals, and in the day of the gladness of his heart.

Chapter 4

Behold, thou art fair, my love; behold, thou art fair; thou hast doves' eyes within thy locks: thy hair is as a flock of goats, that appear from Mount Gilead.

Thy teeth are like a flock of sheep that are even shorn, which came up from the washing; whereof every one bear twins, and none is barren among them.

Thy lips are like a thread of scarlet, and thy speech is comely: thy temples are like a piece of a pomegranate within thy locks.

Thy neck is like the tower of David builded for an armoury, whereon there hang a thousand bucklers, all shields of mighty men.

Thy two breasts are like two young roes that are twins, which feed among the lilies.

Until the day break, and the shadows flee away, I will get me to the mountain of myrrh, and to the hill of frankincense.

Thou art all fair, my love; there is no spot in thee.

Come with me from Lebanon, my spouse, with me from Lebanon: look from the top of Amana, from the top of Shenir and Hermon, from the lions' dens, from the mountains of the leopards.

Thou hast ravished my heart, my sister, my spouse; thou hast ravished my heart with one of thine eyes, with one chain of thy neck.

How fair is thy love, my sister, my spouse! how much better is thy love than wine! and the smell of thine ointments than all spices!

Thy lips, O my spouse, drop as the honeycomb: honey and milk are under thy tongue; and the smell of thy garments is like the smell of Lebanon.

A garden inclosed is my sister, my spouse; a spring shut up, a fountain sealed.

Thy plants are an orchard of pomegranates, with pleasant fruits; camphire, with spikenard,

Spikenard and saffron; calamus and cinnamon, with all trees of frankincense; myrrh and aloes, with all the chief spices:

A fountain of gardens, a well of living waters, and streams from Lebanon.

Awake, O north wind; and come, thou south; blow upon my garden, that the spices thereof may flow out. Let my beloved come into his garden, and eat his pleasant fruits.

Chapter 5

I am come into my garden, my sister, my spouse: I have gathered my myrrh with my spice; I have eaten my honeycomb with my honey; I have drunk my wine with my milk: eat, O friends; drink, yea, drink abundantly, O beloved.

I sleep, but my heart waketh: it is the voice of my beloved that knocketh, saying, Open to me, my sister, my love, my dove, my undefiled: for my head is filled with dew, and my locks with the drops of the night.

I have put off my coat; how shall I put it on? I have washed my feet; how shall I defile them?

My beloved put in his hand by the hole of the door, and my bowels were moved for him.

I rose up to open to my beloved; and my hands dropped with myrrh, and my fingers with sweet smelling myrrh, upon the handles of the lock.

I opened to my beloved; but my beloved had withdrawn himself, and was gone: my soul failed when he spake: I sought him, but I could not find him; I called him, but he gave me no answer.

The watchmen that went about the city found me, they smote me, they wounded me; the keepers of the walls took away my veil from me.

I charge you, O daughters of Jerusalem, if ye find my beloved, that ye tell him, that I am sick of love.

What is thy beloved more than another beloved, O thou fairest among women? what is thy beloved more than another beloved, that thou dost so charge us?

My beloved is white and ruddy, the chiefest among ten thousand.

His head is as the most fine gold, his locks are bushy, and black as a raven.

His eyes are as the eyes of doves by the rivers of waters, washed with milk, and fitly set.

His cheeks are as a bed of spices, as sweet flowers: his lips like lilies, dropping sweet smelling myrrh.

His hands are as gold rings set with the beryl: his belly is as bright ivory overlaid with sapphires.

His legs are as pillars of marble, set upon sockets of fine gold: his countenance is as Lebanon, excellent as the cedars.

His mouth is most sweet: yea, he is altogether lovely. This is my beloved, and this is my friend, O daughters of Jerusalem.

Chapter 6

Whither is thy beloved gone, O thou fairest among women? whither is thy beloved turned aside? that we may seek him with thee.

My beloved is gone down into his garden, to the beds of spices, to feed in the gardens, and to gather lilies.

I am my beloved's, and my beloved is mine: he feedeth among the lilies.

Thou art beautiful, O my love, as Tirzah, comely as Jerusalem, terrible as an army with banners.

Turn away thine eyes from me, for they have overcome me: thy hair is as a flock of goats that appear from Gilead.

Thy teeth are as a flock of sheep which go up from the washing, whereof every one beareth twins, and there is not one barren among them.

As a piece of a pomegranate are thy temples within thy locks.

There are threescore queens, and fourscore concubines, and virgins without number.

My dove, my undefiled is but one; she is the only one of her mother, she is the choice one of her that bare her. The daughters saw her, and blessed her; yea, the queens and the concubines, and they praised her.

Who is she that looketh forth as the morning, fair as the moon, clear as the sun, and terrible as an army with banners?

I went down into the garden of nuts to see the fruits of the valley, and to see whether the vine flourished and the pomegranates budded.

Or ever I was aware, my soul made me like the chariots of Amminadib.

Return, return, O Shulamite; return, return, that we may look upon thee. What will ye see in the Shulamite? As it were the company of two armies.

Chapter 7

How beautiful are thy feet with shoes, O prince's daughter! the joints of thy thighs are like jewels, the work of the hands of a cunning workman.

Thy navel is like a round goblet, which wanteth not liquor: thy belly is like an heap of wheat set about with lilies.

Thy two breasts are like two young roes that are twins.

Thy neck is as a tower of ivory; thine eyes like the fishpools in Heshbon, by the gate of Bathrabbim: thy nose is as the tower of Lebanon which looketh toward Damascus.

Thine head upon thee is like Carmel, and the hair of thine head like purple; the king is held in the galleries.

How fair and how pleasant art thou, O love, for delights!

This thy stature is like to a palm tree, and thy breasts to clusters of grapes.

I said, I will go up to the palm tree, I will take hold of the boughs thereof: now also thy breasts shall be as clusters of the vine, and the smell of thy nose like apples;

And the roof of thy mouth like the best wine for my beloved, that goeth down sweetly, causing the lips of those that are asleep to speak.

I am my beloved's, and his desire is toward me.

Come, my beloved, let us go forth into the field; let us lodge in the villages.

Let us get up early to the vineyards; let us see if the vine flourish, whether the tender grape appear, and the pomegranates bud forth: there will I give thee my loves.

The mandrakes give a smell, and at our gates are all manner of pleasant fruits, new and old, which I have laid up for thee, O my beloved.

Chapter 8

O that thou wert as my brother, that sucked the breasts of my mother! when I should find thee without, I would kiss thee; yea, I should not be despised.

I would lead thee, and bring thee into my mother's house, who would instruct me: I would cause thee to drink of spiced wine of the juice of my pomegranate.

His left hand should be under my head, and his right hand should embrace me.

I charge you, O daughters of Jerusalem, that ye stir not up, nor awake my love, until he please.

Who is this that cometh up from the wilderness, leaning upon her beloved? I raised thee up under the apple tree: there thy mother brought thee forth: there she brought thee forth that bare thee.

Set me as a seal upon thine heart, as a seal upon thine arm: for love is strong as death; jealousy is cruel as the grave: the coals thereof are coals of fire, which hath a most vehement flame.

Many waters cannot quench love, neither can the floods drown it: if a man would give all the substance of his house for love, it would utterly be contemned.

We have a little sister, and she hath no breasts: what shall we do for our sister in the day when she shall be spoken for?

If she be a wall, we will build upon her a palace of silver: and if she be a door, we will inclose her with boards of cedar.

I am a wall, and my breasts like towers: then was I in his eyes as one that found favour.

Solomon had a vineyard at Baalhamon; he let out the vineyard unto keepers; every one for the fruit thereof was to bring a thousand pieces of silver.

My vineyard, which is mine, is before me: thou, O Solomon, must have a thousand, and those that keep the fruit thereof two hundred.

Thou that dwellest in the gardens, the companions hearken to thy voice: cause me to hear it.

Make haste, my beloved, and be thou like to a roe or to a young hart upon the mountains of spices.

The Lady of The Manor

Dear Diary

I know I haven't written for a week, but this new position as lady's maid has done me in. As you know, I've wanted to be in service my whole life and it was my happiest day ever last week when I heard I got the job here at Muckington Manor. I'd always wanted to be under Lady Arruthers-Plushington, or Lady A-P as we call her downstairs.

Yesterday was a right peculiar one. I don't know if it's a typical day here, but I can see I'm going to have my hands full. Her Ladyship rings early, well before we were ready. I thought the upper classes didn't rise for hours! The bell rang and I'd hardly had a wink as it was.

I share with her Ladyship's other maid, Dolly. She snatches all the sheets on the bed and she moans something terrible in her sleep! She cried out again last night . . . 'Oh, Jack! Jack!' I know this is something to do with Jack Ladd, the apprentice gamekeeper. The first time I heard her moaning in the night I teased her rotten the next morning but the horrid little madam pinched me that hard that I never dare mention it again.

I think Dolly is what my mother described once as 'no better than she ought to be'. Needless to say, she kicked me out of the bed claiming it was my turn to get the breakfast things together.

Lady A-P looks beautiful, even first thing in the morning. We laid out her breakfast and brought up her post . . . she receives letters in the nicest handwriting you have ever seen . . . but one of them yesterday, well, it even smelled different. And this is the funny thing, Diary, but it smelled like . . . a man. What I think a proper gentleman smells like, too, not of tobacco and whisky like his Lordship, her dad. Isn't that strange?

Not that I'm not getting used to odd goings-on here – the thing about the upper classes is they seem to think we're invisible. They act as if we're not there but we see and hear everything. But then it hardly matters . . . who would we tell other than other servants?

Jack Ladd even boasts that he's seen her Ladyship in the altogether, ''avin' it' with someone. I went to slap him that time, that's not the way we should be talking I told him, but he grabbed my hand and called me a 'silly little cow' and that I'd 'find out soon enough'. Horrid boy. But this letter . . . she read it, laughed scornfully and tossed it aside on the floor like we weren't even there and off she swept for her bath.

Dolly pounced on it immediately. I begged her to leave it alone – it's her Ladyship's private things – but she fought like an alley cat to read that letter, striding around the room reading bits out. But oh, the language: 'I must have you or I will die', that was pretty, or 'I'm fair blue with need, cruel lady' and – oooh! – 'meet me in the stables at three o'clock'.

Dolly grabbed me. 'We've got to catch them at it! I'd love to see her face! Them upper classes, they think themselves so good and proper and clever. Ha! She's no fancier a scrubber than I am,' she scoffed.

Well, Diary, she was right about the very last words. I wasn't having it. Not her Ladyship! Dolly laughed and pinched me and pulled at my hair. 'The stables. Three o'clock. You'll see what she's really like!'

I shook her off and tried to get her mind on our chores. I at least have some pride in my work! Anyway, there was something about that letter had an effect on Milady also . . . her blood was up. She called for

Jack, saying she was going to shoot something or someone this morning. That gave us a couple of hours to get our jobs done, although Dolly was no help at all.

She will act up so! We were supposed to be making up the beds but that descended into a pillow fight and well, guess who won? And, as usual, because she was the winner, Dolly pinned me to the bed again and did that thing . . .

She hardly put her back into it for the other chores, and I knew we were for it. Dolly's been warned that many times. Her Ladyship gets back, Jack Ladd lolloping behind and leering at me. I don't doubt he gave Milady some sauce as she was spoiling for a fight on her return and, of course, when she realised what a slipshod job had been done this morning she goes hopping mad, her eyes a bit glazed. I was hoping she'd taken it all out on some clay pigeons . . . but clearly not.

I expected her to call for the housekeeper, Mrs Shaw (right strict – she keeps a leather strap in her apron and I know Dolly's felt the back of it) to have her dock our wages but we were told to wait in the library for her Ladyship to discipline us. Well, Diary, I have to say it was jolly different. It hurt something rotten, but . . . I don't quite know how but it made my heart beat all fast but in a way I liked. I know what her horse must feel like now . . . I'll be black and blue for weeks. Thank God the tradesmen's doorbell rang else she might have half beat me to death. The interruption was her Ladyship's delivery. Boxes and boxes of it. Frills, flounces and fancies the like of which you've never seen.

And, oh, she looked beautiful in them. I don't know why she wanted such la-di-da smalls though, she was only going riding in them, or at least so I thought, because wasn't she meeting that friend of hers at the stables?

'You dozy little mare,' sighed Dolly. 'Come on,' she said, dragging me the back way to the stable yard where indeed Lady A-P and a gentleman (who had that scent like off the letter) was doing something . . . right un-equestrian, if you ask me. I begged Dolly for us to leave right away – I didn't want to get caught spying. Only we did . . . by Jack Ladd. I suppose what he then did might be described as blackmail, but Dolly didn't seem to mind in the least and, well, I've had worse afternoons I suppose, although Dolly was a beast with that whip . . . she's had lessons from her Ladyship, I shouldn't wonder. Speaking of whom, she gets back to the house and neither of us is in sight. Not best pleased, I can tell you. Particularly as Dolly had hay still sticking out of her hair, a bit of a giveaway.

Lady A-P knew immediately that we must have been down there and seen what she did and the whip came out again. Dolly was first but she would not confess under interrogation or beating. She'd put Mata Hari to shame, that one. She actually winked at me as Milady brought down the whip over her backside. And because she kept her mouth shut, I was up for the high jump next. Barely a stroke was on me and I screamed, still sore from that morning. I didn't blab a thing, mind, I ain't a squealer. Her Ladyship could have wore herself right out (and I might have felt sorry for her were it not my behind she was tanning). In fact, she only stopped from fatigue, not lack of determination.

'Well, at least I know how to work hard, even if you lazy guttersnipes don't,' she said (and some other things besides – the language you hear from these nobles, really). 'I need refreshment. We will have tea.'

And that's exactly what we did. All three . . . none of her society lady friends, just us. Which I thought mighty strange after that previous performance, but that's them elite, isn't it? Do what they likes. I have to say, that clotted cream stuff does get in some funny places, you know.

Honestly, yesterday, if I weren't being spanked by the Mistress, I was being prodded by the senior maid or something quite other by that gamekeeper lad. All I wanted was a long, hot soak and that romantic storybook I'd sent off for. But no, it was back in the boudoir for Milady's ablutions. She has a right big bath, so big all three of us could fit in it. Her Ladyship says it was custom in their family for the maids to warm up the bed. But all night? Not that I care, it's all work to me. In the morning though – and I could barely believe this – Dolly asked Lady A-P, right to her face, 'Veronica, you seeing that billionaire playboy fella again, then?'

Veronica? I have never heard anything like it! What was she thinking? The impudence! I didn't think my poor behind could take another thrashing, as doubtless I'd be slapped silly as well. But her Ladyship just reached over and stroked her cheek, looked at me and said, 'My dearest Dolly, I don't think so, do you?'

A Satisfied Customer

D ear Agent Provocateur,

You must know me by now. I'm the formal-looking City girl with the red streaks in her hair and the 34DD cup that pops in every few weeks to buy something new. It seems only fair to tell you what I've been up to over the past few months, as it's your underwear that's got me into this situation. When I first came to you I was fairly shy, although I've always had a tendency towards what psychologists call an addictive personality. For instance, a couple of glasses of champagne are never enough for me. From the first taste of the exquisite fizz exploding on my tongue I want to hear those corks popping every twenty minutes. I don't want to be told 'the champagne has run out, madam, but we have some white wine'. I can't stand settling for the mediocre when I've tasted the magnificent.

I'm the same with clothes. It breaks my soul to shop in the high-street chains now I've felt the luxury of fabulous undies next to my skin. And since I discovered your shops, I've been getting bolder with each new item I acquire – coming out of my shell. I love the snug fit of satin stretched over my firm behind, and clinging to my hips. Fastening suspender clips, lacing a waspie, or adjusting my breasts into a sheer

black and pink satin-trimmed bra is such a wonderful girly bother! The feeling of power it gives me is worth all the effort. I don't know how I got by for so long on commonplace cotton when this world of glamour was waiting for me.

Being a goal-oriented person, I set myself the challenge that with each new item I added to my collection, my exploits were to become increasingly daring. My experiments began with your sheer black bra – you know, the one with the naughty slit just where the nipples poke through. It was so thrilling the first time I wore it under my work clothes, and felt my smart cotton shirt rubbing across the sensitive flesh. I caught the eye of a few suits on their way to work that day, especially the ones who pressed up against me in the packed tube carriage. They just couldn't prevent their eyes from flashing to my chest, and I did nothing to dissuade them. In fact, I loved it. As did my boss. I was making a presentation to the entire company later that day and I could see his mind was focused more ardently on the great mystery of my suddenly hard nipples rather than on our client's needs. He's become noticeably more amenable towards me on the days I wear my peep-hole bra. It's amazing what a pair of perky breasts can do.

✳ ✳ ✳

I started to spend time posing in front of my bedroom mirror, imagining I was one of the models in your catalogue. I couldn't wait to try out my next purchase: the demi-bra and knickers. I first wore them a few weekends back while visiting my boyfriend Rob's parents, who live in the country. We went for a stroll in the fields near their house while his mum and dad prepared Sunday lunch. I'd been teasing Rob mercilessly and he'd accused me of flirting with his dad, which I shamefully admit was true. But I couldn't help it. He's a wolfish alpha male of the world; reminds me a bit of Bill Clinton when he was president. You know the sort of thing – in his late fifties but still with all the drive and desires of a younger man. Anyway, his whole body seems to come alive whenever I'm invited to their house. His hand against the small of my back during the arrival and departure embraces always communicates a very intimate affection. I don't think Rob's mum has noticed anything. I'm not that much of a bitch that I'd flaunt it in front of her.

But Rob's got my number. He can see right through my feminine wiles, yet they also inflame him to a fever pitch. He's more than happy with my new-found confidence. So, anyway, I'd been flirting with his dad and Rob said he was going to 'teach me a lesson' on our walk when we came upon a stile at the corner of the field. I'd marched a little way ahead, showing off, lifting my skirt and flashing him a view of my new underwear. I leaned over the stile, which was positioned at just the right height to pivot myself over it, and began fooling around. Rob was immediately behind me and, before I could collect my senses, he had pulled my skirt up and was spanking my satin-covered buttocks. I was squealing and begging him to stop but this only spurred him on. With no one in sight, and with me bent over the smooth wood of the stile, Rob whisked my pants down and began applying sharp, stinging strokes of his hand to the flesh of my cheeky pink bottom. I knew I shouldn't have said it, but in the throes of the moment I thought I might as well go for broke: 'I bet your dad would like a go of this,' I said between laughter and gasping for breath.

This got him really riled up, and he gave me such a telling-off – for being a slut, for not behaving like a young lady, for getting wet while I was being spanked. There was nothing else for it, he said: I was going to get fucked over the stile like a rustic peasant girl who'd teased the farmer just that bit too far. I had every opportunity to pull my knickers up and run away while Rob was releasing himself from his trousers but of course I didn't. I wanted his eight inches of heaven every bit as much as he wanted to drive it into me. It was a really rough quickie – saucy and dirty, with both of us saying the filthiest things to get us to our goal: a mind-blowing orgasm in the open air.

I'm sure his dad knew what we'd been up to. Over Sunday lunch he remarked rather laconically on my healthy complexion. I wanted to say, 'You should see my other cheeks,' but I bit back my impulse and smiled coyly instead.

So, over the course of the past few months my body language has become increasingly bold – suffused with sensual promise, where it used to be swift and businesslike. I've become very aware of what I've got, and what it can do. So it was really playing with fire when I ordered up my latest treat, a set called 'Gangster'. The moment I eased those pleated-edged, fire-engine-red satin suspender briefs over my bottom I knew there was going to be big trouble.

We'd been out on the town, my two best girlfriends Ellie and Jo and me, and it was one of those Friday nights with a wild atmosphere, when everyone seems hyped up and primed for something to happen. The moon was a fat pearly disc in the sky as we hit the City bars and began drinking shots in rapid succession. We were in a lively mood, egging each other on to confess wilder and wilder stories. I admitted my shameless flirting with men on the tube, in shops, men everywhere. I was flirting in the bar too, flashing looks at a very nicely dressed legal eagle at the other end of the room. I knew he was a barrister or a lawyer – as are all the well-turned-out blokes around that area on a Friday night. He looked fit under his suit, had a thick glossy head of dark wavy hair and rimless designer glasses – a thoughtful intelligent type with a killer body. There was no evidence of a wedding band or a girlfriend in tow. I had to have him! I gathered my energies and concentrated on sending him my best sexual smoke signals.

And of course my pals spotted straight away what I was up to. 'What's come over you?' they asked. 'You've turned into a wild woman!' And that's when I unbuttoned my top to show them my Gangster bra and they shrieked in delight, laughing and saying, 'Well, you'd better live up to the name then, girl!' And they were right. It was too good not to be used. And after a couple of champagne cocktails I felt bold enough to take on the world. A quick visit to the bathroom and I'd stripped down to my undies but concealed my treasures under my belted knee-length mac. Suddenly I was a sexy spy or undercover agent ready to make her sting. I applied some smoky eye shadow and sticky red lip gloss and I was ready for a hold-up. Except my target wasn't the local off licence but a certain man with a briefcase full of court reports.

On my return I gave my friends a flash of my skimpy outfit under my coat and there were, naturally, gasps of astonishment and giggles all round. I sat smouldering at the bar, my attention drifting from my companions' conversation and into my own imagination of what it would feel like to run my hand into his suit jacket and around his waist, feeling the crisp cotton of his shirt and the firm abs underneath. My friends kept pulling me back into their chat but I was keeping one eye on him all the while. His occasional glances in my direction kept me eager for action. Then, after about forty-five minutes, during which time I'd had another two cocktails, I saw him retrieve his coat and make a move to leave. I was not prepared to stand for the audacity of being ignored. He should at least come over and introduce himself. My brazen mind came up with a plan – I would follow him out into the night. With my coat around me, no one need know how little I was wearing.

'Drink up quickly,' I ordered my pals. 'I've got a mad idea.'

They were buzzing on my bravado and up for a laugh so the three of us grabbed our belongings as I gave them instructions. Outside we tracked him as he weaved his way through the drinkers gathered outside pubs in the warm September night. His route would take him past some of the narrowest, oldest streets in London, where rakes and harlots of centuries past would flit between coffee houses and plot their various debaucheries. I had my own dastardly plan hatching as we kept our distance behind him, trying not to giggle, then he turned into a narrow passageway past a seventeenth-century church.

Running to catch him up, I sprang in front of him and stood there feeling strong and sultry, Ellie hanging behind.

'Remember me from the bar?' I asked. 'I need to settle a bet. Would you mind answering a couple of questions?'

He ran a hand through his lustrous hair and, with annoying confidence, replied, 'Why not, sure, go ahead.'

'First, are you a lawyer?'

'Yes, I work at the Chambers over there.' He pointed to the west.

'So, I was right.'

'What else?'

'Do you like adventure?' I asked, unbuttoning my mac to flash the red satin of my underwear like jewels glinting in the dark.

His eyes fixed on my suspender briefs as I ran my hands suggestively over the fabric. He dropped his bag onto the pavement and rather self-importantly said, 'I take it you mean adult adventure, rather than 'trekking in the jungle' adventure?'

'Oh, very much so,' I said, making obvious my intent. His eyes were glued to my hand as I snaked it down between my legs. His tone changed. His voice lowered.

'I saw you in the bar. I was going to come over but I was embroiled in conversation with a client and it would have been unprofessional to abandon them, and then I realised the time and I had to –'

'Stop making excuses!' I said. 'You haven't answered my question. Do you like adventure?'

'If it's the kind I think you mean, then yes. Any man would.'

I snatched his bag from the ground and threw it to a surprised Ellie.

'What's going on?' he protested. 'Hand that back! There's important papers in there.'

'Well, you're going to get some adventure tonight,' I said, laughing, a wild feeling beating in my heart. I grabbed him by the coat and pinned him up against the alley wall. 'You're going to come with me. Just be nice and do what I say and you'll get your papers back.' I whisked the scarf I'd been wearing earlier from my pocket and tied it around his head as a blindfold. Then I pulled him upright and frog-marched him along the alley, giggling and high from the adrenaline coursing through my aroused body.

I hailed the cab that appeared suddenly and ordered my unseeing captive into the back. I grabbed our bags from Ellie, blew a kiss to my friends, who stood there looking slightly shocked, and we were off, speeding into the night. It was that quick.

I told him I had his bag and he calmed down, especially when I ran my dew-soaked fingers under his nose and let him suck them. He swiftly got hard, so hard, and I was pleased to see that the danger and the surprise of the situation was turning him on. Revelling in the power I had over him, I felt emboldened enough to grab his cock right there in the back of the cab. His erection was bone-hard and pleasingly thick. The way it poked lewdly at the expensive fabric of his suit trousers sent the moisture gathering between my legs. I was so wet and excited that I wanted to straddle him and take his meaty girth into me there and then, but I knew I had to prolong the tease. It would be worth the wait to see him beg.

I couldn't believe what I'd done, but sometimes, when the moon is full and desire is strong enough, anything can happen on one of those crazy London nights. By the time we reached my flat he was under my spell and we were both radiating the adult perfume of arousal.

'I've never done this before,' he said croakily, as I pushed him gently into my living room. 'I don't make a habit of being abducted by female perverts.'

'Shut up,' I ordered. 'Just do as I say and no one will get hurt.' My language was sharp and dominant. I was taking a huge risk but I wasn't going to wuss out of what I'd started. As they say, fortune favours the bold. 'And keep the blindfold on. You'll carry out my instructions to the letter, if you know what's good for you. First, you're going to strip for me.'

He stood by my sofa and shrugged off his coat, then his suit jacket.

'Now the shirt,' I instructed. 'And be quick about it.'

His slightly trembling hands fiddled with the buttons until he – somewhat gracefully, I noted – eased the shirt over his beautifully defined shoulders.

'There. That's better.' Now I get to see you as an object of my lust, I thought. How liberating it was for me to have him unseeing. I no longer had to be careful where my eyes landed. Without having to make pretences to a demure, feminine gaze, I could feast my voyeuristic pleasure by staring at him for as long as I wanted. He was a handsome specimen, too: toned, tanned, just enough dark hair across his chest to be pleasantly masculine, strong arms and a neat stomach. I had chosen well.

The pair of killer heels I was wearing gave me a rush of sexual power. Coupled with the satin underwear, yet still I kept my mac on, I couldn't fail to feel devastatingly female, dangerously predatory. My own body was turning me on as much as the sight of his, yet I knew it was time to

let him feel me. I slid over next to him and insinuated my body against him. His hand went straight for the curve under my buttocks and he grabbed a handful of my firm, satin-encased flesh. Instantly I felt the response I wanted, pressing itself into my abdomen. Then he was moving, grinding against me with slow, determined pressure.

'Please,' he whispered, 'please do want I know you want to do. Making me wait like this is torture.'

I liked the idea of the tortured barrister, driven to the brink of embarrassment and made to perform to my liking. But he was going to be made to savour his longing. I had an idea that would add even more fuel to my fire. I whisked the belt from my mac and deftly seized his wrists to tie them together behind his back. Now he was blind, constricted and subordinate to my whims. He didn't struggle. His fat erection flexed inside his trousers and I ran my hand proprietarily over his flesh as he pushed against me, whispering entreaties of desperation.

I had him kneel down so that his face was level with my sex. The panties were tight and he would have to perform great agilities to give me pleasure. For a moment I wasn't sure I could stand the frustration, but on my command his hot breath targeted my cunt and he began to probe for me with his tongue, snaking under the elastic to find the essence of my need.

Watching him work for me like that was magnificent. Here was this man of the world reduced to a sexual servant, pleasing me, abjecting himself for the glory of my impending orgasm. I didn't want him to bring me to climax like that, though. I was too lubricated by my own juices and in need of his hard flesh in me. But to see the pulsing and thrusting of his cock, straining for attention and constricted by his trousers, almost brought me to the point of no return.

The belt tying his hands behind his back was long, and I was able to lead him by his bonds into my bedroom, where I pushed him down on the bed. Finally, I removed the blindfold. He looked so fuckable and gorgeous with his hair mussed up and perspiration covering his throat. As I finally, slowly, undid the belt of his trousers I felt exultant, wanton and very pleased with myself. I relished the idea of this important, professional man looking undone, dishevelled, debauched, under my control.

As an expert of tease I knew just how far to take him before stopping, leaving him pleading with me to continue. He kept telling me how he'd never known anything like this before, asking if I was mad? Wondering when I was going to let him go. Of everything I did, the one thing that really hit the spot for him was the sight of me bringing myself off, as he lay there with his cock stiff and shining from my mouth. The great thing was, I didn't need to take off my satin two-piece until the very last minute. And after I had tipped myself into that gorgeous abyss, when I was aching for the feel of him inside me, it was with the full knowledge that I would be releasing a man taken to the point of desperation. And he didn't disappoint. He went at me with the full force of a brute, yet he was skilful with it, moving me around into different positions to achieve maximum depth. His thrusts were deep, yet slow and deliberate, and I loved the way he kept running his hands through his hair and over his own body. My captive brief was a right little narcissist!

And when he was almost there, ready to release the joy and tension, he pulled out of me, straddled my chest, and made me watch him. I had a full dirty close-up of his beautiful fat cock ready to blow.

'I'm going to come in your face. This is what you want, isn't it?' he said, as the cream shot from him and splashed my hair and my lips and I gave myself over to the delirious adult fun of it all, laughing freely.

❉ ❉ ❉

And I'm still laughing now. In fact, both of us have had quite a fun time talking about how I've changed over the months he's been my boss and how pleased he is that he set up an account for me at your shop. We've been telling each other our fantasies since the beginning of the year and he's been most appreciative of the details, but everything moved up a gear last week, when he handed me my instructions for our kidnap scenario in a sealed envelope. I have to say, his acting abilities were superb. Ellie and Jo would never guess we knew each other. It's my turn next. I've already booked the hotel for our next assignation – on his credit card, of course. I'll be lounging in my luxury suite awaiting room service, and a very satisfied customer.

360°

Boys, no more than boys, thought Samantha irritatedly, as she swam slow silent lengths, her hair fanning out beneath the surface of the cool blue pool. It had been a long day. At twenty-seven she was one of the older models working on the shoot, and she usually prided herself on the serene self-assurance that years of experience in the industry had given her. Nothing fazed her, usually, but then usually there was nothing – no one – to distract her much from her work.

The calm under the water broke briefly into cacophony as she lifted her head to take each breath. Then silence again, closing over her as thick as fog.

Sometimes, it would be quite nice to take your work home with you. She tried and failed to dispel from her thoughts the group of photographers' assistants she had worked with that day: a glittering shoal of beautiful men in a sea of gorgeous women. Damon was six foot two with messy dark hair and sexy black spectacles. Mark was tanned and athletic-looking, muscular even, with short blond hair. Will was not yet twenty, slim with an intelligent face, and Saul had the most beautiful blue eyes and wore retro sweaters that clung to his taut frame. Mostly Samantha had concentrated on the work, on what the photographers were trying to achieve, but there was a lot of waiting and watching to be done.

She had the pool to herself now. The other girls were near, but did not intrude on her evening ritual. Only the heady, summery fragrance of juniper and cucumber snaking over the water from feisty gin and tonics, and the relentless rhythm of one disco record after another, disturbed her peace. Samantha would go over to them, but needed this solitude first, to regenerate herself enough to rejoin the bubbling throng at the end of each day. This was day fifteen: the job must be costing the client a fortune, she thought. Fifteen days so far, modelling endless underwear and swimwear for a glamorous superlabel, who were in commercial collaboration with a luxury car brand. The sports cars were elegant and desirable and each one cost about the same as Samantha's West End studio apartment. Fifteen days multiplied by seventeen beautiful, practised models, plus one sprawling villa and countless staff running to and fro daily with fresh flowers and coffee; pressed linen; chilled champagne. Samantha had come a long way from her parents' Welsh terrace cottage. She smiled to think of it, and ducked her head once more beneath the surface of the water.

That day had been draining. Modelling was hard work. Sort of. What was hard was the dragging of the hours: trying to enjoy the enforced stillness, the lack of privacy. Much as she resented the distraction of beautiful boys, and sometimes girls, she was grateful for it too. Sometimes she was totally in the mood to be touched and pampered: to have her hair stroked and brushed and her face made perfect with gorgeous potions. Other times she felt dangerously out of control, and restless.

✻ ✻ ✻

Luella stood on one foot then the other, trying to relieve the ache from a day's standing. A long glass of gin and tonic was beginning to float through her body and make everything feel more easeful. Luella had been 'spotted' seven years before, waitressing in a spectacularly busy restaurant in Cornwall in the middle of a long school holiday, and had never looked back. But being on her feet all day was still not her idea of fun.

She was happy at least that they had managed to shake off the clients that night. As the fortnight's shooting drew to a close, the men at the car company were growing increasingly insistent that they throw the models a drinks celebration to thank them. Luella could think of little worse than doing unpaid overtime feigning interest in monologues from overenthusiastic corporate man-bots.

Some of the other men on the shoot, though, maybe. Were they cute to start with, or had the slow pace of the days drawn more attention to some of the other faces at the studio? In any case, all of the girls were doing what they could to make the time pass more interestingly. The models had largely convinced the clients that the need for beauty sleep was no myth, and that they all retired religiously to bed soon after nine each night in order to look their best for the next morning's shoot. But in truth, they had been doing anything but. Nine was when the girls began their night's entertainment. Some took hired scooters into town and found the biggest, hardest club they could, and came home joyfully senseless with exhaustion. Others would go for long twilit walks, or nestle into sand dunes to watch beach barbeques teeming with laid-back surf boys.

Others, and Luella was one of them, usually retreated to the huge daybeds scattered poolside, the uninterrupted view of the sea providing the most beautiful backdrop to the pool's azure water, and began slow, exploratory kisses with whichever of the other models was around.

It had started on the very first evening. The atmosphere was too heady, too erotic to ignore. The heat of the day gave way into balmy night, and Luella found an unexpected bliss in the arms of a dark-haired Ukrainian girl called Xana. She barely spoke English, it seemed, so was subjected to less chat from the client. Her eyes were black with mischief as she slipped her slender arm round Luella's waist and brought her mouth to hers, biting Luella's lip gently. Ripe roses and lavender, juniper and cucumber: her head swam with powerful fragrances, and her body melted. She lay back, and let Xana undo the buttons on her shirt dress to trace patterns on her bare skin. Her touch was gentle but sure; her eyes never left Luella's.

✳ ✳ ✳

Xana had always been quiet. Not necessarily shy, but quiet. And this often meant that people assumed she had nothing to say; that she thought nothing, or – on a lot of jobs – that she simply couldn't speak

English. In many ways, her nature was a blessing. Spoken language often led to difficulties and misunderstandings, she'd noticed. Body language, facial expressions, were easier for everyone to read, if they concentrated.

She was enjoying this job. Two weeks had passed at this blissful place by the sea and the working days passed quickly for her, if they started a little early for her tastes. The light: she knew you had to catch the light. But mainly at the moment she was interested in the dark. Come evening she sought her pleasure with predatory focus. The trick was not to seem too eager, but to approach with languor and confidence. She was having the time of her life. The memory of boyfriends she'd had in the past left her cold now: she had discovered far greater pleasures in recent years exploring the bodies of other beautiful women. She loved to spend hours just kissing, getting hornier and hornier just touching someone else's tongue with her own. The women smelled good, mints and perfume, and their skin was as satin-smooth as her own. And when things did progress, when Xara could bear it no longer and stroked her way down a girl's body from breasts over a flat brown stomach to an eager, slippery cunt, the pleasure outweighed anything she could remember from her past. She loved the awkwardness other models sometimes showed; often they had never slept with a woman before, but modelling made you horny and open to experimentation. There was something about the constant physical attention, being touched and handled all day long, being around other gorgeous girls – often in a state of nudity – that made you very physically aware.

Last night, for example. Xana had lain quietly next to a young model with short blonde hair, who after a few minutes' intense kissing suddenly rolled her over and began to plant tiny kisses all across her belly and hips before parting her legs and tonguing her ready pussy. This was rare, and Xana loved her confidence. She could tell that the girl had not done this before, but guided her with touches and moans. She always kept her pussy entirely bare, and could feel every lap of the girl's tongue as it ran up and down. In the end she put both hands in the blonde's hair to keep her still as Xana came in great waves, oblivious for the moment to anyone else.

This evening, the final evening, was to be different. Struggling to perfect the last pictures, the photographers had given the girls the day off on the understanding that they would finish the shoot that night, at the models' villa. These were two older, male photographers who had long worked together on major campaigns like this one. They wanted the shoot to look beautiful, sultry, exotic: they wanted to capture the chemistry between the models, show how good it made women feel to wear the label's designs. They had brilliant product shots, and some gorgeous individual images, but they intuited that the models felt inhibited at the studio. The clients would keep turning up for the most spurious of reasons, and the photographers saw how the girls reacted to these interruptions. Most importantly, these two wise men saw how some of the girls had begun to relax around the edges of the shoot, to smoke with and giggle with their young assistants. The photographers announced to everyone that they wanted to work at the villa instead that evening in order to finish the shoot no matter what, and they left it at that.

Late in the afternoon, Samantha's solitude in the pool was complete. When she lifted her head clear of the water this time, no sound came rushing at her. Every other girl was inside, catching a nap or beginning to prepare themselves for the shoot ahead.

Most girls, that is. Luella and Xana were tussling on the Egyptian cotton sheets of the huge bed in Luella's room. Xana had come in on the pretence of borrowing some make-up, but when she had pushed Luella back onto the bed and begun to kiss her Luella found she was in no mood to resist.

Xana was in a boisterous mood. The languid caresses of a few nights before were replaced by passionate kisses, bites and exploring hands. She quickly brought Luella to a point of weakness, so that she was desperate to come. 'More,' breathed Luella. 'Like that. Touch me like that.' She was anxious as the girl withdrew her touch.

'Patience, darling!' smiled Xana. She was off the bed and looking around the room, much to Luella's irritation. Minutes later, she returned and sat astride Luella's body with an array of props. 'Wider,' she instructed, as she began to tie assorted silk scarves and stockings around

Luella's wrists and ankles, before wrapping and knotting the other ends around the four corner posts of the bed. She took pity on the squirming girl and knelt down briefly, burying her face between Luella's slim white thighs. 'You look lovely like this,' she offered. 'Very defenceless!'

Luella's eyes were shut and she took no notice of Xana's words. It suited her to think she could not speak. In fact she wished she would stop altogether right now – Luella cried out in pleasure as Xana brought her close again and then backed away, before it was too late.

'Please,' she begged. 'Please, I just want to come . . .'

Xana put her fingers to her lips. 'Shhh, darling. You'll thank me, I promise!'

Rifling through and rejecting the other props she had brought to the bed, Xana moved off and opened cupboard doors and drawers. 'Aha!' she announced, waving a purple vibrator from Luella's bedside drawer.

Luella smiled at her. 'My friend,' she explained. 'Bring my friend over here.'

Xana smiled too as she looked over her spread-eagled lover. Her heart was beating fast. She loved to play and she loved this girl's open, sexy manner. How beautiful she looked, her breasts pale and firm with her arms tied tight above her head, her thigh muscles taut, the soft mound of fur between her legs so enticing. The room smelled sweetly of sex, and the sun was falling away from the day, leaving shadows on the bed and in the corners of the darkening room. She leaned over and stroked Luella, who was calmer now but still horny, still impatient to start again. She ran her nails lightly over Luella's breasts, the cute pink nipples, and pinched them lightly. She trailed her hand all the way over and down and then ran her fingers lightly over the girl's clit. Luella moaned and opened her wide thighs further still. Xana ran her thumb gently over the silky clit and slipped two fingers deep inside her cunt, then began to slide them in and out, ever so slowly. Luella bucked and tried to hurry her, but Xana would not be rushed. She watched the pink flush rise in her lover's cheeks, watched as her nipples grew hard and her cunt grew wetter still. She had to stop herself from reaching down and touching herself. Not yet.

Xana picked up the vibe and rubbed its length gently against Luella before pushing it slowly and gently deep into her. She switched it on and it began to buzz, and then she began to slide it rhythmically in and out of Luella's cunt. Her moaning grew louder and her hair was damp against the fine cotton. 'I wanna come,' she mumbled again, and Xana said nothing but bent down and put her tongue gently on Luella's clit as she continued to slide the vibe slowly in and out. Luella's breath came harder and then she was coming, finally coming, twisting in pleasure for endless seconds beneath Xana's tongue as she fucked her.

Now it was Xana's turn. Luella lay hot and exhausted but Xana clambered over her body. 'I hope you don't mind,' she said, as she kneeled over Luella's face and lowered herself gently to her mouth. Tied tightly, Luella had little choice, but Xana began to free her hands, and she shook them out before raising them to roam over Xana's round breasts, which swung and bounced as she writhed on top of her. Xana was almost silent, panting as she gyrated her hips before coming all of a sudden as Luella pinched her nipple hard and licked her pussy tenderly. Xana collapsed beside her on the bed, grinning widely.

'That was fabulous!' she announced in her strong accent. She rolled onto Luella and kissed her hard before rolling herself off again. 'Come, let's get ready,' she suggested, and the two girls began to brush each other's hair in readiness for their work ahead.

✳ ✳ ✳

Samantha appraised herself briefly in the mirror. She had finished her hair and make-up herself and was pleased with what she saw. She was practised now at doing this, and had picked up endless tricks over the years. There was something nice about getting herself ready now, at her own pace, as opposed to the stress of a usual shoot. She was wondering what to wear when she was disturbed by sounds coming from the other side of her bedroom wall. Always difficult, overhearing the sounds of sex. Invariably you were on your own and were made to feel lonely, and annoyingly horny, by the noises. Samantha couldn't make out the mumbling voices or the moans but assumed they must be to do with Luella in the next room.

She liked the look of Luella. She had lay down with her on the daybed at dusk recently and remembered suddenly the feel of her mouth, her sulky lips and the mint slip of her tongue on Samantha's own, and on her neck. She remembered the touch of Luella's fingers and began to touch herself without even thinking about it. She ran it over in her mind again and again, fingering herself gently and then more urgently, kneeling in her bathrobe and dreaming of Luella's searching fingers rubbing her clit as they kissed. Yum. The moans in the next room grew louder and Samantha imagined what might be happening. All these women . . . The boys from the shoot entered her thoughts again. She couldn't help herself. She pictured them: any of them, all of them, idealised, shining with youth, untethered finally from their strict apprenticers. The moans from next door grew louder, and Samantha let her imagination run riot, seeing Luella in there alone, then with the men, eight greedy hands roving over and inside her body, taking it in turns to fuck her, stroking her tenderly then making her come again and again with cocks, fingers, tongues. She remembered vividly the warmth of Luella's naked skin next to her own, Luella's saucy expression as she slid her fingers for the first time into her eager cunt, and Samantha began to moan with pleasure.

✳ ✳ ✳

The shoot looked messy from the start. Good messy. There were bodies everywhere. The photographers arranged them one by one, draping the models artfully over chaises longues, sunbeds, one another. The swimwear was flimsy, and the photographers had ordered everyone – including those modelling the lingerie – into the water first, so that the fabric glistened wetly and transparently. The light was beautiful: golden sun filling the lens, now dipping, dipping, and the women were bathed in fading sunlight and gorgeous shadow.

A shoot was perfect when the models felt utterly adored, admired, lusted after. This was the responsibility of the photographer, although he might delegate it to his assistants, openly or otherwise. Here the men had taken care hiring their help, and chosen as their apprentices young men who were thoughtful and enthusiastic, but also somehow louche and beautiful. And as the photographers ran the shoot, they were cruel to everybody, cunning as foxes: forcing the boys to pay such intimate attention to the models that both models and assistants were growing excited and frustrated. The photographers ordered their helpers to adjust bikinis, move the girls' positions, stroke more oil onto their skin, even reapply the models' lip gloss. They forced them close to the girls, but not close enough.

Champagne ran as water and the women grew bold in the face of adoration and attention. They became pliable, posing freely, arching their backs more than ever, pouting lasciviously, reeking with sexuality. They giggled and laughed, stretched and teased. They were having fun, their inhibitions and professional skills forgotten, replaced by a natural wantonness that was a joy to watch. The photographers shared glances and worked on, thrilled with what they were able to capture. The models barely noticed when they stopped shooting.

It was not clear when the dynamic shifted. The women were flirting, and the men were working, and then things changed and the models knew they had gained power. First they stopped posing, and then they were teasing the boys. Samantha was first with a camera. It was so liberating to be capturing the images, controlling them, for once. Since her teens, Samantha had been the object: subjected willingly to the male gaze, the consumer's gaze. Now, looking through the lens, she felt immediately more powerful. She toyed with Will, and she was strong and persuasive, and smelled of sex and heat, and he crumbled. Laughing, pushing him easily to the ground, she made him kneel as Luella peeled off her bikini top before him and tied the band over Will's eyes. He reached up with eager hands to stroke what he could no longer see, slipping his hand up across Luella's inner thigh and hooking a lucky thumb into her bikini bottoms. That was the tipping point, right there. Once Will touched Luella, once the blindfold freed him from all obligation and he made that intimate contact, there was no going back.

A blonde girl with flicky 70s hair and very white teeth watched as the scene unfolded before her and made the smallest of aroused groans at the sight of Luella parting her thighs for Will. She was dressed in the tiniest of lingerie sets, her generous breasts spilling over the top of her balcony bra and flimsy knickers barely covering her bottom. And others

were watching her. Xana moved in first, expertly and imperceptibly closing in behind her before bending to kiss her neck. Xana let the back of her hand trail down the blonde tresses and over the girl's right breast, and let it linger there, catching Damon's eye as he looked on with frank desire. She did not drop his gaze as she began to stroke the girl's breast through the material, and smiled wickedly as she felt the nipple harden at her touch.

Damon thought for two beats before moving towards the women. He did not know what he was going to do, just that he could not stay away, could not be happy just to watch any longer. The two weeks of work had started out like any other job, but as time had gone on he had found himself thinking less about photographic technicalities and more about high round tits and silky hair. He had found himself looking, watching, but that was suddenly not enough. Xana was almost as tall as he was and looked up from the blonde's collarbone and delicious breasts to kiss Damon full on the mouth. She had not kissed a man for a very long time, let alone one so young and hungry, and it felt great to have that wash of greedy male desire hit you so hard. Damon touched the blonde as they kissed, tentatively at first, and then he joined Xana in caressing her breasts, freeing them from their lacy bra and tugging at the little lace panties. The girl between them groaned and squirmed with pleasure as hands ran over her perfect skin, and resisted not an inch when Xana held her so that Damon, hurriedly casting off shirt and jeans, could grasp her firmly around the waist before sliding himself deep into her silky, hot pussy.

Samantha lowered the camera, grinning with delight. She cast a predatory glance around the room before sighting Mark and Saul. Both were pinned back on sunbeds, arms tied tightly behind them, naked from the waist down. Despite their nerves, they could not help but show off fantastic, straining hard-ons while models laughed and danced wickedly and suggestively in front of them. Samantha watched until she could watch no longer then, picking up the camera, she began to move over towards the two men.

Xana watched her happily from her new position on one of the chaises longues, then looked back down at Damon, his dark curls

buried between her thighs. She concentrated on the feeling of a good-looking man's mouth on her cunt, and then she began to come as the blonde girl stroked her hair and tenderly bit her nipples. It was going to be a beautiful night.

Quietly now, Samantha watched and filmed, watched and filmed, and as the sky grew black she felt pleasure beyond compare knowing that all this was hers for ever, all the beautiful people trapped like butterflies in a jar, her beautiful, filthy, home-movie souvenir.

The 17ᵗʰ-century Punk Poet

As the wicked John Wilmot, 2nd Earl of Rochester, has found a place in the dark side of this tome, we reserve space here for his contemporary, the incomparable Aphra Behn. Her life, she proclaimed, was 'dedicated to pleasure and poetry': a poetry which called for equality of the sexes and free love (and never missed a chance to poke fun at an arrogant male turned impotent).

England's first professional female writer, one of the most successful Restoration playwrights and poets, Royalist spy (code-named 'Astrea') and firm supporter of James II, she was also a friend of the most famous of the Libertine poets, Rochester himself. She was widowed at a young age (although many believe that she made the marriage up in order to raise her status). Whatever the identity of 'Mr Behn', he disappears from historical record in 1666, whether gathered by the plague or abandoned in real life or imagination.

When James II failed to pay her for her espionage trips to Holland, Aphra kept herself out of debtors prison by writing plays. This commercial exploitation of her own skills led many to name her 'the Ingenious Mrs Behn' and many of the crueler male tongues at the time to brand her 'a lewd harlot' or 'punk' (whore) poet. These barbs did little to put her off her stride because she wrote play after play for crowded theatres.

During her lifetime she was notorious, successful and famous: she knew and wrote for Nell Gwyn, John Dryden, the Earl of Rochester (immortalised as the rake protagonist 'Willmore' in her most popular work *The Rover)* and the Duke of York. Beneath many of her plots runs her quiet anger at the lack of power allowed to contemporary women. As Virginia Woolf wrote, 'All women together ought to let flowers fall upon the tomb of Aphra Behn, for it was she who earned them the right to speak their minds.'

Her romantic disposition was not only turned towards men, as *To The Fair Clarinda*, first published in 1688, shows. Indeed her themes were so explicitly sexual that in print they were first attributed to Rochester.

Truly a woman after our own hearts.

Love Miss A.P. x

To The Fair Clarinda, who made love to me, imagin'd more than woman

Fair lovely maid, or if that title be
Too weak, too feminine for nobler thee,
Permit a name that more approaches truth,
And let me call thee, lovely charming youth.
This last will justify my soft complaint,
While that may serve to lessen my constraint;
And without blushes I the youth pursue,
When so much beauteous woman is in view.

Against thy charms we struggle but in vain
With thy deluding form thou giv'st us pain,
While the bright nymph betrays us to the swain.
In pity to our sex sure thou wert sent,
That we might love, and yet be innocent:
For sure no crime with thee we can commit;
Or if we should – thy form excuses it.
For who, that gathers fairest flowers believes
A snake lies hid beneath the fragrant leaves.

Thou beauteous wonder of a different kind,
Soft Cloris with the dear Alexis joined;
When e'er the manly part of thee, would plead
Thou tempts us with the image of the maid,
While we the noblest passions do extend
The love to Hermes, Aphrodite the friend.

Two Anonymous Poems

Eighteenth-century England: an Age of Reason but also an age
that wore its heart on its silken sleeves. Passion, desire and
seduction pervade its prose and poetry. If only we were a
time traveller . . .

Love Miss A.P. x

She lay all naked in her bed,
And I myself lay by;
No veil but curtains about her spread,
No covering but I:
Her head upon her shoulders seeks
To hang in careless wise,
And full of blushes was her cheeks,
And of wishes were her eyes.
Her blood still fresh into her face,
As on a message came,
To say that in another place
It meant another game;
Her cherry lip moist, plump, and fair,

Millions of kisses crown,
Which ripe and uncropped dangled there,
And weigh the branches down.
Her breasts, that welled so plump and high
Bred pleasant pain in me,
For all the world I do defy
The like felicity;
Her thighs and belly, soft and fair,
To me were only shown:
To have seen such meat, and not to have eat,
Would have angered any stone.
Her knees lay upward gently bent,
And all lay hollow under,
As if on easy terms, they meant
To fall unforced asunder;
Just so the Cyprian Queen did lie,
Expecting in her bower;
When too long stay had kept the boy
Beyond his promised hour.
'Dull clown,' quoth she, 'why dost delay
Such proffered bliss to take?
Canst thou find out no other way
Similitudes to make?'
Mad with delight I thundering
Throw my arms about her,
But pox upon't 'twas but a dream.
And so I lay without her.

I gently touched her hand; she gave
A look that did my soul enslave;
I pressed her rebel lips in vain:
They rose up to be pressed again.
Thus happy, I no farther meant,
Than to be pleased and innocent
On her soft breasts my hand I laid,
And a quick, light impression made;
They with a kindly warmth did glow,
And swelled, and seemed to overflow.

Yet, trust me, I no farther meant,
Than to be pleased and innocent.

On her eyes my eyes did stay:
O'er her smooth limbs my hands did stray;
Each sense was ravished with delight,
And my soul stood prepared for flight.

Blame me not if at last I meant
More to be pleased than innocent.

Allegra

Allegra steadied herself at the doorway. She felt slightly fuzzy
with alcohol, a fact that few looking at the tall, confident
woman, who held herself with such assurance, would have
been able to guess. Allegra's manner was always welcoming yet
no one could mistake the touch of frost in her flawless conduct, her
unapproachable beauty.

She had, in point of fact, just knocked back three glasses of
champagne. It was a peculiar habit she allowed herself once the music
festival she organised was under way. The drink calmed her nerves
(irritation rather than shyness) and eased the flow of conversation with
the endless stream of strangers that came into her orbit. This much was
true and was how she would rationalise it if anyone caught her. More
essentially to Allegra, however, it was a little present to herself. This gift
allowed her to absorb the first half of each performance using her
senses rather than rational thought – eyes closed, a private smile
dallying at the sensuous edges of her curved lips.

And she needed it now for she was a little irritated. The handsome
and charismatic Hungarian conductor, almost twice her age, with whom
she had been flirting harmlessly for the last five seasons had this year
selfishly brought his wife. Allegra had of course smiled generously (as
the conductor had noted) though not warmly (a fact not lost upon the
wife) and immediately given up her seat in the dress circle to this

unsolicited addition to their number. As she swept off down the emptying corridor, she used a practised hand to snatch a glass from the waiter's tray as he scurried past. A reward for my professionalism, she thought. And then added a silent 'Damn him'. It had been a Pyrrhic victory to see Barto wince when she gave up her seat. She knew very well that he had planned to lean his knee heavily against hers during the performance as he had done every year since they had met. Silly old fool, she thought as she paused outside the 'royal box'. Then she sighed at the door: the box had notoriously bad views and missed all the pleasing effects of the new acoustic system. It was therefore always empty.

As she paused she heard the applause for the conductor who must have just walked on stage. The noisy welcome intensified as, she imagined, the renowned pianist took her place at the piano. They were to perform that most romantic of Scriabin's scores: the concerto in F sharp minor. She must hurry; it was one of her favourites.

Allegra slipped into the darkened space as the clapping ebbed away. Using her hands, she found her chair as her eyes became accustomed to the half-light. She was about to sit when a hand brushed against hers. The effect was electric. She was too composed to cry out but she was agitated to discover she was not alone. Who could this be? She had studied the seating plan most carefully only an hour ago and these chairs had not been assigned to anyone. She turned and peered into the gloom. It was a man, that was all she could tell. He had his back turned as he laid his jacket carefully over a chair. The audience was hushed now. Allegra quickly took her seat, annoyed to have her composure and her privacy disturbed. Forget it, she thought, and closed her eyes, breathing deeply, allowing the warm champagne waves to roll over her again. In the silence of the moment, she smoothed out the velvet folds of fabric in her skirt, shuffled slightly and raised her face a little as the horns ushered in the first extended chords of Scriabin's strings.

As the momentum of the first movement grew, Allegra melted into a sea of thought and colour. Just like the composer, Allegra saw notes as colours in that strange sensual swapping that synaesthesia brings about in the mind. Visceral experience could conjure a riot of

complementary sensual experience in her head: sounds could be revealed as taste; touch could become colour; images could become smell; and making love? Well, making love could be an astounding melee of touch, images, colour and sound. And orgasm? Almost mind-blowing. Allegra smiled a private smile.

She was now swimming in her own pool of sensory delight. As the bright notes of the piano tumbled over the rising melancholy of the strings, Allegra perceived the music as a mass of blue light which vacillated and pulsed through violet to red to blue and back again. The mists of the champagne were now at their thickest and Allegra's heart was overrunning with happiness.

Just then, as the first movement was coming to its swirling climax, her unknown companion, who had until this moment been sitting silently behind her, shifted his chair. He did not actually touch her, but he was so close that Allegra could sense the proximity of his knee to the small of her back. Allegra was confused, her senses agitated by the music and now this rude interruption of her personal space. She tried to remain focused upon the music and her inner world but the awareness of his body began to burn through her concentration. She clicked her tongue with annoyance, knitted her brow and tried to remain detached, but it was no good.

So preoccupied was she with the position of the trespasser that at first she was not aware that the music had stopped. Suddenly the silence of the short interval seemed to burst into her consciousness and the void of the auditorium, hanging there expectantly, forebodingly. Allegra held her breath. It only served to exacerbate her awareness of how little space there was between her and the intruder. It was then that she felt his warm, light breath on the back of her neck. It made her feel strangely semi-naked. The rhythm of his breathing was even, yet seemed gently insistent. Allegra sank into her imagination again, perceiving the ebb and flow of his exhalations as cool water splashing over her, dissipating into a million lustrous fragments as it hit the skin. She closed her eyes again and the soft opening bars of the second movement mixed with the alcohol and the myriad colours coursing through her body as she allowed herself to become lost in the flood of sensual experience. She at last succeeded in cutting out her

awareness of the man beside her. That was until she became aware of the pressure of his knee against her left thigh.

Despite her warm and muzzy state, all was suddenly made clear to Allegra. It must be Barto! Had he orchestrated the whole annoying seat-shifting thing in order to be alone with her? Allegra smiled again. What did it matter anyway? She was happy to have him to herself again. She enjoyed their flirtation. She allowed his leg to continue to press against hers, and then, after a while, she began to return the pressure, but softly; she didn't want to give him too much encouragement. These were the unspoken rules of their dalliance. Allegra settled down to enjoy the evening, her heart quickening slightly, her breathing deep and full.

Just as the music began to lull the audience with its elegiac sweetness the piano suddenly crashed in abruptly with rich insistent chords. Allegra coughed slightly and shifted in her seat and all of a sudden, at that precise moment, he had moved his chair. He was now even closer. She shivered. He had pulled himself forward slightly but she still couldn't see his face out of the corner of her eye, and annoyingly he no longer rested his leg against hers. Allegra hated to admit it but she ached to close the gap between them. Slowly, she let her leg fall against his. This too was a well-rehearsed part of her ritual. At this point, Allegra knew, Barto would return the pressure. She waited in anticipation. But he did not. She was about to cough slightly, to remind him of his duty, when his hand slid smoothly over her velvety knee. She stiffened slightly. This surprise was not unwelcome, as long as it didn't signify anything else. They both stayed locked like this for a moment as the notes of the piano tickled and danced about the air. Then his fingers too began to tremble, not, Allegra keenly noted, in a nervous way, but in a delicious insistent rhythm. Allegra, wrapped up in her own private internal recital, was very happy to let this play continue. That was until she realised that his repeated strokes had begun to pull her skirt back across her thighs, indeed the hem was now rising slowly above her knee. As the music swelled so too did her sudden urge to open her legs and pull his hand into her.

This could not go on!

She flicked out her hand, blocking him from moving any further, and as she did so she felt the skin of a much younger man than Barto. She withdrew her hand urgently then returned it immediately as his fingers quickly began an inquisitive foray under her hem, running like warm silk over her stockings. What on earth . . .? Allegra's fingers shook as she clamped both hands down over her skirt to hold his outrageous hand captive. What should she do? She had to stop this madness but at the same time her restrictive pressure had also succeeded in pressing that electric touch deep into her thigh. It was a delicious problem. His hands possessed an extraordinary energy. He could only be a string player, she thought. But did it matter? What did matter? She didn't know any more. She knew nothing except that she didn't want this to stop. She shouldn't be letting this happen. When she opened her eyes she saw the orchestra she had booked, and the faces of some of her most important clients dotted along the dress circle, she remembered her professional responsibilities; but when she closed her eyes to sink again into the place where the crashing themes of the orchestra and the kaleidoscope of colours pulsed and faded and deepened as she felt the weight of his hand on her thigh, she couldn't give a damn. For a moment she was torn, her breath shallow and expectant. Then, in a sudden decision that surprised her, she released the pressure on his hand and let her own slowly and deliberately fall away from her lap. He now had free rein.

Allegra stole a furtive glance about her. To her right, the people in the dress circle had almost to look through the edge of their box to see the stage. Any strange movement that she made would immediately draw attention. What was she doing? She steeled herself. Whatever her thoughts were now, it was too late to change the course of events. She stretched out her long leg to brace her stiletto shoe against the balcony and slipped slowly, surreptitiously down in her chair, tilting her hips to meet the lovely movement of his fingers. As she did so, her skirt rose higher and his hand, previously constrained, was at last free to explore her. Which he did, quickly and urgently.

She jumped as he dragged a nail along the line of her suspender and she opened her legs slightly, aching for him. In the sensual confusion that followed she imagined a thousand burning strings ran up the flesh

85

of her thighs and into her pussy. She pictured herself naked as a cello in his hands. He would gently pull her head back to reveal her neck and she would feel that wonderful vibrato movement of his fingertips. Then with his right hand he would take his bow and draw it across her breasts, across the nipples, sawing back and forth as they tightened beneath his strings. It was a mesmerising fantasy.

The music soared and wheeled and at last she felt the pressure of his finger between her legs. She opened her eyes slightly and through her lashes she could just make out the silhouette of his aquiline face as he leaned closer towards her. No one would be any the wiser, she thought, as he watched the orchestra with an expression of calm concentration. He seemed engrossed in the music. She too knew that her face gave nothing away, but when his fingers played and lingered over the lace material of her underwear all burned beneath her cool exterior. Allegra swallowed – she was very aware that her pussy was soaking wet. As at last he slipped a finger beneath the material he turned his face to hers. Surely this would draw attention to their illicit liaison? She closed her eyes tightly as if this could protect them from discovery.

His cool breath began to fall over her cleavage that rose full and pale above the tight tailoring of her velvet jacket. Allegra raised her right hand and allowed the nail of her fourth finger to scratch a fine line from her collarbone to the deep valley between her breasts. And as his stroking became more insistent back and forth between her wet folds she bit into her bottom lip and gripped his forearm, holding him to her, digging her nails into his taut flesh. She could feel the muscle and sinew beneath her grasp extend and contract as he began to circle her clit. She refused to release him and pulled herself closer to him, holding her breath, hoping no one could see how her body had begun to shake, how her stomach contracted, how her head fell back as the rising orgasm began to draw her insides up in an inexorable progress towards the explosions of colour and shapes in her mind. The music had reached its shuddering conclusion. She started suddenly as applause broke out across the auditorium. It was over. Allegra hung her head, collected her thoughts and let go of his hand. She pulled a programme protectively over her knee as she smoothed down her skirts again.

As the soloist and orchestra stood to accept the cheers of the audience, Allegra felt her companion rise from his seat. She remained where she was to compose herself, however desperate she was to meet this stranger. At last she stood and turned and came face to face with him. Indeed this was not Barto. No, this was another, younger, stronger, more handsome . . . Allegra could not stop the flow of adjectives rushing into her thoughts. What an idiot, she chastised herself, for acting like a quivering schoolgirl. He reached for her hand and lifted it to his mouth. As he kissed it, she added 'soft-lipped and strong-fingered' to his list of attributes before she pulled herself together. It was the young Spanish cellist; she recognised him now. She was leaning forward slightly, her lips parted, an expression of what must have been childish expectation playing across her face, for he smiled as he stooped lower over her hand, which she tried without success to stop from shaking. After what seemed like a lifetime, he raised his eyes and spoke to her. It was almost inaudible above the clamour from the audience. Allegra could only think that it had sounded like, 'I want to fuck you.'

'I'm sorry?' she said weakly.

'*Allegro con fuoco*,' he said, and kissed her hand again. Allegra snapped back into focus now. She was not going to be reduced to a mute imbecile by such a young buck, however well he had just got to know her.

'Alive and fiery?' she mused. 'Are you referring to my name or the performance?'

'*Your* performance,' he said simply, pausing to hold her gaze. Then he took his leave. Allegra rarely found herself speechless. She stood there for a moment, perplexed. She hated unfinished business. After a second or two she straightened herself and strode out of the box towards the foyer where so many people – clients, friends and admirers – were waiting for her. She was aware of the sea of smiling faces that turned to her as she walked but she did not stop to greet them, nor did she slow her pace until she had reached her office. There she carefully closed the door and sat at her desk. She opened her laptop and began to compose an email to a Spanish agent:

Dear Carlos. It was ridiculous that we were unable
to find space in our programme for Joaquin de
la Fuente this year. As we are one of the most
important festivals in the social calendar and
he is obviously set to become one of our most
talented musicians we must ensure that we procure
him for next year. Please can we book him
immediately before anyone else gets their hands
on him? In fact, to be on the safe side, should we
pencil him in for the year after as well? I am sure
that it will prove to be a lasting relationship.
On a sadder note, I feel that Barto's long tenure
here may be coming to an end as he may have
given us all he can. May I get back to you once
I know what our commitments are?

Yours truly

Allegra

Essensual Reading

I f you are reading this side of our compendium then I assume you are in a softer frame of mind. So my mind conjures with what in Miss A.P.'s extensive library of erotica might satisfy your curious minds. There is a panoply of taboo-breaking sensual reads that have fuelled our darker moments but there is still enough on the shelves for us if we simply want to be tickled pink . . .

As I stroke the spines of my favourite texts, from the *Song of Solomon* through *The Delta of Venus* to *L'Armande* and beyond, my finger quivers with anticipation, all the more for knowing intimately the contents of each well-thumbed page. If your mood is more sex kitten than sex vixen, then may I recommend some passages you may have overlooked in your rush to find the naughtiest bits in the school library.

A quick hit has its place in my heart but, frankly, when looking for literary stimulation, the long slow burn often leaves the most lingering impression. I must profess that very little has haunted my hazy moments as strongly as the erotic undertones of nineteenth-century England. What can be more tantalising than the achingly slow foreplay between Mr Darcy and Elizabeth Bennett in *Pride and Prejudice*? A little over thirty years later, in the same year, two books were published that rocked Victorian sensibility to its crinolined core. Their effect still resonates today, indeed, the very teenage yearnings of Miss A.P. herself were shaped by the cruel obsessions, and that ever-present hint of danger, in the brooding sensuality of *Wuthering Heights*. The thwarted passion in *Jane Eyre* still has the power to light a thousand pyres on which countless schoolgirls have thrown their girlish innocence.

Of course there is countless classic erotica (such as the poems of Ovid and Sappho) that may light scholars' fires but would have trouble lighting the smallest scented candle in the sensually sophisticated girl's boudoir. For that, my eager readers, turn to the novel, whose birth ushered in a medium in which sensuality could work out its ardour. Ensure that you own one of the first examples: John Cleland's *Fanny Hill: or, the memoirs of a Woman of Pleasure* (1748–9). Every girl should have her as a friend on her bookshelf:

> *Her sturdy stallion had now unbutton'd, and produced naked, stiff, and erect, that wonderful machine, which I had never seen before, and which, for the interest my own seat of pleasure began to take furiously in it, I star'd at with all the eyes I had.*

Fanny was withdrawn from her ardent public not long after publication and didn't reappear (legally) for another hundred years in the UK. However, in the United States it was banned until 1959, along with DH Lawrence's *Lady Chatterley's Lover* (1928) and Henry Miller's *Tropic of Cancer* (1934). Lady Chatterley won't shock you today, but she could usefully prompt some very rousing Mistress-and-Servant fantasies. Read Henry Miller for a veritable fuck-fest, or, for more texture and 'description' (much to her anonymous patron's chagrin), turn to the prodigious outpourings of Miller's lover, Anais Nin:

> *Her blood was fired now. By his slowness he seemed to have done this, at last. Her eyes shone brilliantly, her mouth could not leave his body. And finally he took her, as she offered herself, opening her vulva with her lovely fingers, as if she could no longer wait.*

(Anais Nin, The Delta of Venus)

By the 1970s there had been a veritable explosion of the explosive read. Even the good girls knew *Emmanuelle* (1975) …

> *… she whimpered softly without knowing the exact cause of her distress. Was it the finger that was probing so deeply inside her, or*

the mouth that was feeding on her, swallowing each breath, each gasp? Was she tormented by desire or ashamed of her lasciviousness? She was haunted by the memory of the long, arched form that she had held in her hand, magnificent and erect, arrogant, hard, unbearably hot. She moaned so loudly that the man took pity on her. She at last felt his bare penis, as big as she had expected, touch her belly and she pressed against it with all the softness of her body.

During the last quarter of the twentieth century the marketplace became flooded, so browse the shelves of your nearest bookshop and take your pick. Our particular favourite of recent times is the anonymously authored *L'Armande*:

Lowering my panties, he put his cheek on my buttocks, spreading the crack with his fingers and making room for his nose. I was wet. Then he took a small flask from one of the shelves, removed a drop of oil, and perfumed my anus with it, massaging it for a long time, to the point that I forgot my trepidation and my muscles began to relax as his knowledgeable hands became more focused, I had no idea what he wanted to do to me but was wishing that he would just do it and certainly not stop the circular motion that was driving me wild, opening me up for him, as my vagina discharged its joy in long translucent strands.

The floodwaters of this kind of fiction, in the twenty-first century, seem just as unlikely to abate. Modern-day genres are growing. There is something for all tastes: harem, S&M, Coming of Age, homosexual – seek out, for instance, Jane Delynn's popular lesbian classic, *Don Juan in the Village,* whose heroine trawls the world looking for the much longed-for, ideal love, garnering sexual encounter after encounter of every imaginable kind in her (ultimately fruitless) search.

The recent growth in erotic literature, however, has left Miss A.P. yawning. Better writing for women should harness the essential elements of good literature: plausible point of view, empathetic character, well-crafted prose, narrative pace and imaginative plot. Many recent publications, which claim to wear the laurel crown for women's erotica, are, we often feel, little more than cynical publishing ploys that mistake 'shock' tactics for erotic drive. We prefer to get our literary thrills elsewhere – often hidden between the covers of literary fiction.

The story of repressed erotic love, for instance, caught up in the long, frustrated relationship between Ennis and Jack in Annie Proulx's *Brokeback Mountain* was beautifully portrayed in Ang Lee's film. The original short story, however, is a masterpiece of tight erotic prose:

> *A hot jolt scalded Ennis and he was out on the landing pulling the door closed behind him. Jack took the stairs two and two. They seized each other by the shoulder, hugged mightily, squeezing the breath out of each other, saying, son of a bitch, son of a bitch, then, and easily as the right key turns the lock tumblers, their mouths came together, and hard, Jack's big teeth bringing blood, his hat falling to the floor, stubble rasping, wet saliva welling and the door opening and Alma looking out for a few seconds at Ennis's straining shoulders and shutting the door again and still then clinched, pressing chest and groin and thigh and leg together, treading on each other's toes until they pulled apart to breathe and Ennis, not big on endearments, said what he said to his horses and daughters, little darlin'.*

The core of sexuality that burns through the pages of Michael Ondaatje's *The English Patient* may not bring the immediate relief that hard-core works will deliver, but the weaving of the female body with the exploration of a topographical landscape is powerful in the extreme. The themes of the book are summed up in Katherine's excruciatingly sad farewell letter:

> *We die rich with lovers and tribes, tastes we have swallowed, bodies we've entered and swum up like rivers. Fears we've hidden in – like this wretched cave. I want all this marked on my body.*

And hidden in many a manuscript is a piece of unique description that can inject new fantasies into your erotic play:

> *After some moments, he relinquished her hand and laid it down on her breast . . . He bent over her and took her foot in both his hands. He caressed the foot, seeming to examine every tender inch of it and then he moved very gradually towards it, holding her leg aloft for a moment, like a dancer's leg, and then reaching down and taking out his sex, which was erect, and then bending her knee and bringing her leg down until her foot touched his penis and then starting to rub*

himself against her foot. And now Harriet saw the habitual sadness
of his face transformed by an expression of pure wonder.

But if much of this is to you just so much milky froth that only double espresso will do, please turn immediately to page 105 of the Dark Side for darker essensual gratification. We leave you, however, with our favourite erotic literary ending: Molly Bloom's famous orgasmic soliloquy that finishes that otherwise often indecipherable work by James Joyce, *Ulysses*:

> *. . . I was a Flower of the mountain yes when I put the rose in my hair like the Andalusian girls used or shall I wear a red yes and how he kissed me under the Moorish wall and I thought well as well him as another and then I asked him with my eyes to ask again yes and then he asked me would I yes to say yes my mountain flower and first I put my arms around him yes and drew him down to me so he could feel my breasts all perfume yes and his heart was going like mad and yes I said yes I will Yes.*

Inside My Knicker Drawer

A s any of my followers will know, there are frequent missives posted on the website by our saucy agents around the globe. They have attracted quite a following (and a few copycats I can attest!). Here are a few of my favourites....

Love Miss A.P.

x

A Stormy Berlin Night . . .

Standing in front of my bedroom mirror half-naked and breathless with anticipation, my wild, dark hair is wet, messed up and clinging to my face. I have just run back home from the underground station in the thrashing Berlin winter rain, my Katy red shoes dependably getting me home in the downpour. My clothes are soaked through, but I don't care – I can't wait one more minute to try on my newest purchase, which has just arrived today.

Throwing off my storm-weathered dress and stockings (apart from my pearl necklace) I ceremoniously slip into the sleek dark-plum gorgeousness that is my new Nikita lingerie set. I stand there in the soft glow of my bedroom light, my olive skin slightly damp and am mesmerised. My breasts sit in my new bra like two ripe fruits ready for the plucking as my necklace slithers around my neck and chest like lithe fingers navigating itself around this undulating landscape.

I slowly start to place the string of pearls between my wet lips and am transported back to the memory of yesterday at work, where I had a sensual encounter with a darling young man who came into the shop. He had lingered by the A.P. shop front a few times before, but I had never really paid much attention to this tantalising creature with dirty blond hair and electric-blue eyes until that moment. I naively thought he was a cute but rather nervous customer plucking up the courage to come in and buy some sexy lingerie for his girlfriend.

Finally he strode up to the till point and asked if I could advise him on a fragrance; of course, as the professional A.P. girlie that I am, I obliged without hesitation. I volunteered my wrists to him, on one hand spraying the classic A.P. fragrance. He gently held my wrist in his hand and slowly raised it up to his nose, his lips briefly grazing my perfumed skin. I could see a tattoo peeping out at the nape of his neck; and anyone who knows this A.P. girl well enough knows how hot and bothered I get seeing ink on flesh, yum. I was enjoying the tingling sensation so much I immediately offered up my second wrist, generously spraying Maitresse upon it, to which he responded similarly.

Before he left he slipped a little square package into my hand and departed looking back at me with a naughty smile. On further inspection it was a music compilation CD he had made. The front cover won me over with the 1940s-style pumps and seam-and-heel stockings – certainly a man with taste. Looking at the CD inlay there written in black marker pen was his address and a time for that evening.

I spent the whole day counting down the minutes till I was off work in anticipation for the later encounter . . . . I mean, it would be rude not to turn up, right? OK, I was completely intrigued and greedily wanted more of that divine sensation he had left behind in his wake. Later that evening I made my way to the address, which was only a couple of blocks away from my own apartment.

It was a cold and windy evening; my dress kept blowing up over my legs as I entered the dark East Berlin apartment courtyard. As I mounted the creaky wooden stairs I could hear the echo of my shoes click-clacking against the boards and was accosted by the damp, cold smell of the stairwell. I checked the apartment number and slowly approached the door; it was already slightly ajar. Though there was a chilly draught blowing through the stairwell my body was warm with anticipation and my lips were tingling (I had also just applied some Titillation, which may have also contributed).

As for what happened after I entered his room, let's just say that the evening developed from the scintillating first encounter to sizzling second with hot, wet breaths against more than just my wrists. You never know, perhaps the lucky lad may have a third rendezvous that might include the official debut of my delicious new Nikita lingerie set . . . I'll get my paddle out just in case.

Kisses from Femme Fatale xxx

Santa, Baby . . .

There's something very distinguished and alluring about a gentleman of a certain age; especially if he has promised you the world if you would just be a good little girl for him! Easy – I'm always very, very good, I assure you! At what, I won't divulge at the moment. We're talking about something far more important, namely this older man in my life. He's got a style all of his own, his own business, and is generous to a fault if you do all he desires. I've written and received love letters, but this one takes up a little more time each year. Sean Connery will have to wait until the New Year to be back on my mind . . .

Dear Santa . . . Baby . . .

I realise that you may have already heard a rumour that I've been a naughty girl. Well, you and I know that, while this may be true, I'm naughty in the best way possible and that I truly deserve the Gwendoline corset with long Duchess gloves. I've been planning to wear them with the bottom half of my Nikita

set – you know, the suspender belt and cheeky ouverts? If this letter convinces you maybe I can show you?

I don't mean to tease the boys. Really, I don't! I've been an angel all year. I can't help what happens when I bend over to pick up something I've dropped, or when I stretch for something up high and one pesky button pops off revealing the latest edition to my (ever-expanding) lingerie drawer! What would you have me do? Think of all the fun I've missed trying to be good for you?

I suppose the best thing for me to do would be to wait to speak to you in person, Santa cutie. I do hope you'll be impressed by my newly trimmed . . . er, tree. I'll be waiting patiently on the bearskin rug by the fire with two glasses of VVSOP cognac to keep us both warm while we thrash it out. I utterly promise that I'll be good that night. I'll even make a special purchase just for you, and give you a lap(land!) dance in a black Top Hat quarter-cup string. You just promise me that, after you've peeled off my silk stocking, you'll fill it up?

Brianna O'Baby, Your Emerald Agent!

The Beautiful and the Damned

As a few of you may know, this Agent Provocateur lass is a sucker for all that is 1930s and 40s glamour and when the 'Swingin' Ballroom' dance evening came to Berlin last week it was the perfect excuse to do what I do best: dress up to the nines with my highest heels, my Ruby Woo red lipstick, and of course my foxiest Esme bra and knickers half-heartedly hidden underneath the silk ruffles of my Bordeaux red dance dress.

A.P. leaped at the chance when the opportunity came about for us to collaborate with the Admiralspalast theatre (in the heart of Berlin's bustling Mitte district) for a night dedicated solely to swing music, high fashion, and old-school sophistication. The recipe was 30s glamour, champagne galore, handsome men in tailored suits, beautiful women coiffed and preened, hours of live swing music, tap-dancers, an absinthe bar, cigarette girls and on top of that whole shebang a whole lot of A.P.

thrown into the mix. The result was a fabulously elegant if somewhat debauched evening.

The Admiralspalast theatre itself has an idiosyncratic history. During the 1920s and 30s it was a pleasure palace of sorts, hosting within its parameters a bathhouse, restaurants, a speakeasy, the world's first indoor ice-skating revue, and of course a grandiose Art-Deco theatre housing up to 1700 people at a time. Oh, and by the by, the surrounding area also had the highest concentration of prostitutes in Berlin. It was revamped and reopened last year at the same time as Agent Provocateur opened its first shop here in the city. Coincidence? I think not!

After hours of getting ready I met my fellow A.P. ladies at the theatre, where a table was waiting for us positioned in the centre front of the ballroom dance floor, with a bottle of champagne on ice just squealing for us to pop its cork. There were already pairs on the dance floor twirling and spinning around in a dizzying display of proficiency. I caught a glimpse of a couple of customers who had come into the shop earlier that day to purchase a few items for that night – now they were furiously dancing in their seam-and-heel stockings and suspender belts, which peeked out with every twirl. It was as if we had walked in on a scene directly taken from an F. Scott Fitzgerald novel.

On stage the star of the evening, Andrej Hermlin and his swing orchestra, churned out the tunes accompanied by our two beautiful A.P. representatives for the evening, Polly and Tallulah, who, appropriately, sat on swings on either side of the stage as the orchestra played. They swung seductively back and forth dressed in black Sandy bra and knickers, champagne-and-black seam-and-heel stockings and pompom mules. They were a pure visual treat, and as the swings were made of see-through Perspex, a cheeky (excuse the pun) glimpse of their derrières was the cherry on the cupcake.

I myself, in my gradual champagne-infused stupor, was gazing unashamedly in lovesick abandon at the most gorgeous creature that evening, a man known as Herr von Eden. He is the well-known designer of exquisitely tailored suits, with a string of boutiques in Berlin, Hamburg and Copenhagen. With his powdered face, jet-black hair

slicked into a side parting and pencil-thin moustache softly grazing the rim of delicate lips, I was lost. If this was *The Great Gatsby* then Jay Gatsby was standing right before me at that very moment.

The evening merrily meandered on with a spectacular performance from Miss Polly Rae, who was flown in from London by A.P. to perform for us at the event. She breezed on stage with her ruby-red lips against her porcelain skin and dark hair, strapped in tightly (by me!) into a one-off gold-edition Diva corset, then sang a breathy rendition of 'Through with Love'. She was a sight for sore eyes, all the gentlemen staring at her lustfully. Later that evening she treated everyone to a surprise striptease, provocatively peeling off the layers of her Jackie lingerie set as the A.P. logo was projected above on the blood-red velvet curtains behind her. At the end she stood there in her stockings, thong, black nipple pasties and a smile as the thousand-strong crowd cheered out for more in ravenous applause.

We neared the early-morning hours and the crowd slowly dwindled to the last fifty or so people, including myself, who were intent on dancing till the sun came up. I myself was impressed that I had managed to dance all night without falling over or slipping a disc in my new 12cm-high peep shoes, though I did have the support of a rather dashing young man who I wiled away the remnants of the evening with. I later found out that the gentleman I was swaying across the floor with for the last hour or so was actually a Latvian porn actor – what are the chances, hey?

The lingering memories of that evening left me with the thought that if F. Scott Fitzgerald were there that night, he would have noted that we truly were the 'Beautiful and the Damned'.

Femme Fatale

Wedding Belles

My undercover investigations recently took me to the very wicked Temple Bar where the best of British Beauties come to play for one last time before they get hitched! Inspired by the abundance of bars and nightclubs in Dublin's 'cultural quarter', gaggles of girls strut their stuff and spend most of their time doing what girls do best . . . shopping and socialising! Temple Bar, being notorious for its hen and stag parties, does not disappoint.

Whatever you 'stags' out there might do, nothing can compare to the lengths us girls will go to in order to stand out from the crowd! Think Britney Spears' bridesmaids in their matching pink-velour tracksuits following her nuptials to Mr Federline, and you will get my point! I even experienced this phenomenon as I tottered off the LUAS on my way to work at eight-thirty the other morning . . . and they had pink suitcases too! It's great fun to watch the ladies pass in their 'L plates' and veils. They terrorise groups of boys with their alcohol-induced games, and barely remember a thing the following morning.

That's when they come into our little Aladdin's cave, and where better to go than Agent Provocateur, in the finest department store Ireland has to offer, Brown Thomas. Especially now that we've come over all romantic (with a devilish twist!) and designed some of the most spectacular wedding lingerie and accessories a blushing bride could dream of? There is nothing I would love more than the thrill of seeing the look on my new husband's face as I peel off that virginal dress, only to reveal the super-sexy corset with my seamed white stockings! Or to just finish him off straight away with the ivory nipple pasties with baby-blue tassels, matching tulle tie-side briefs, and pompom mules?

We have a fantastic time here listening to sordid tales of previous nights as friends collect Swarovski-covered whips, innocent garters, and not-so-innocent ouverts. With bright smiles they regale us with stories about naked laps of their hotels, strippers, and much worse! You can't even have a quiet meal in Temple Bar without some sort of circus continuing around you. A fireman, who burst onto the scene as I sat in the Thunder Road Café enjoying dinner with a friend one evening, captured my attention. In front of the entire restaurant, and with the enthusiasm of a bride at a Vera Wang sale, he proceeded to disrobe . . . He didn't look like he was putting out any fires in the crowd the night I was there! Shrieks and hoots from the ladies told me that he and his banana sidekick were very much appreciated. I would love to have seen where those foxes ended up that night!

But Agent Provocateur does not let you rest once you have found your Adonis. We now have the fabulous Cupid maternity ranges for the aftermath! What would you do without us? Luxurious lingerie to lure him in, followed by a dash of ivory-white to make him glad he asked, and then a taste of Cupid to keep both your fires burning during those 'I-feel-like-a-basketball-has-attached-itself-to-me' months!

So congratulations and good luck to all of those taking the plunge, and be sure to keep us Dublin Agents posted on your naughty antics!

Until next time . . . live long and provocatively!

Briana O'Baby, Your Emerald Agent!

Esther's Hands

E sther was neither inordinately vain, nor proud of any part of her physique other than her beautiful hands. She had a general attractiveness that was without vanity or affectation, but when it came to her hands' care and maintenance she had always indulged time and attention. They were internally charged with a physical strength that was perceptible at the surface of the pearl-smooth skin and were elegantly weighted, with long-jointed, finely manicured fingers. She loved to stroke, rub and feel things and, correspondingly, since she centred her life around tactility, her flat was draped and furnished with tastefully coloured fabrics: plain damask, brocade curtains, chenille throws, raffia mats, linen coverings and, in her bedroom, raw wild-silk sheets. Her reading matter was similarly eclectic, being dictated by her attraction to vellum, calf and morocco-bound books.

It was as well that Esther was fortunate in this attribute since she worked as an assistant in an up-market gentleman's bespoke footwear shop in London's St James' area – a vocation that required a high degree of manual sensitivity. Her job, mainly, was to take the measurements of her client's feet, demonstrate a range of shoe leathers and styles and – if called upon during a fitting – to provide a brief yet vigorous foot massage, always conducted over the gentleman's woollen or silk stockings (according to the weather). Esther found her job rewarding and felt that, of the three assistants at the shop, hers was the most concerned and thorough service. The proprietor, Mr Dobbyns, was a clubbable man who rarely felt moved to visit his establishment before midday – if at all – and so was happy to delegate responsibilities to his well-remunerated staff.

Esther found many of the shop's gentlemen clients appealing and was particularly attracted to those men who maintained fastidious standards of tasteful grooming, which in fact was most of her customers. However, she was rather too meek and lacking in confidence to respond to the occasional hint (sometimes a strong hint) of a pass at her. Whereas Esther's professional efficiency sometimes made her appear remote (and perhaps led the men to believe she was being constant to a partner), in fact, she was generally disappointed in love and secretly longed for the thrill of passion. In her private moments she often caught herself indulging in the kind of fantasy which she very much doubted she could ever bring to realisation.

✳ ✳ ✳

One day at work her favourite, most valued and lavish customer came into the shop, a Mr Hinton, who was well established in the world of luxury imports. The very epitome of the poised, slightly dissolute 'silver fox', Esther would often enjoy engaging in conversation with Mr Hinton to draw upon his knowledge and love of exotic textiles and furnishings. He was a charming man with a rather suggestive, lascivious look around his twinkling eyes and, taken all in all, had something of the roué about him: a type Esther found alluring even if she was too demure to let on. However, she often caught a glance from Mr Hinton that seemed to imply that he could sense her hidden depths; that in fact, he considered her to be corruptible and perhaps, yes, why not, potentially depraved beneath her carefully contained surface.

Today, after a discussion of the relative merits of Kashmiran velour over traditional velvet (Mr Hinton opined that the latter was usually too heavy to be of much use), Esther sat him down and set to fetching the catalogues of shoe designs and a thick book of leather and suede samples. After some lengthy deliberation Mr Hinton ordered two pairs of expensive lightweight tan-calf Oxfords that he felt might be suitable for an upcoming business trip to the Far East.

Upon completion of the fitting and arrangements Mr Hinton, as usual, requested that Esther massage his feet. Retiring to a divan at the rear of the shop, Mr Hinton reclined while Esther pulled up a stool, took a stockinged foot to rest in her lap and set to, coaxing the muscular stress from it. As she rubbed and kneaded, Mr Hinton settled deeper in the divan and shut his eyes, a blissful smile of enjoyment occasionally flickering across his lips. Esther couldn't help but notice that her massage strokes were – at the ends of them – turning into sensual caresses and at one point Mr Hinton opened an eye and arched a brow as her hands wandered rather further up his trousers than was necessary.

Hastily changing feet, Esther started again, kneading Mr Hinton's instep. As her hands once more began to caress northwards inside the loose-fitting trouser leg, the palpitation of the lump in Mr Hinton's groin was impossible to ignore. The shop was spacious and fairly quiet and, furthermore, they were slightly obscured by a convenient marble counter, so Mr Hinton's growing arousal remained unnoticed. However, Esther felt that her ministrations had strayed too far from being a professional massage, even as she seemed to have lost the ability to direct the hands foraging inside Mr Hinton's trouser leg where they had now reached above the knee and were rubbing his inner thigh. Mr Hinton himself had reclosed his eyes and was affecting insouciance, even though his lips had slightly parted and his breathing had noticeably quickened.

Pulling herself to with a jolt, Esther managed to suddenly wrench her hands from Mr Hinton's trouser legs. As she did so, however, they froze in front of her in midair for seemingly ten seconds or more before descending with deliberation in an arc, to mould themselves to Mr Hinton's knees. He was wearing a beautiful light-wool flannelled suit and Esther marvelled at the texture and quality of the expensive cloth. In some turmoil, however, she attempted again to remove her hands from Mr Hinton's person, but to her startled dismay found they simply would not respond to her bidding. Indeed, they had resumed their soft, caressing motion over the surface of the trousers, working up the lithe, strengthened thigh and spreading in circular, sensual patterns of stroking.

By now, Esther felt she was losing control. Amazingly though, her intimacy with Mr Hinton was still unobserved by the other people in the shop (who seemed locked in profound discussion). Mr Hinton had sunk deep into the divan and Esther took a large gulp of air as her hands simply refused to remove themselves from his person. His penis was now fully and unmistakeably erect and he'd opened his eyes to lock with hers in a conspiratorial smile as if to dare her to continue her ministrations.

Sitting forward on her stool as her hands moved round to Mr Hinton's hips, Esther caressed inwards, over the luscious flannelled cloth, with slow deliberation to the tops of his inner thighs. As Mr Hinton shifted to open his legs slightly, she could feel his balls stirring beneath her thumbtips as if churning with agonising desire. From there, her palms brushed over his groin, softly stroking either side of his fly-flap that by now was bulging with the tumescent erection pullulating beneath it. Esther realised she was losing all restraint and she could feel her vulva swelling up against the cotton of her knickers. Placing each hand to rest either side of Mr Hinton's straining cock, she very gently stroked up and down his lower abdomen, her thumbs and index fingers pressed either side of his cock's shaft.

Mr Hinton groaned and Esther, terrified of discovery, once more attempted to throw herself back and away from him but still her hands remained as if glued. By now, though, she could feel her insides melting as she squirmed and rubbed her cunt against a corner of the stool. Esther decided in a moment of lucidity that hastening the situation to its resolution would be her best strategy of concealment and so she placed her right hand directly over Mr Hinton's cock and gathered it through the soft materials of his clothing in a firm clasp. As she did this, her left hand broke off – again with seeming autonomy – to yank her skirt up, pull aside her knickers and insert two fingers into her swollen, moist flesh.

Esther could feel her body tightening to propel her into an orgasm even as she furtively glanced behind her arched back to check that the shop was still oblivious to the tryst she was locked in. Her right hand was still stroking and pulling gently at Mr Hinton's cock from over his

trousers and she could sense that he was extremely close to release. Calibrating the stroke inside her knickers in time with that of the hand wanking Mr Hinton, she felt herself coil inside. Maintaining the regular rubbing rhythm, at the same moment that Mr Hinton's cock held its rigidity for a beat or two before tipping into a pumping action, her clitoris stiffened and she met him in climax, feeling waves of ecstasy rushing in tremors through her body as a darkening stain spread through the creamy-smooth, willow-grey flannel of Mr Hinton's pleated trousers.

✳ ✳ ✳

Esther was left feeling completely baffled by this encounter, since it seemed as if she had been somehow possessed during it; certainly she would not normally have considered acting in such a way even though, admittedly, she had occasionally fantasised along similar lines. It wasn't as if she was particularly repressed sexually: in her relationships, she'd felt she was quite an actively expressive partner. However, outside of the bedroom she had always aspired to restraint and moderation, traits which, along with propriety, she held to be healthy and desirable but certainly not erotic. She did not want to explore her sexuality outside a safe and appropriate setting and dreaded – much more than being discovered having public sex – the loss of self-control through pure lust.

One night over dinner with her best friend Amber, a far more sexually emboldened woman she turned to in such moments of hesitancy, Esther outlined her predicament whilst describing the peculiar sensation of losing control of her hands, quickly glossing the events in the shop featuring Mr Hinton. Amber laughed uproariously and, indeed, seemed to choke for some time after the climax of Esther's tale. Composing herself to pour out another glass of the Chablis they were sharing, Amber questioned Esther as to what on earth it was that could trouble her? OK, she had given a man a hand-job in the course of her day's drudgery, and as to losing control of her hands: well, consider the centuries past when 'wandering hands syndrome' was a tolerated, peculiarly masculine failing.

Time to catch up, said Amber; and if that meant taking matters into one's own hands (she couldn't restrain a giggle that was so infectiously

lewd that Esther simply had to join in) then so be it. Indeed, many was the time when she had espied a handsome stripling parked up against a bar and had simply marched over and ordered a drink while turning to face the fellow and cup his balls in her hand as a none-too-subtle signal for him to proceed to buy the drink for her. (It was unlikely that this strategy had ever failed since Amber was one of the most exquisitely poised and beautiful women on God's wide earth.) There followed a few choice tales from Amber as the bottle emptied that really set Esther purple with bashful confusion laced with something else . . . but what was it? Of course, she knew full well, even as she had to admit to herself: it was desire.

Not long after Esther's encounter with Mr Hinton (whose business trip, fortunately for her continued employment, had taken him to the Far East for six months or more), she had welcomed one of the shop's more esteemed, patrician customers and had actually patted his backside as he stepped up to the shoe-fitting area. The man, quite elderly although in stern health, seemed surprised at this gesture but had taken it in good humour while Esther had mumbled an apology and blushed down to her roots.

Nor were her roving hands limited to the shop's customers. A cinephile, Esther regularly went to see the latest films alone and one evening, soon after her hands had developed their peculiar autonomy, she found herself in a darkened, half-full cinema watching a newly released Samurai movie. This was her favourite film genre since she always received an erotic charge as the heavily armoured Samurai warrior – usually a darkly violent solitary figure – vanquished endless lines of opponents with his *katana*, the beautifully curved sword that was often ceremoniously unsheathed very slowly and which Esther longed to touch; to feel the cold, sharp metal of the blade. Midway through the film during a particularly protracted duel in a forest, Esther found the swift, athletic movement of the Samurai, wearing a compelling, grotesque mask, just *so* irresistibly visceral that her hands hitched her skirt up past her hips and sneaked inside her knickers, her fingers rubbing the tops of her inner thighs and masturbating the curves and lips of her pussy in time with the flashing swordplay.

While she did this, some innate sexual alert gave Esther an indication that a group of young men in the row behind were fully alert to her peccadillo, and this heightened her arousal as she climaxed, squirming and arching her back, hoisting her knees over the seat in front as her fingers probed and caressed her vulva, which contracted and sucked them in deeper. As soon as she had come, Esther quickly recomposed herself to abruptly exit the cinema, leaving the lithesome Samurai warrior literally suspended in midair.

✳ ✳ ✳

Another time after work Esther was on the usual packed and endless tube-ride home, pushed into a corner and spooned into a man behind her. Unable to turn enough to see the man's face, she could see, however, looking down, that his suit was of good-quality light cashmere and noted his rather prominent wedding ring. Despite gathering all her resolve not to do so, she let herself gradually lean a bit more heavily into the man than was strictly necessarily. After some time like this, Esther felt her hand reach behind her to rub the edge of the man's trouser-pocket flap between her fingers until, as the train lurched, she accidentally brushed against his fly-hole. As she murmured an apology from the corner of her mouth (she was still too tightly squeezed to look round), Esther felt the man slightly relax his posture, a small bashful movement which she instinctually took as an invitation for her to continue.

At the next station, even more people squeezed onto the train, and as it moved off Esther's hand reached stealthily behind her back and sought out the unknown man's engorged prick through the thin wool of his trousers, rubbing gently on it so that it stiffened further to become seemingly as hard as a metal bar. All the while, the man's passiveness gave no indication to the surrounding passengers as to what was occurring, which served only to embolden Esther further. Desisting for the pause at the next station (where, again, no one got off) until the train recommenced, Esther realised she was now in a high state of excitement as she reached behind her to rub the man's cock through his trousers again.

Pressed back by the crowd, she pushed her other hand into the pocket of her own suit trousers which, she now discovered, had a

fortuitous small hole (which she'd meant to have mended) that allowed an unobstructed finger to push the elastic of her knickers aside and to press and flick at her clitoris. As the train rocked, Esther's hand behind her back unzipped the man's trousers where, to her delight, she discovered that he was wearing a pair of gossamer-thin, silk boxer shorts. A small button clasped the opening of the shorts but Esther dextrously undid this, slipped her fingers between the silk and grasped the man's penis like a stolen jewel which, illogically, felt simultaneously both diamond-hard and meaty to the touch.

Esther held the man's cock inside his silk pants for more than a minute as the carriage shunted about whilst also fingering her cunt in sway with the train. After steadily wanking the man for a while, she reached further behind to caress and fondle his balls as lightly as her feverish fingertips could manage. The disruption of stopping and starting the man's masturbation continued for several more stations, each one a maddening, teasing interruption of her hand's regular stroke, until, finally, during an extended sway around one of the tunnels' lengthier curves, Esther felt the man's first spurt of hot ejaculate squirt up her wrist and she could feel him squirm behind her, attempting to hide the wild inner excitation that was gaining release through spunking all over Esther's one hand whilst, through the hole in her pocket, she felt her own sex juice gushing over the fingers of the other.

At the next station, Esther pushed through the crowd to leave the train and wait for the next one, resisting the urge to turn and see the man's face: somehow, the encounter seemed perfect in its anonymity and she marvelled at her audacity as she wiped the man's still-warm come off her hands – her uncontrollable hands – with a silk handkerchief.

❋ ❋ ❋

Esther's employer, Mr Dobbyns, was an avuncular, bibulous man who despite rarely visiting his premises could not help but notice, when he eventually did, that Esther seemed to have recently discovered a well of confidence and poise that, consequently, had seen her sales overtake that of her two fellow employees. Taking Esther aside one day Mr

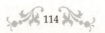

Dobbyns asked her for an opinion on the quality of a recent batch of silk hosiery that had been delivered from Japan. Esther had been struck lately by the decline in the quality of the cloth and gave Mr Dobbyns her considered opinion that the gentlemen's socks, particularly, were not of their previous quality.

'Exactly,' said Mr Dobbyns. 'We need someone to go over there and check what's going on with our suppliers in Tokyo. I simply can't make any headway trying to speak to the merchants over the phone. The whole thing would be much simpler if we sent someone over there. You could use your discernment either to buck-up the current lot, or to find a new outlet. So will you do it, my dear?'

Esther was taken aback. A visit to Japan to visit silk factories and select the cloths for Dobbyns' celebrated gentlemen's undergarments? Of course, she assured her employer, the whole thing was incredibly exciting and she'd be delighted to do everything she could to make s ure that the Dobbyns standard reverted to its former excellence!

'Super!' said Mr Dobbyns. 'We have one of our revered customers – Mr Hinton, you know? – out there at the mo and he'll help to get you around and provide new contacts if needed . . .'

Esther assured her employer that she would indeed sort the predicament out and did he have a date in mind for her to embark to Japan?

'Well, my dear,' said Mr Dobbyns, 'I was rather hoping you might be available to leave tomorrow, instead of coming in to the shop?'

✳ ✳ ✳

'Oh, for God's sake,' drawled Amber at the emergency kitchen summit that Esther had called for that night as the cork popped from the second bottle. 'Just what the fuck is wrong with you? You have flight tickets to Japan leaving tomorrow afternoon, you have an all-expenses-paid trip to Tokyo for a week to fanny around the silk shops picking bits of cloth . . . and the only problem is that you have to meet up with some guy that you fancy? Please tell me you snatched the damn tickets away with half of old Dobbyns' hand!'

Esther looked down at her own hands. She considered Amber's jocular words carefully. Yes, she had indeed accepted the task of going to Japan, had collected her flight tickets and her case was half-packed. But she was also due to meet up with Mr Hinton and, given the developments at their last encounter, she felt some trepidation and embarrassment about doing so.

'Look,' Amber continued, 'just go there, pick your itsy-bitsy bits of cloth, let Mr Stinking-Rich Hinton lavish you with gifts and, if the move strikes, give him a good seeing-to. And if not, then not, darling!'

Esther stroked the rim of her tulip glass with an index finger until it sang an exquisite, pure note. Straightening her back and lifting her head she looked straight into Amber's eyes for the first time since beginning this evening's angst-a-thon. Esther smiled winningly for a moment before frowning and looking down at her hands. 'Mmm,' she said, 'I wonder if the cherry blossoms are out at this time of year?'

✳ ✳ ✳

Esther felt that the endless, bewildering suburbs of Tokyo were the nearest thing imaginable to being teleported to a distant planet as a taxi took her to the accommodation that Mr Dobbyns had booked and which, typical of his generosity, turned out to be a luxury hotel in the heart of the Shibuya district. As she checked in, the concierge handed her a note from Mr Hinton proposing that she meet him for dinner during her visit and would she call him to arrange it.

Esther put a decision about meeting Hinton on hold as she spent the next few days in paradise, visiting the textile markets of Kiryu and the Raw Silk Exchange in Yokohama. At the latter, she had revelled in a day of sensual onslaught as she felt and stroked hundreds of cloths from the sheerest gossamer fabric to the roughest, rawest silk imaginable. At one point, a draper had pulled down a ream of silk and spilled it to the floor for Esther's delectation: a beautiful oyster colour, its texture was pure cream and it was all that Esther could do not to strip her clothes off, dive to the floor and roll around in it. She resolved at one peak point to form a company – perhaps with Amber? – and make her fortune importing these astonishing textiles to London. The practical business, to locate a double-weave silk suitable for manufacturing gentlemen's socks, was in fact easily concluded after locating a merchant who spoke English and who was appalled at the scribbled prices and the quality of the sample from Mr Dobbyns' previous supplier.

On the fifth day, enjoying her trip immensely, Esther finally called Mr Hinton and arranged to meet for dinner. She arrived in a clinging silk dress that she'd bought that morning, a rather more flattering garment than she was used to, accentuating her waist before softly falling down to just above her knees. The dress was of a pearl grey and so light that despite its discretion, it revealed Esther's supple curves and held her breasts so well that she'd decided not to wear a bra. And so she felt almost naked upon greeting Mr Hinton at the appointed sushi restaurant that had recently been awarded three Michelin stars. Shown to a beautifully spartan private room they kneeled at their low table as women in traditional kimonos served up an astonishing train of over thirty miniature courses, one after the other: seared belly tuna, marinated clams, sea urchins, spider-crab legs and – Mr Hinton assured her since his Japanese was excellent – an octopus's appendix, each dish more delicate and elegant than the last.

During this amazing repast the conversation with Mr Hinton was relaxing and pleasant and he had managed to make her feel at ease. An attentive listener, he was particularly encouraging concerning Esther's plan (sketchily outlined) to found a silk emporium in London. The saki was kicking in a little and at one point, as Mr Hinton leaned over to enumerate the ingredients in a particularly elaborate dish, Esther felt her hand jump up and brush over his wrist. Mr Hinton was gentleman enough to overlook this, since she had blushed so deeply, and conversation quickly returned to all things Japanese; Esther, lightening somewhat, confessed her love of Samurai cinema. There followed a learned and entertaining history of that clan during the Edo period from Mr Hinton, and Esther caught herself marvelling at what a wonderful evening she was having, quite the most convivial she had ever enjoyed.

Eventually, Mr Hinton called for the hostess of the restaurant and paid the astronomical bill while speaking to her in Japanese. Esther couldn't help but notice that the hostess giggled slightly before beaming

at her in apparent amusement. As she went off, Mr Hinton requested that they remain a little longer and taste a particularly rare Japanese liqueur and perhaps, yes, to watch a little floor show, a traditional demonstration that the hostess had now gone to arrange for them.

Intrigued, Esther remained to sip at her liqueur. The conversation had just returned to Japanese feudalism and the Shogunate when she caught herself looking into Mr Hinton's eyes and smiling conspiratorially as they re-experienced the erotic charge of their encounter in the shoe shop. And then, suddenly, a door sprung open to one side. To Esther's utter astonishment two Samurai warriors in kimonos marched into the room. Bowing low to each other, they stood off before blindfolding themselves by a black velvet ribbon beneath their satiny top-knotted hair. As Esther watched in astonishment they set to, flashing their *katana* swords about, seemingly locked in some sensory, muscular argument since they appeared to rely purely on the sound of the sword's *swoosh* in order to dodge it. Clearly this wasn't a fight to the death but a demonstration of swordsmanship, and in between lunging at each other in the close room, the warriors would toss a silk kerchief above them and blindly slash about, cutting it in half.

Esther was quite overcome by this display, feeling a return of that curious itching surge in her hands and, more pointedly, an exciting enervation in her groin. Still, the Samurai warriors flashed and clashed their swords together with unnerving synchronicity, quite dangerously close to Esther and Mr Hinton in the small room. One extended salvo seemed impossibly thrilling until, with an almighty swish, one of the warriors missed his fellow's blade and slipped with his sword so that it nicked the tip of Esther's shoulder. Startled, Esther watched as a thin trickle of blood seeped from her shoulder and ran down the silk cup of her dress, over her breast, to form a drop of blood hanging from her nipple. The Samurai, having removed their blindfolds, conferred in rapid, guttural Japanese, seemingly castigating each other for the missed stroke. Mr Hinton leaned over the table in concern, but Esther waved him away.

At the moment the blade had made contact, Esther had felt the curious, lustful sensation in her hands that she'd had before and she

was amazed to watch a finger lift, point to the Samurai who had cut her, and crook and flex at him in the universal sign of beckoning. The warrior did as he was bidden and came over to kneel before Esther. Looking into his eyes, Esther slipped her shoulder strap down to reveal her breast; taking the Samurai's head in her hand she lowered his mouth onto her bloodied nipple, which he began to lick and kiss. As he did so, Esther felt her other hand steal to the sword at his side and she could feel her excitement rising as she stroked the cold metal blade of the Samurai's *katana*.

Mr Hinton moved to the side of the room for a more advantageous view and looked on in amazement, since it was intended that this be a titillating floorshow only, a piece of mild erotica between two actors that he knew could be added to the evening's fare and which had been quickly arranged by the restaurant's hostess for Esther's and his delectation. Evidently, Esther realised from his expression and with some surprise that Mr Hinton hadn't expected the exhibition to take this turn, to go quite this far. But still, her hand slipped from the *katana* to steal slowly between the gap in the bowed warrior's kimono, where she discovered him to be naked, feeling between his thighs to cup his balls.

After some minutes, Esther's hand beckoned to invite the other Samurai to come over too and, standing both of them before her, motioned them to shed their kimonos, before squatting to sit perched on the edge of the table before them. Reaching out to the naked warriors, Esther gathered the Samurai's stems to her. At the periphery of her vision she was aware that Mr Hinton was watching avidly, hawklike, as she took both men into her mouth.

After sucking the Samurai in this manner for a time, by now utterly aroused, Esther popped the cocks from her mouth and, turning, leaned over the low table, her hands hitching her dress up and yanking her knickers down. The first warrior (who had accidentally cut her) took a kneeling position behind Esther and pushed his cock between her legs, entering her slowly to fuck with long sweeping strokes. As he did so, her hand reached between and behind her own legs to cup his balls and then stretch a finger, inserting its tip into the Samurai's anus as he stayed constant, fucking her with deep, sinuous thrusts. The texture just

inside the Samurai's rectum had the slightly moist sleekness of satin and she felt his sphincter muscles relax as his cock swelled up to a final surge, and he pushed her further across the table as Esther dug the nails of her free hand into his muscular buttocks that were filmy with sweat, pulling him into her as he stroked her arse in turn and came deep inside her convulsing cunt.

Remaining prostrate over the table, Esther was still drawing breath as her hand beckoned to the second warrior to replace his mate. Obediently, he came over to adopt a kneeling position behind and between her thighs. Esther reached behind her, grasped his cock and pushed it inside her. Looking to her side she met Mr Hinton's eyes and, since he looked back kindly and admiringly, she could see he was enjoying the spectacle very much. Licking a forefinger again, Esther reached behind through their legs to press and circle the rim of the Samurai's anus in rhythm with her other hand that now was urgently rubbing her clitoris as the man fucked her with mounting, tempestuous urgency. If the expenditure of the second coupling was of comparable brevity to the first, it was of no less intensity as Esther pushed her finger deeper into the Samurai's arse while they fucked quicker and harder, knocking the crockery from the table about them as they came together while Mr Hinton looked on admiringly. Very evidently, he once again had a dark stain spreading in the front of his trousers.

❋ ❋ ❋

At the airport, Esther was about to head into Departures after thanking Mr Hinton for his hospitality and guidance during the visit. He had assured her that he would indeed pursue some contacts to facilitate her in setting up a company with Amber. Esther was glad to hear this but felt awkward and bashful, half-wondering if the outrageous events of the night before were all a private fantasy that hadn't truly happened. However, Mr Hinton rested a hand on her arm and spoke softly to her: 'My dear, last night you gave a worldly, mature man the most thrilling ride of his life! I thank you from the bottom of my heart for allowing me to witness such an exquisite display.'

Esther kissed Mr Hinton on the end of his foxy nose, smiled sweetly, sighed, and turning, strode towards the Departures lounge, deciding at that moment, in fact, to set up her own business independently of either Mr Hinton's or Amber's assistance since, quite literally, she felt that she held the whole wide, blessed world in her own hands.

How To ... Do It

S o you have read some of these erotic tales. Go on. Admit it. In your mind's eye you put yourself in their place, didn't you? You imagined what it would be like; wondered how it would feel, how it would taste. You did. I know you did.

In your own head you can go anywhere, do anything, create fireworks! But, in real time, are you the star of your own show? Do you have what it takes to induce a night, a day or, let's aim high, a week of unrestrained, mind-blowing passion? Of course you do. But it's surprising how many of you allow yourselves to be rushed headlong towards the main event without so much as a tickle or a kiss. Shame on you, girls! I have heard you complaining to each other about your lovers' lack of attention in certain areas, yet have you really made it clear what works for you? Have you whispered it in their ear? Have you shown them? Truthfully now: do you really (really) know what you need?

Don't answer that. I will save you the embarrassment and assume that you know all the basics. Of course you do . . .

The most important tool in your box of tricks is confidence; indeed if that's *all* you've got you can still get a long way. What else might you need? Good girl: imagination and an open mind. Add a sense of adventure to the mix and heaven's the limit. But variety being what it is,

I would always advocate having a few tricks up your sleeve (or in your drawer). Here are three that work rather well . . .

How to Talk Dirty

Never done it? Take your lips to their ear, close your eyes and say what you would like to hear. Whisper. Guide them. Urge them. Plead with them.

Try it.

'Cup my breasts . . .'

'Lick my nipples . . .'

'I love it when you fuck me.'

'Oh, please fuck me . . . please fuck me . . . please fuck me.'

Or a particular minxy favourite of mine: 'Oh, please don't! Stop! . . . Oh, please . . . don't! Oh, stop! Oh, please . . . please . . . please don't stop! Oh!'

Naughty Miss A.P. Tell me I am a naughty girl. I am a very naughty girl. Are you going to spank me?

How to Give a Good Spanking

Learn to invite your punishment: have I been a bad girl?

If you want to take it further than a smarting thwack across the buttocks before your lover penetrates you from behind, then find time to discuss your needs and your limits a long time before you invite your punishment. Where can they strike? Where can't they? What level of pain is truly pleasurable and what is not? And decide on a safe word or signal in advance so that anyone can stop at any time – should they want to. And essentially, don't use the word 'stop' as a safe word (for reasons which I am sure that you understand).

Let's formalise this. I like the whole ritual.

Tell me to take off my clothes. And fold them.

Insist I assume the position. Buttocks must be bared and available! Across your knee . . . bending over the kitchen sink . . . lying over the billiard table? Your choice.

Perhaps you might spank me through my clothing first to show me your intention, but once you hit my bare flesh I will at first feel the pleasurable warm tingles as the skin reddens and smarts. Keep the rhythm even, the strokes light. Then just as I am beginning to relax into my punishment, vary the pace. Surprise me. Shock me. Then tell me to take it.

Spank me harder. But keep me guessing.

Now tell me why I deserve it.

Next time it's your turn.

How to Give a Good Blow-job

Look him in the eye. Tell him, without words, what you intend to do.

Don't apologise – use your tongue to trace a trail to his shaft. The wetter the better.

Enjoy the theatre – you have to be invisibly visible. There is nothing more off-putting than a lot of show or a lack of enthusiasm. Imagine you are making your own video, crouch like a tiger but don't look as if you will bite! You've got to create a carefully designed balance between dominatrix and servant of pleasure: get that right and you can err on either side to great effect.

Use your hands, as well as your mouth, lips and tongue. Don't just suck. And certainly don't blow! Lick him, breathe upon him, cup his balls, hold him in your mouth. Most importantly, reassure him that you revere his cock (and, by the way, if you don't, you should – *seriously*) but don't let him get complacent – you should always retain the edge. After all, you are in control here; use it, or lose it.

And please, I am not interested in any argument of whether you spit

or swallow. Such conversations really are beneath you. Anyway, a girl has to have a few secrets.

While we are down here: a useful string to your bow . . . Learn how to place a condom in your mouth with the tip facing inwards and position it behind your teeth. Press your tongue against the tip. Lower your head onto his cock and, using your tongue, press against the head so that the latex covers it. Tease him a little by running your tongue over the head. Keep the condom in place with your tongue and pull your teeth back, letting the ring fall from your lips. Push it down as far as you feel comfortable, taking his engorged shaft to the back of your throat. Finish by stroking the condom down with your hands if you prefer, using your tongue elsewhere as you (and he) please.

Realisation

So, what now? Dress for success: as thousands of erotic works concur, the appearance of the semi-clad body is often more arousing than the naked flesh. Everybody loves to unwrap a present.

Take that final look in the mirror; aim that puff of scent at your well-maintained cleavage and . . .?

Go and work your magic upon your heart's desire.

Well? What are you waiting for?

'Perfect'

Lena had spent the twenty-five minutes since she woke up in a dazed panic of showering and throwing together a passable work ensemble, but as she approached the front door of her apartment she slowed down. She paused for a moment, centring herself. Then with a satisfied smile, she slipped each of her bare feet slowly, delicately into the brand-new stiletto heels that were standing elegantly, like sentinels, in the hallway. She straightened up and looked down admiringly at the crisscrossing straps of bottle-green leather against her caramel-brown skin. OK, so perhaps they had been a touch out of her normal price bracket, but sometimes a girl has to indulge herself. Grabbing her bag, she slammed the door behind her, grinning at the way the shoes seemed to coax her into sashaying down the stairs.

The morning sunlight streamed in between the buildings like it only ever does in New York City. Lena strode down the familiar SoHo streets briskly, while taking appreciative deep breaths of the warm summer air. It was going to be another hot one, she could tell already. She was grateful that her office building was only a few blocks from her apartment, and decidedly more air-conditioned. As she rounded the corner in front of her office, she caught sight of her striding reflection in the glass front of her favourite boutique. The shop window was elegantly bedecked in lacquered black, framing an envy-inducing skimpy ensemble arranged on a mannequin. She shrugged – at least her legs were looking fabulous in these new heels. Just as she was formulating a plan to swing back by the store at lunchtime, a cigarette butt rolled over, narrowly missing her toes. She looked up, irritated, but her frown was ironed out by the sight of a tall, artfully dishevelled specimen of manhood leaning against the wall a little way ahead. He had clearly flicked the still-smouldering stub, but he didn't apologise. Instead, he ran an entirely undisguised gaze up and down her slim physique as she walked past and into the building.

She felt like she'd been struck with an almost physical jolt of electricity. Part of her had wanted to fire off a sharp remark towards him – the kind she usually reserved for wolf-whistling road workers – but on this occasion something about the guy held her back. She quickly shook the strange feeling off as she got out of the elevator and pulled open the opaque glass doors of the upmarket real-estate bureau, Mandeville Klein.

'Hi Marta,' she called as she breezed past the reception desk towards her office.

'Lena, babe, hold up. You have someone coming up to see you for a preliminary.'

'No. C'mon, seriously?'

Lena stopped, rolled her eyes and swivelled on her heel back to Marta's desk. The receptionist nodded.

'I'm afraid so. They're on their way up right now, actually. I guess Jeff must have arranged it last night after you left . . .'

'Does he not realise how crazy my client list is already? He can't keep dumping this shit on me.'

'Sorry, doll, I tried to tell him.' Marta grinned, in a manner that suggested she hadn't tried particularly hard. She shrugged, handing over the files to Lena. Then she leaned in with a conspiratorial air.

'Actually, Le? Apparently this guy asked for you *specially*.' Giggling, she leaned back, snapping some gum that had been hidden between her back teeth. Great, Lena thought, another sweaty business suit with

a rundown of mundane 'must-haves' for a serviced apartment block. Scooping up her things, she hurried into her office to straighten up before the client arrived. A moment later, the intercom buzzed. She jumped.

'Ms Scott?'

'Yes, Marta.'

'Mr Murphy is here to see you now. Shall I send him in?'

'Yes, please do, thanks Marta.'

Lena frowned at the intercom – there was something a little odd about the way Marta spoke, as though she was barely containing some kind of smirk. Lena shook her head and took a swig of the day-old glass of water that sat next to her computer, her face twisting into a grimace just as her door opened. She nearly choked.

There, framed in the doorway, was the Cigarette Guy.

He almost had to stoop to fit inside it, he was so tall. There was not even the slightest suggestion of a suit – he was dressed almost head-to-toe in faded black to match his short, ruffled hair. Black T-shirt, thin cotton brushing against his torso, slender but muscular, tanned arms emerging from the sleeves. Worn-looking jeans filled out just right, like a second skin. Scuffed brown boots picked out the warm brown of his large, penetrating eyes. As Lena stared, struggling to find her voice, he stepped inside the office and proffered a sinewy, strong-looking hand.

'Ms Scott? I think I saw you outside, didn't I? I'm Cole. Cole Murphy. I hope they let you know I was coming to see you?'

He looked back over his shoulder inquiringly. His voice was deep, like burned oak and honey. He had a thick Irish brogue. Lena attempted to clear her throat.

'Sorry, yes, come on in. Sorry.' She cringed at her flustered speech. Taking a deep breath, she remembered where she was and started again.

'Mr Murphy. Yes, I'm afraid I haven't had a chance to go over your

requirements. Perhaps you could run me through what you're looking for?'

'Well, I need a new apartment, is the long and short,' he exhaled, slumping into the seat opposite her desk. 'Something with a bit more space. My lawyer, Harvey Sampson, said he'd used you.'

Lena only vaguely recalled the client, and she was a little pissed off at this guy's general air of arrogance. Still, she began to nod – but Cole cut her off.

'And I've seen you around here. You've usually got some other rich bastard trailing after you, looking positively overjoyed that you're about to take a hefty percentage on his overpriced real estate. I thought I might like to join that club.'

At that, Lena's eyes flicked up from her computer screen. Her delicate features tightened defensively, but her look betrayed a certain curiosity despite her growing annoyance. Cole gave a short chuckle and shook his head, his gaze remaining locked on her.

'Not to worry, Ms Scott. I'm not a stalker. It's just an occupational hazard. I make art, so when something . . .'

He paused, leaning forward.

'. . . or *someone,* catches my eye, I can't help but take notice. Particularly when it's right across the street from my studio.'

Suddenly his name clicked in Lena's mind – *Cole Murphy*. She had seen posters with his name up all over the area; he'd had a show at a gallery nearby. She'd caught his eye? Lena shifted in her seat. Heat seemed to be radiating from him, across her desk and over her body. She did her best to ignore it. Instead, she slowly leaned back in her leather chair, crossed her long legs, and returned his stare.

'Right. I thought your name sounded familiar, Mr Murphy.'

He doffed an invisible cap, his gaze relentless. A wry smile spread across Lena's face.

'Well, I'm not going to lie – those gentlemen certainly are satisfied by

the time they part with their cash.' She hadn't meant to sound so suggestive. Somehow it just came out that way.

'So, Mr Murphy. What kind of space are you interested in?'

✳ ✳ ✳

At 8.45 a.m. the next day, the sun was already burning hot. Lena rounded a side street towards the factory conversion that contained the first apartment she was planning to show the enigmatic Mr Murphy, but found he had beaten her there. Twenty charged seconds passed as Lena strode towards him in what felt like slow motion, smoothing down her sleeveless, belted dress. But despite the echo of her heels against the pavement in the quiet of the morning, he kept his gaze, cloaked in dark, retro-looking sunglasses, straight ahead. His lean frame rested against the large iron door to the building and a cigarette, almost burned down to the filter, nestled between his lips. He held a pad in one hand, a pencil poised above it in the other.

As she reached where he was standing, she noticed that the paper was blank.

'Nothing inspiring you this morning, Mr Murphy?' she said in an even tone. She was determined that today she wouldn't let being in his vicinity muddle her.

Cole held up his hand and turned towards her by way of response. He was so close that the end of his cigarette was only inches from her face. Without saying a word, he took a step back, and then ran the pencil quickly across the page, nodding to himself. She couldn't really tell where he was looking behind the blacked-out lenses of his sunglasses. Finally, as Lena stood regarding him, arms folded and portfolio tucked under one arm, he spoke.

'You can call me Cole, you know. Ms Scott.'

She nodded.

'OK. I'll remember that. Are you ready to go in?'

'Absolutely, Ms Scott.'

She retrieved the keys from her handbag and opened the main door to the building. She started to go in, but noticed he was waiting, pulling down his sunglasses a fraction and looking up at her from underneath dark eyelashes. She turned back around to disguise her spreading grin.

'Call me Lena,' she said.

As they walked up the steep concrete steps to the third floor, they stayed silent. The sound of footsteps reverberated up the stairwell until they reached the door of the apartment, both panting slightly from the effort. Lena could smell the scent of Cole's laundry detergent as the warmth rose off his skin and through his T-shirt, mingling with the oddly intoxicating smell of his sweat and cigarette smoke. Almost unconsciously she lingered for a moment, breathing him in before opening the door.

The space was cool, dark and empty. Lena stepped aside and gestured for Cole to go in ahead of her. He crumpled his pad in half and nestled it into his back pocket, slipping the pencil behind his ear absent-mindedly. As soon as he entered, he began shaking his head. Lena had flipped open her leather portfolio binder and was about to start pitching, but stopped short.

'What do you think?' she asked. She tried not to stare too hard at the triangle of tanned chest that appeared as Cole tucked his sunglasses into the neck of his T-shirt.

'No. It doesn't feel right. Something about it's not . . .' As he walked back towards her a couple of steps, his voice trailed off. He seemed suddenly distracted. Lena stood blinking at him, one hand resting on her hip, keeping her expression neutral. He frowned slightly at her then sighed quietly and looked away. She noticed a tiny trickle of sweat inching over the muscles in his neck, and found that her tongue was tracing across the roof of her mouth, like a reflex. The air felt thick. He looked up at her again, and then cleared his throat.

'Well, as I stand here I think it might be growing on me . . . maybe just a little?' He raised an eyebrow at her. 'But it just feels like it's not quite right. A little bit too cold.'

The corner of Lena's mouth twitched ever so slightly, but she nodded.

'No problem, Mr Murphy. Cole. I have one or two others that perhaps might be more suitable. Perhaps tomorrow lunchtime –'

She thought she saw a faint look of disappointment cross his face as he cut her off.

'Sure. Tomorrow lunchtime. Send me the details.'

And with that, he put his sunglasses back on and strode past her out of the apartment and down the stairs.

✳ ✳ ✳

Lena broke into a trot as she realised the time. She said a silent thanks to the weather for suggesting her wedge sandals, with their secure ankle straps – far more conducive to running than her usual footwear. Still, she reached the building ten minutes later than they had scheduled. To her surprise, Cole was nowhere to be seen. Breathless, she took the opportunity to gather her loose curls away from her face for a moment, fanning herself with her portfolio case.

'Mmm. It is hot, isn't it?'

His deep voice, straight into her ear. It made her jump, and she stumbled slightly. Cole reached out to catch her, one hand on her elbow and the other on the small of her back. She wriggled self-consciously, feeling the damp through her cotton dress. He pulled his hand away and ran a finger suggestively across his lips, licking them briefly with a devilish smile. It did nothing to help cool Lena down.

'I'm feeling better about this one already,' he said after a moment. He squinted up at the brown brick building.

The apartment was on the ground floor, a warehouse-style open-plan inside which Lena's own place could have fitted in twice over. She felt certain that the space would be more than enough for a single guy. Though she suddenly frowned – she had, after all, only been assuming that the apartment would be just for him. She found herself suddenly impatient. As she watched Cole wander around the apartment, studying its nooks and crannies, she heard her agitated voice echoing out

through the vacant space, in spite of herself.

'Perhaps you could let me know if this is something approaching the type of thing you're looking for. Or would you prefer something completely different?'

The question hung in the air as Cole turned and looked back at her. She immediately felt wrong. Her heart was pumping fast. It was like she was rushing something more than just his decision on the apartment and she wished she could take the last moment back. But Cole seemed to sense this too. He walked up to her silently, his brow furrowed. With the back of his hand, he slowly, very gently, brushed down the length of her bare arm. Blood seemed to be pulsing around her body so hard her skin felt like it was vibrating, and the ache of his physical touch sent a shimmering energy down her core and into . . .

'You're right,' he said. 'This isn't it.'

✳ ✳ ✳

Dusk, three days later. Lena had shown Cole four more apartments. In each one, he found some flaw. As she approached each building to meet him, Lena felt a growing sense of frustration that was definitely more than concern over her commission. But she couldn't quite put her finger on it. She had been nothing more than utterly professional with him, but somehow every time she was near Cole, she felt as though she was like a synchronised swimmer – making graceful movements above the water whilst kicking furiously below.

She drew close to the last building on her list, and nerves danced in her stomach. If this wasn't the one, then there was every possibility that Cole would decide to go elsewhere – that whatever was happening between them would end. They arrived at the block almost simultaneously. Cole leaned over and kissed Lena on the cheek. It could easily have been passed off as a friendly client greeting – she had, after all, been showing him properties all week. But the spark of panicky excitement that Lena felt course through her indicated that wasn't all it meant.

The apartment was a penthouse, and so, amid some unusually polite chitchat, they entered the old-fashioned elevator together. The gates slammed shut with a loud bang, and just at that moment, Cole leaned forward and whispered something in Lena's ear, something she couldn't quite make out. But she thought he said . . .

I don't know if I can take this much longer.

She turned around, feeling her chest rising and falling, her eyes locked dead into his. Suddenly the elevator jerked to a halt. They had reached their floor. She turned back again and undid the gates, feeling Cole's breath ever so slightly tickling the nape of her neck. She broke away and stepped into the apartment. Despite having the specs in her binder, even she was slightly taken aback.

Stretching from the floor to the ceiling in the open-plan living space was a series of enormous windows, exposing a breathtaking view of the city beyond. The floors were warm dark wood; the sound of their footsteps almost sank into it. Lena strode towards the windows in a beam of dying sunlight and spread her arms in a gesture of defiance.

'Well. What can I say? If this isn't it then I don't know what is.' She grinned confidently to hide any signs of the butterflies fluttering up into her chest.

Cole inhaled deeply, staring at her. Lena realised her arms were still spread out, and she dropped them to her sides. The light shimmered through her almost-sheer blouse and cast a shadow onto the wood floor in front of her. She coughed, not sure what to do or say next.

She didn't have to do anything.

Before she knew what was happening, Cole had taken two, three, four steps towards her. There was barely space between them, but he was just far enough away that they weren't quite touching. Lena let her bag and portfolio case drop to the floor. Cole reached an arm out and pressed his palm flat against the glass behind her, leaning down next to her face. Involuntarily, her mouth opened just a fraction, air racing in and out of her lungs. Then his voice, a low rumble, almost breaking with yearning.

'Lena . . .'

A tiny sigh escaped her lips as she felt the tip of his tongue, just barely, tracing behind her earlobe and down her neck to her jaw line. His breath was hot against her skin, moving across it in waves. He lingered for a moment, then, achingly, stepped away again. She tipped her head back and let out a groan. He laughed quietly, and then spoke again.

'Take off your clothes.'

Lena hesitated.

'I want to paint you.'

'Mmm,' she growled from the back of her throat. Her voice felt hoarse. 'You want to paint me?'

But then her fingers were at the top button of her blouse. Cole folded his arms in front of him, his bottom lip resting ever so lightly between his teeth. Lena slowly undid all of the buttons and slid her blouse down her arms. They prickled with goose pimples, despite the heat. She kept her eyes on him, but Cole's gaze was already moving around her chest and down towards her stomach. She began to feel her nipples stand to attention, straining against the silky material of her bra. She felt for the zipper at the back of her pencil skirt, turning around and looking back over her shoulder teasingly as she eased it down and stepped loose of the garment. She started to slip one arched foot out of her patent-leather pump, but then stopped, leaving the shoes on. She turned back to face Cole. He had knitted his fingers together and was resting them behind his neck. She could see the material of his T-shirt moving back and forth rapidly in the twilight shining through the windows.

Standing stock-still, she reached behind and snapped open the fastener on her bra, letting her round, full breasts bounce free. Cole swallowed hard, moving towards her just a fraction. She bent down and pulled her panties past her hips, shimmying them down to the floor and stepping to one side. Cole's eyes ran over every inch of her.

'Turn around.'

The room had been nearly silent, punctuated only by the jagged rasps of their breathing, until he spoke. Lena did as he said, then waited. Quietly he came up behind her, and a flood of heat pulsed into her as she felt his warmth, through his clothes, against her naked skin. Pressing closer, he took each of her wrists in his hands and stretched her arms up above her head. Using the weight of his body, Cole eased her towards the windows and placed her palms against them. Lena found she was standing on her tiptoes, straining to get somewhere. She felt Cole move his hands down her arms and into her hair, pulling it up, away from her neck. Then, again, his tongue. Starting at the nape of her neck, he licked down her spine in tiny strokes, all the way down to the dimples in the top of her bottom. He moved slowly back up, then down again, all the time licking, licking, his hands still in her hair then moving down to her shoulders. After what seemed like forever, she felt his fingertips tracing down her body, just skimming the sides of her breasts then down and around her to her stomach, then back up and over the peaks of her nipples, fleetingly, then away again and down, down . . .

Suddenly, Cole stood up, put his hands on Lena's hips and spun her around towards him. She tilted her face up, her fingers digging into the back of his neck as she pulled his mouth towards hers. His tongue moved, strong, urgent against her own, swirling, then back out and all around her chest, his lips moving against the skin on her shoulders, kissing her breasts, sucking at her nipples, his fingers flickering against her skin. He was right – Lena felt like she was being painted with hundreds of tiny brushes.

Then in one swift movement, Cole slipped his hands under her buttocks and lifted her. She wrapped her legs around his waist, her naked body pressed against him still fully clothed. He took several strides backwards, holding her effortlessly. They were in the kitchen. He eased her onto the work surface, his tongue still deep in her mouth. Breaking away, he reached one arm towards the freezer nearby. He rummaged around and after a moment, he pulled out an ice cube, glistening between his fingers. She grinned and shook her head, but he popped it into his mouth. She shut her eyes.

Then sharp cold against the skin at the base of her throat. Slowly, his lips moved down towards her chest. Ever so slowly. Balancing the ice on his tongue and edging it, painfully slowly, down across her breast and

then lower. The ice was melting against her skin. The freezing water escaping from his lips. Faster now. Trickles edged towards her belly button, and then out, and downwards ever further, followed closely by his tongue. And then, just when she thought she couldn't take any more, she felt his mouth, a mixture of hot and cold, but unmistakably wet . . .

Gently at first, and then, as her hips began to rock back and forth, harder and harder, Cole flicked his tongue against her hard clit. He knelt down on the kitchen floor and took long, luxurious licks up the whole length of her pussy as she lifted her leg up and rested it over his shoulder. She started trembling as she began to climax, her hands tangled in Cole's hair, her eyes squeezed shut. But he wouldn't let her. Just as she was about to come, he pulled away again. He stood up, and she opened her eyes. He was wandering around the kitchen, arms folded in mock contemplation of the room. Unsatisfied. She smiled.

Somehow, outside it had become night. Lena slid off the work surface, and exhaled. She strode past him, heels softly clattering against the wood floor. She walked through the living space and pointed towards a room at the far end. Glancing over her bare shoulder, in the pale twighlight coming through the window through the window she noticed that Cole was straining against the front of his dark denim jeans.

'Perhaps the master bedroom might clinch it for you?' she said throatily.

Cole took off his T-shirt, exposing his lean torso. Unbuttoning his jeans, he pushed them and his boxer shorts over his long, hard penis and stepped free. He followed her. But just as he reached her in the vast, empty bedroom, Lena pushed past, strode back out and into the open living area. His eyes followed.

'Like what you see?' A smile played on her lips. 'I know I do.'

She walked leisurely back towards the large show windows, faced them again, and pressed her nude body against the cool glass. She felt his eyes on her, she bathed in them. Then in the reflection she saw Cole approach her. A moment later, his hands were reaching down in between her legs. She could not have been any wetter. He spread her wide with one hand and finally, gently, unbearably slowly, he eased his hard cock inside her with the other.

Lena arched her back and groaned.

A deep, guttural noise escaped from Cole's throat. He waited there inside her for a moment, then reached around and began to play with her. She could barely gasp for air as Cole slowly began to grind deeply into her pussy, the heel of his palm pushing against her abdomen, fingertips dancing at her clitoris. Her eyes locked to his in the reflection of the glass, their naked bodies writhing against it for the entire world to see if only they would look up.

He bit her ear and began to thrust harder, one hand slicking her own juices around her swollen clit, the other pressing down on her waist. The glass began to fog. She cried out louder and louder, begging, shouting his name, but now Cole wouldn't stop. He thrust deeper and deeper and deeper until they both could hardly stand up. Together they crumpled to the hard floor, he behind her still, their knees knocking and rubbing painfully against the wood, but neither could feel anything other than the rush, the profound ache of release. Lena's entire body froze as she suddenly was overwhelmed, and she came harder than she ever had in her entire life.

Then she slumped down and spun around under Cole, pulling him down on top of her, gripping him over her, her nails breaking his skin, and he entered her again, she was soaking wet, and he hunched over her, snarling almost, her legs locked around him, heels of her shoes digging into his lower back, until wave after wave of orgasm shook her for what felt like an eternity, and with a strangled cry she felt his come pulsing into her, and her name in his voice ringing out into the empty space . . .

Cole pulled Lena close.

'OK . . . Yes . . .' He curled his body around hers on the floor. 'Perfect.'

Agent Provocateur is back with a selection of some of today's finest erotic writing.

Soixante neuf, a wonderful concept: something for everyone and a thrill at every turn. So too with this book, there is a story for every mood, whether you feel like a sex kitten or a naughtier vixen, complete with stunning images from David Bray that will stimulate your own fantasies.

Find a quiet corner and plumb the depths of this side of the book for stories that push the boundaries and explore your darker side…

Happy reading

Love Miss A.P. x

Agent Provocateur

Soixante Neuf

PAVILION

First published in Great Britain in 2009 by
PAVILION BOOKS
10 Southcombe Street, London, W14 0RA

An imprint of Anova Books Company Ltd

Design and layout © Anova Books Company Ltd, 2009
Illustrations © David Bray, 2009
Text © Anova Books Company Ltd, 2009, except:
Text © Agent Provocateur for *Lady of the Manor*, *L'Appartement* and
Inside My Knicker Drawer
Text © Ashbourne Welles for *Julia at the Glory Hole*, *Sixty Nine* and
Esther's Hands

Commissioning editor: Emily Preece-Morrison
Project editor: Kate Oldfield
A.P. editor: Jess Morris
Copyeditor: Ian Allen
Authors: Neo, Angelina, Ashbourne Welles, Susanna Forrest, Annie Blinkhorn,
Vita Rosen, Saffron Mayhew, Sareeta Domingo, Sarah Griffin, Bassma Fattal
Illustrator: David Bray
Jacket and page design: Georgina Hewitt
Typesetting: SX
Production: Rebekah Cheyne

A CIP catalogue record for this book is available from the British Library.

ISBN 978–1–862058–38–5

Printed and bound by Mondadori, Italy

10 9 8 7 6 5 4 3 2 1

This book can be ordered direct from the publisher.
Contact the marketing department, but try your bookshop first.

The Dark Side Contents

Brought To Heel

The details were very specific. A pre-paid cab would deliver direct to her office in Knightsbridge, she would text a designated number to acknowledge receipt and the cab would disappear. Seffy Hall – only her family called her Persephone – looked at her watch. Ten minutes. Obviously she wouldn't be greeting the taxi personally, whatever the instructions said. That's what PAs were for. But if Laura wasn't back from her break soon there was the rather nasty chance that she, Seffy, would indeed have to make her way four floors down to street level.

Eight minutes.

Why isn't Laura answering her mobile?

Six minutes.

How long does it take to get a skinny latte?

Four minutes.

Well that cab will just have to wait.

Two minutes.

Hold that lift!

Ninety seconds later Seffy swept past the neatly turned out old man

at the security desk and blinked as the unexpected daylight hit her usually protected eyes. She felt naked without her Chanel shades. They were the first thing she picked up before leaving the office. The holy trinity of accessories: sunglasses, Blackberry, purse – in that order. But in the rush she'd forgotten all three.

Where's that cab?

The words were still forming in her mind when the traffic slowed and a London taxi – totally black, no garish advertisements along its doors – pulled up in front of her. It was empty, even though the 'for hire' light was off. The passenger window wound down and the cabbie called out.

'Your name Hall?' he asked in his cheery East End accent.

Seffy nodded and heard the door locks click off. She opened the back door and climbed in. There taking up centre spot on the three rear seats was a pink box elaborately bound in pink and black lace ribbon. Without sitting down, Seffy scooped up the package and was about to crawl back out of the cab when the driver called out.

'You'll be texting first, Miss?'

Shit. The Blackberry. Seffy could picture it inside, on the desk by the Apple Air, right next to the shades and the purse.

'I left my phone upstairs,' she said.

'Then the box will be staying with me, love.'

Seffy studied the driver's face. Probably in his mid fifties, casually attired and by the looks of it suffering more than most from the effects of the smoking ban. He looked like a kindly, if a bit out of shape, uncle but there was something in his eyes that said, 'Don't even try to make a run for it.'

As if he could tell what she was thinking there was a loud clunk and the door locks re-activated.

Seffy sighed and put the box back on the seat.

'You'll wait here?' she asked.

8

'For a while,' the driver replied. 'I was told if they weren't picked up by quarter to then they had to go back.' They both looked at the digital counter affixed above the windscreen. 'That gives you about eight minutes by my reckoning,' he said. 'Sorry.'

Another clunk and the doors were unlocked again. Seffy took a deep breath and climbed out. Eight minutes. *That's doable. But when I get my hands on that Laura…*

She was back at the cab with three minutes to spare – this time wearing her sunglasses which obviously caught the driver out. As she tapped on the window he hurriedly threw his *Financial Times* down onto the spare seat and covered it with a copy of the *Daily Star*. Neither of them would be talking of this moment again.

Sixty seconds later Seffy was waiting once again for the lift, clutching the pink box to her chest. *That was close.* The repercussions if she'd missed the delivery were not worth thinking about.

A voice interrupted her thoughts.

'Hello, Seffy,' said Laura, a waifish beauty who made the black tartan pinafore look work. 'Don't normally see you down here in daylight hours.'

Memo to self, Seffy thought. *Find a new PA.*

✻ ✻ ✻

'My God, they are beautiful.'

'I think I'm going to die.'

'I'd break my neck if I tried to walk in those.'

A small but immaculately dressed crowd was gathered around Seffy's desk. Two men – one obviously straight, one not – and four women, all her junior but too entranced by the red stiletto heel shoes in front of them to respect normal work boundaries.

'Where did you get them?' one asked.

'Well I don't think it was Clarkes.'

'Haven't you seen Clarkes' new fetish line?'

Sniggering.

'They must have cost a month's wages.'

A month of your wages, perhaps, Seffy thought.

Then: 'Can I try them on?'

That was too far. 'Zoo time's over,' Seffy snapped. 'Jaison, that Dior account's not going to manage itself, is it?' A handsome Latino looked as though he had been shot and backed away. The others took their cue from him and soon Seffy was alone. With the most expensive pair of fuck me shoes she had ever seen.

Her phone rang and caller ID did its trick. *It's him.*

Two rings. Three rings.

She had never got past six before. Never dared.

Four rings.

And she couldn't do it now.

'Seffy Hall,'

'Hello, Persephone.' The one person outside the family to use that name. 'You cut it fine today. I thought you were rejecting my little present.'

'Staff issues,' she replied, momentarily lifting her eyes from the shoes to glare at her PA on the other side of the spacious room.

'Are they beautiful?' the voice asked.

'You know they are.'

'How do they feel?'

'I haven't tried them on yet.'

'No, but how do they *feel*?' He emphasised the last word and Seffy knew what he meant. Cradling the phone under her chin she reached out with both hands and lifted one shoe. A quiver ran through her. She closed her eyes.

'They feel soft,' she said quietly into the receiver. 'Soft but firm. Strong, really.' She ran her finger tips around the toe and up to the cupped front. With her other hand she drew a finger down the curved back to where it scooped inwards like a swan's neck and tapered to the savage needle of the stiletto. Seven inches of heel at least. Maybe eight. 'Dangerous,' she added. 'I wouldn't want to be on the wrong side of these.'

No words came back down the phone line but he wasn't silent. Seffy could hear breathing, fast and quite heavy. She imagined the man with the phone pressed so tight to his head that his ear hurt.

'What sort of person wears shoes like this?' he asked.

'A bad person.'

'Are you a bad person, Persephone?'

'No, I'm a good girl.'

There was a noise, like a stifled cough. Seffy opened her eyes and saw Laura turn hurriedly away. *Reality check.*

'I can't talk now,' she said into the phone.

'Of course you can.'

'I'm not alone.'

'I'll send another cab then. Box them up. Shall we say 15 minutes? Shame,' he added. '*Shame.*'

Seffy paused.

'Wait.' She covered the mouthpiece and barked to her assistant. 'Laura, time for your lunchbreak.'

'I don't do lunch.'

'Well time for *my* lunchbreak then – and what I really fancy is a break from you. Close the door on the way out.'

Laura knew not to argue with her boss when she used that tone. 'Shades, Blackberry, purse,' she muttered to herself and then trotted out

of the office, ego wounded but image intact.

'Where was I?' Seffy said as the office door clicked shut.

'You were being a good girl.'

'Oh yes. I was, wasn't I?' Seffy closed her eyes again and let his voice take her from the office.

'You were being too good to wear such naughty shoes. You were feeling bad because you'd already touched them. And you have touched them, haven't you, Persephone?'

'Yes, I have,' she whispered. 'I've stroked them.'

'Stroke them for me now. Pick one up, stroke it slowly with the back of your hand.' He could hear her doing it. 'Stroke the instep slowly down your face. Let your cheek kiss the soft leather. It is soft, isn't it, Persephone?'

A groan.

'Now the other side.' He paused. 'And now lower. You want to feel that softness, that firm softness, pushing against your neck, don't you? You want to be bitten by the leather, don't you? You want it pricking your skin. You want its mark.'

Seffy's head leant back heavily against the side of the shoe as it pushed against her nape, sending goose bumps down both arms. She was the one holding the shoe but it felt like she wasn't in control. It was listening to the voice from the phone. *Responding.*

Just like her body.

'Tell me what you see.'

Seffy's eyes were closed but the images were clear.

'Hands. Running over me. Caressing me, pulling off my clothes.'

Memories or dreams?

'What else?'

'Tongues. Licking me. All over. I feel them through my shirt. But my

12

shirt is being undone.'

'Love the shoe, Persephone, make it yours.'

And she did. Her tongue explored the toe, the sole, the vamp, the sides, the back. And then, with audible delight, she tackled the heel.

'It's so sharp,' she whispered, oblivious to whether her voice could be heard down the line. 'So smooth, but so powerful. Vicious.'

Almost unconsciously she let her hand reach along her lap. Along the top of her thigh, pressing softly, barely touching the expensive fabric of the black Chloé skirt. More by sense than feeling she followed its touch as though not in control of her own limbs. And even before it hovered between her legs she gasped.

'You're cheating aren't you?' the voice said. The instant silence told him he was right. 'No hands, Persephone. No hands.'

She groaned again. But obeyed and withdrew her palm. At the same time she lowered her other hand, the one holding the red slice of eroticism, and felt the top of the heel press hard where her hand had just been.

'That's better, isn't it?' Cupped under her chin, the phone picked up every little utterance, every urgent breath. Little animal noises, instinctive, visceral. Seffy at that moment was oblivious to everything. But he knew what she was doing. And he knew how it made her feel.

'Give in to it,' he instructed.

She hooked the thumbs of both hands inside the shoe and pressed its back down between her legs. The toe, almost as angular as the needle heel, stood upright and proud. But mobile. It wavered as the top of the heel gyrated.

'Tell me what you're doing.'

Nothing.

'Tell me what you're doing or I will hang up.'

'You know what I'm doing.'

'But how?'

Seffy told him. She told him how she was manoeuvring the widest part of the heel around the unseen outline of her pussy, just there, so with every sweep of her hands she felt a stab of pleasure as her clit yelped with interest. With pleasure.

With the desire for more.

She told him how her breathing was getting heavier, but he knew that. She told him how she let one hand take control of the shoe to alter the angle of the pressure as she ground down. She told him how the spare hand was stroking her left breast through the starchy touch of her wide collared shirt. About her nipple, anxious for contact. About her lips, craving more. About the swelling in her pussy, the building of… *oh, oh.*

And then she couldn't say anything. Not for a while. A minute, almost.

He might have said something, she didn't know. The first words – the only words – she heard next were perfectly clear.

'Wear them tonight.'

✳ ✳ ✳

'Did I tell you to sit down?'

'I'm sorry.'

'Did I say you could stand up?'

Again, 'I'm sorry.'

They were in an apartment overlooking the Thames. It wasn't exactly penthouse but it was penthouse 'style' according to the estate agent. Normally that meant expansive layout, stunning views. Tonight it meant a torturer's playground. Stunning views of a different kind.

Persephone Hall stood at the panoramic window and stared out across the river to the trendier north. The other side had the postcode; she had the postcard views. The chimes of Big Ben, the bell inside St

Stephen's tower at the Houses of Parliament, struck seven. It was dusk. Car lights flickered across Lambeth Bridge to her right and Vauxhall Bridge to her left. The wheel just past Westminster Bridge subtly changed its colour from blue to green.

But she wasn't watching any of this.

She was watching the reflection in the window of the man hovering warily behind her. He called himself David but tonight he was Slave.

Seffy turned round. She was wearing a pair of gravity defying red stiletto shoes. *The shoes from her office*. They fitted perfectly, like he knew they would. They wrapped around her feet. She didn't wear them. They were part of her. And they dominated her look. Transformed her. Already slim legs were suddenly toned and powerful. Elongated muscles, tight calves, long, majestic thighs.

It wasn't just her body that was transformed. At work she had staff, she had responsibilities, she was the manager. Some would say she had power. The chain of command, the private office and the title confirmed it. But this was different. She looked different. Her eyes were on fire. Her smile was knowing. Her body was ready. This was real power.

And it was all down to the shoes. It had to be.

She wasn't wearing anything else.

Her dark brown hair swung loose about her exposed shoulders. She was five foot two without heels – five nine in these incredible creations. Their influence continued up from her thighs, past her taut stomach to her small but upturned, pert breasts. She wasn't smiling. Her lips wore lipstick in the same colour as the shoes and they meant business.

But David didn't know this. He was blindfolded. Fully dressed in a business suit, dark blue, discrete black lines, that season's Paul Smith collection, bare feet, no jewellery or other adornments. Just a black velvet eye mask tied expertly around his head.

He didn't see the vision in front of him. He didn't see the shoes that had cost him, including elaborate delivery, more than £700.

And he didn't see what was in her hands.

If he had, he might have thought it was some kind of stick. But not one made of wood. This was pure ivory. The cost of smuggling it into the country had been thousands alone. Its purchase price took the transaction into the realms of the obscene. And on closer inspection it would be revealed as not a stick. It was a giant, sabre-like shoehorn.

He couldn't see it but David the Slave was about to find out what it felt like.

'You've had your hair cut,' Seffy said.

'I did it for you.'

'I hate it. It's too short. You look like a squaddie. You like orders? You want to be bossed around? I'll give you orders.'

Seffy walked around room. It was large and open plan. Two giant crushed velvet sofas formed a V around the riverside views. A white, clean kitchen area stood at the other side. A chintzy mirrored bar area, replete with chrome stools, expensive liqueurs and spirits from all around the globe, formed the only other furniture. Three curved steps, sunk into the middle of the room, gave the feeling of round, concentric levels plunging into the floor.

'Make yourself comfortable,' Seffy said. But as David edged gingerly to where he knew the sofas should be, she interrupted. 'Not there. Walk backwards. I want you on the floor.' She paused. 'On the steps.'

He knew from memory that two strides backwards would find the stairs. They didn't go anywhere. They just gave the impression of depth into the faux penthouse apartment. Carefully he stepped backwards, letting his bare feet feel the descent of the first stair, then the second, and the third. Reaching the safety of the lower level he dropped obediently to his knees. Then lowering himself slowly forwards he rested his chest against the steps themselves so shoulders and head were the only features on ground level.

Perfect, Seffy thought.

She walked towards him, the deep carpet masking her tread. David couldn't see her and he didn't hear her. But he smelt her. The

unmistakeable aroma of unworn leather. Box fresh, even treated for elemental wear, its richness filled his nostrils. He inhaled and made the mistake of lifting his head from the floor.

'Down,' Seffy ordered, and pressed the ball of her shoe flatly against David's head. It hit the carpet with an audible thump. She didn't release the pressure at all. If anything she shifted her weight and trod harder. David groaned. Very real pain was beginning to seep through his consciousness. His breathing was more urgent. He couldn't smell the shoes any more. All his concentration was on combating the pain in his head.

'Are you going to obey me now?' Seffy asked.

'Y-y-yes,' the Slave coughed. The sudden brutality of her movement had caught him out.

'Pardon?' she barked and increased her weight.

'Yes, Mistress!' he screamed.

'Good boy,' she said and took her foot away. His first instinct was to bring his hands to his head to comfort the throbbing ache. But he didn't dare.

'You've done well, Slave,' Seffy said. 'You should be rewarded.'

As she spoke Seffy pushed her left foot along the carpet until it had manoeuvred underneath David's face. The vamp of her foot was pressed against his mouth and nose. 'You can lick me now.'

He didn't need to be asked twice. Seffy watched as his tongue worked all over her shoe. Slowly, methodically, covering every inch. She could see how much he enjoyed it. The fact he couldn't see only heightened his sense of smell and his sense of taste. Without thinking he moved one hand to touch the shoe. Immediately he realised his mistake and stopped but Seffy let it pass. Watching him flinch in expectation was thrill enough.

She slapped the wide end of the shoehorn into her other palm. The snap of contact sang cleanly throughout the silent room. The sting focused her mind. Reaching down she tousled the prone man's dark

hair with the ivory tip and heard him react with something like pleasure. Then she drew its curled back slowly around to the front of David's head and pushed down so it rested on the toe of her shoe. His tongue, his busy tongue, flickered over it. A second later he ran his mouth up as high as he could reach then back down.

In a hearbeat Seffy jerked the ivory implement sideways then flicked back in sharply.

Thack!

The two-inch width slapped crisply against the Slave's cheek.

'Shoes!' she said crisply. Then smiled as his face, clearly smarting, fell back to her foot.

At the same time Seffy felt a pulse of enjoyment at the top of her legs. She had enjoyed that act of correction. She had enjoyed it a lot.

Resting her left hand on her hip, with her right she dragged the shoehorn up the inside of her own leg and closed her eyes to maximise the physical reaction. She felt every inch of her inner thigh explode as the cool ivory passed. When it reached the V at the top of her legs she let it rest. Just its proximity made her flush. *What if I...?*

But no. That was not for her to do.

Not when she had her Slave.

'Enough!' she instructed, pulling her foot sharply out from under David's caresses at the same time. With a quick, fluid motion she moved down the steps till her outrageously adorned feet were planted firmly either side of his waist. Then reaching back for balance Seffy eased herself down onto the top step. Her legs were outstretched, straddling the Slave's torso. Her stomach was close enough to his head to feel his breathing.

And her pussy was just a few tantalising centimetres from his mouth.

Three things happened next. With her left hand she caught the nape of David's neck and forced his face downwards. With her right she brought the ivory shoehorn stinging down onto the man's backside. At

the same time she said, 'What are you waiting for, Slave?'

He had been waiting for instructions, but he didn't dare say anything. He couldn't. His nose was pressed hard against the svelte runway style hairs of his mistress's bush. His tongue was enveloped in the hot grip of her pussy. Her hand against the back of his head guided his work. He wanted to be gentle, to lace his tongue against her syrupy sweetness and tease her to climax. But Seffy's needs were too urgent. She craved pressure, she wanted rough brush strokes not delicate lines. That was for another time.

She arched her back and rubbed herself against the hardness of the man's tongue, his nose and even his clean-shaven chin. It all worked for her. She needed comfort in more places than his tongue could cope with. By rolling her hips she raised her pussy in long upward sweeps against him and felt his entire face trail down her, alternately flicking and stabbing and kissing her screaming clitoris. But it wasn't enough.

She needed more.

Planting one foot firmly on the carpet next to his right hip, she lifted her other leg until the crook of her knee was hooked tightly behind the Slave's head. Only then, only when her right shoe was resting on her left thigh did she remove her hand from the back of his head.

She was nearly there. She could feel so much of him inside her sensitised lips, more than he wanted. She could feel him squirming beneath her, his hands anxious on the ground, trying to get purchase. Trying to get air to his mouth. He was a beaten wrestler, desperately beating the canvas floor in submission.

But Seffy didn't care. She let her body fall backwards till her head was on the carpet. The action pulled her legs up and with it the Slave's face. She heard him gasp for air but a second later she'd constricted her legs again and he was silent. He needed to save his energies for her.

But not for long. She writhed and she bucked and when she heaved her pussy up his face was sucked down, all of it brushing indiscriminately against her.

So good, so good, so near.

Her hand tightened around the shoehorn and she smacked it down hard against the floor. It missed his shoulder by inches. She didn't care.

'Bite me, Slave, bite me!'

But he didn't need to. The rigid angles of his handsome features had done enough. They'd surfed against the softness of her pussy again and again and she could hold back no more.

With every wave that washed over her she jerked her hips into the air. Her stiletto pierced deep into the carpet with each surge. Her cries were shrill and short.

And then the Slave felt his necklock loosen. His face was free. He could feel the wetness coated all over. Without touching it, he knew his blindfold was as damp as his mouth. She had used his whole face. She had denied him air. She had nearly snapped his neck. She had force fed him her incredible pussy. And he could tell without checking that he would have a welt from the shoehorn on his arse for days.

But he wouldn't change a thing. Well, maybe one thing.

He pulled off his mask and stared at the naked woman lying in front of him.

'I suppose you want to have some fun now?' Seffy said, smiling.

He nodded. If he didn't get out of that suit soon he would burst.

A whip of ivory flashed against his shoulder.

'Think again, Slave. Other shoe. Lick. Now.'

A Night in the Life of a Domme

This is the first surprise. People think of people like me – well, who knows what they think, but I suspect it has a lot to do with black leather, high shiny heels and red lipstick. And the word 'dominatrix'. And I can be all of these things, on any given day, but usually I am Mistress Penelope, and I am a Domme, and it is not my job but my *life*.

The girls who get it wrong are those who think of BDSM – bondage, discipline, sadism, masochism – as a fancy way to make money from your body. But I think, when it works, it is because BDSM is your first and only love. Of course, you need partners to play with. I personally need bottoms – submissives – to play with, because I need to be queen bee, or top. But I know plenty of charming women who get their kicks – and their living – not from being Dommes, because they are completely neither capable nor desirous of it – but from being true subs. They are in charge, and pick their clients and lovers, but past that they are absolutely not in charge. Once you understand, it's simple.

Take tonight, for example. I'm going to Mistress Clare's for a while – for three hours, to be precise – and she is your classic sub. She just loves to be bound and spanked. Hard. I've experimented with it in the past but I have never really enjoyed the sensation of being so restricted. But Mistress Clare likes nothing more than to be tied up and humiliated. It's a

very common thing. And what a lot of people can't appreciate is how sexy it can be. I think it's a fantasy lots of very young girls have, and they either grow afraid of it and shake it off, or they grow with it and it can be a wonderful thing. As I say, I don't like to be tied up myself. But I can't tell you how exciting I find it to be the one tying a girl – or even a man – up. But girls more – their more rounded bodies are perfect for it. I start with the wrists, usually. Most people struggle to start with. You tie the wrists together – I like to use a silken rope, but some people particularly request the roughest ties, and that's fine too. I prefer to tie the wrists behind a person's back while they are still dressed. Then I tie a gag over their mouth – they have to bite down on it – it's making me excited just to think about it. Quite often I make them bite down on a pair of knickers first, if I think they'll enjoy it, and then tie over that. Lots of women look at their most beautiful at this point. They are excited, anticipating what lies ahead, but they are also scared. They can't be understood verbally any more, so their eyes become extremely expressive, imploring you to stop, or take care of them. Of course, you do no such thing.

There are safe words, I should say here. There is a kind of code in our community that all BDSM practices must be safe, sane and consensual (SSC), and generally they are. And most people have heard of the use of safe words, I think, which do help ensure that people adhere to SSC practice. I have written contracts with several clients (and I always write a contract with a slave) based around the use of safe words. It's a very tricky area, because British law does not recognise the legality of hurting anyone, but to try to make things clear BDSM professionals often set out in writing the client's (or their own) permission to cause them pain, humiliation and discomfort – to whatever level he or she wishes – up until the use of the safe word. Then in our eyes it becomes a crime to mistreat someone after that.

Of course, it is made tricky by the fact that a lot of clients like to wear gags, masks or ball gags, so they can't use a spoken safe word, and then we have a safe gesture, like a tap on the hand or a pinch or something. And if they are totally immobilised, we have to know what to look out for in their eyes. It's a very tricky business, and takes a lot of training. Very dangerous just to crash in and start whipping, biting or spanking people, for example. Let alone some of the edgier ('Edge') practices.

So tonight, once I have made myself at home at Mistress Clare's, and before her other guests arrive, I will tie her the same way I always do: I will gag her and tie her ankles together, and then tie her ankles behind her to her wrists – it is quite a complicated knot – and then I begin to cut her clothes open. She gets through hundreds of pounds' worth of silk and lace dresses, corsets, lingerie and stockings every week, but that's how she likes it, and she has admirers falling over themselves to buy her replacements. She looks amazing, with her dark curls, her voluptuous breasts spilling over as I cut open her shirt and then her bra, and often I just push her over so she is kneeling, exposing everything, and that is the view that greets her guests as they begin to arrive.

All of my clients are regulars and I am really very fond of them. Tonight I am taking a cab to Mistress Clare's, but afterwards briefly I will welcome a client to my flat. It's my place of work but it's also my home, and I don't really feel the need to make a distinction between the two. I have a boyfriend, but he loves what I do and is quite involved. I do keep my toys and tools tidied away – I have the most beautiful bespoke leather cases, velvet lined, with drawers made to fit each particular item, so I can keep them pristine. But there's no hiding the whipping chair, or my special punishment throne. There is only so much a throw can conceal, as we discovered when my boyfriend's conservative parents came for dinner once. I am not sure they believed that it was a modern interpretation of the Eames classic.

My boyfriend. People are often intrigued, or surprised, when they find out I have a partner. They assume that I must keep my life separate from him or her, or that, conversely, he/she must be one of my slaves or subs. But the simple fact is that he's unthreatened, and likes hearing about what I do. In fact, I met him through a colleague of his, now an ex-client of mine. It's like any relationship in that we enjoy sharing the tribulations of our jobs with one another, but while I am interested in hearing about the FTSE – he's a City trader – he is more interested in hearing about my footsies, and my clients' various obsessions with them . . .

I remember my first foot-worship client and I recall feeling amazed that somebody would be so happy – and reward me so handsomely –

just for the privilege of kissing and licking my feet. Now I am unfazed even if they only want to look at them, and at the other end of the scale I am an expert at foot oil massage – *with* my feet rather than on my feet (although I love that too). It is quite surprising the amount of people who turn out to have a kind of fetish in this area, and it is one I find quite charming.

I digress. I said my boyfriend was involved, and he is, regularly, but I should clarify that I've only ever involved him in one particular way, and he will help me out in this way later tonight. The word 'cuckold' has fallen mainly out of use now, but in my world it is still extremely prevalent. I have several male clients whose absolute passion it is to be humiliated and teased about my preference for another man, or men. These cucks, as I affectionately call them, are sometimes very useful and enjoy driving me home from a hard night of tormenting and then being forced to watch as I greet my boyfriend with the most passionate of kisses. He loves it and I love the mixed, slightly pained look on my client's face as he waits obediently to be dismissed. That may sound cruel, but actually to these men it is a true kindness, as it fulfils a deep need in them – it gives them much pleasure to be tortured in this way. They tell me graphically in their letters and emails how much they enjoy watching me being kissed and fondled by a real man, knowing they are beneath me. It's complex, I grant you. But then again – once you understand, it's simple.

I suppose there is a lot of scope for abuse in this job. There is a lot of power involved, and it can go to your head. I've seen it happen. Even the most dedicated women sometimes get carried away by the demands you can easily place on your adoring clients. There is a trend now for 'tribute lists', which I personally don't go in for: much like a wedding list, you can create a fantasy shopping inventory of all the beautiful or filthy objects you could ever want. If my clients have a specific item or outfit they want to involve in our sessions, I'm happy to make suggestions and supply practical details (size, stockist, etc.). But overall, I think it's enough of a bonus that my clients pay me for the kind of antics and lifestyle that I love: for me it's too much to demand that they fund my own equipment or my costumes and running costs too.

Having said that, I do embrace the use of slaves for all sorts of favours. I have three at the moment – that is about the maximum I can run at any one time – and they are extremely competitive; they adore being set against one another. I have them collect my dry-cleaning; wash and polish my floors; buy my groceries; even do my admin. Carrying out any of these tasks puts them in a state of complete arousal and is of great benefit to me too! I often picture Slave H floating blissfully up and down the aisles at the supermarket, each item in his basket adding to his pleasure.

These domestic errands provide lots of opportunities for punishment, too – if, for example, any of the slaves bring me the wrong product or brand, or take too long over a task, or do not complete it to my satisfaction, they can expect to be beaten or at the very least chained up and made to reflect on what they've done. Just yesterday I asked Slave M to iron a pile of my most delicate items. He did it beautifully, as he always does, but he took the liberty of then hanging each item in one of my wardrobes for me. He begged me not to punish him and claimed he just could not resist the urge to touch the collection of leathers, rubbers, laces and silks he knew he would find in there, but I would hear none of it and strapped him to the kitchen door handle for an hour before beating him fiercely with a paddle. We were both invigorated after that and shared a pot of tea to give his reddened skin time to calm down before he went back to his wife, happy and relaxed.

Marks are a tricky one, actually. When I first meet a client, we have a really in-depth practical discussion about their precise limits, and what they might need to hide from whom, by when. These often change as a sub progresses, and that is part of the growth of our relationship. There's a guy I'm seeing tomorrow who has come on in leaps and bounds; a year ago he would never have dreamed of being able to enjoy half the practices he can now. We started off very mildly, but I suspected his shoe fetish – for starters – was something he might want to explore in a more extreme way. Now when he emails me to set up a particular scene – this is something I do with most clients, incidentally, so that as soon as they arrive I have the right equipment all prepared and we are in our roles straight away – more often than not he begs for stiletto trampling all over his body, and I mean *all* over. It helps that he

dumped his vanilla girlfriend, so he now has no physical constraints, bar his own pain threshold.

That is the thing in the end, I think. BDSM is so welcoming and so respecting of people's tastes and preferences that it becomes more idyllic than a lot of other relationships. I have had partners in the past who haven't dealt well with my lifestyle, even though they found it arousing, especially at first. And those people have always had to go. There's a BDSM emblem, a triskelion, that symbolises the rules well. It has three divisions, and represents in a very complex way the various divisions of three of BDSM, (like the three-way creed of behaviour - safe, sane and consensual, or the division in the community between tops, bottoms and switches). But overall what I like the best is that the all-embracing circle represents unity, the oneness and love within our community. Everybody wants to be loved and respected. And if you can find a way of achieving that, and getting your rocks off too, you've got it made.

Speaking of which, I need to go and choose my outfit for this evening's escapades. I'm going to be in head-to-toe rubber. Now that's a look you don't need an iron for . . .

The Conversion

As she watched the yellow Transit van pull up outside her house, Charlotte's heart sank. Another day of drilling, banging, shouting and mess was about to commence. And it wasn't even seven o'clock in the morning.

She let the dusty curtain close and walked out of the lounge towards the sanctuary of her kitchen. How had it come to this? Her husband had left her shortly after the birth of their second child, but not before he'd insisted on hiring the most attractive au pair he could possibly find. Watching that slender, beautiful, raven-haired Polish girl stroll around her own house was a permanent reminder to Charlotte of how much she'd lost. But she couldn't do anything about it. Jack and Harry adored the girl. And so did she, really. Libka wasn't just gorgeous, she was thoughtful and generous too. Everything Franco hadn't been.

His loss.

Things had changed when he'd gone. For so long Charlotte had wanted to extend their Georgian terrace upwards. 'Nobody has a loft any more,' she'd told him. 'We need the extra space.'

That wasn't strictly true – even less so now there was one fewer body in the home. But since she was making Franco pay through the nose for his infidelity and treachery and emotional torture and all those other things she'd accused him of, she was getting her conversion done

now. She may have lost the war but she would win this battle. *If it killed her.*

Unfortunately that's just what it felt like was happening.

It was Carla's fault. She'd promised her spare house in the country months ago. 'It's yours, darling. I'm there for you. We all are.' All the renovations had been planned around its availability. Charlotte, Jack, Harry and, yes, even Libka, would just move there for eight weeks. And then Carla had withdrawn the offer.

Well, Charlotte didn't need her. How bad could a couple of months of building work be?

On the first day she found out.

It was a relief her mother lived so close and could take the boys. But Charlotte refused to move out herself, not when she could just see them there every day. And since her mother detested the very idea of au pairs – 'in my day we looked after our own children' – Libka didn't go either. For a second Charlotte saw a way out of her jealousy problems.

'Libka, I fully understand if you want to find a new home. It's been wonderful having you, but I won't stand in your way.'

Annoyingly, Libka had refused to go. Charlotte sighed and added 'loyalty' to the girl's list of qualities.

So they'd stayed together. The frumpy old woman and the goddess. Charlotte knew that's how the builders must think of them. 'That's if they even notice me at all,' she thought.

She heard the front door open and the sound of the three men enter. What was it about builders' boots that made them sound like robots marching on a tin roof? And why did they have to talk so loudly? Just as well the children were at their grandmother's. No one could sleep through this.

No one, that is, except Libka. Charlotte had never known anyone able to switch off so efficiently. That girl could nap standing up. If there was a moment to snatch forty winks, she took it. Great for her, of course – but it meant that Charlotte was often the one responding to the

bedtime cries of the children while the hired help slept through. 'That could almost be a black mark,' she thought happily.

'Morning, Missus,' the voice of Dan the chippy called out. 'He doesn't even know my name,' Charlotte thought. Two other voices, both older, mumbled hellos as they stomped up the wooden staircase.

Charlotte stepped out of her hiding place in the kitchen and smiled. 'Morning, boys,' she called out cheerily – trying to pretend she liked being up this early, that it had nothing to do with the stress of the physical upheaval around her – but the men were already out of sight. They never ventured into her domain on the ground floor. That had been one of the rules. She'd installed a kettle and toaster in the spare room upstairs – that would be their kitchen. There was a guest bathroom up there as well. The men had no need to stray downstairs except to leave and enter. Charlotte had even moved her bedroom downstairs for the summer. She wanted nothing to do with the men. She just wished she didn't have to see them at all.

But that wasn't strictly true. As much as she detested the layer of dust that coated every item of clothing in her carefully polythene-sealed wardrobes, as much as she was driven mad by the daily invasion of three uncouth strangers, she had found herself hovering in the hallway whenever she heard footsteps descending. It might, after all, be Dan. He was the youngest, the most tanned, the nicest of the men. He was the one who wore white vests like John McClane while his colleagues hid underneath sensible blue boiler suits. He was the one who had muscles like beans in a pod, bursting to get out.

He was the reason Charlotte stationed herself at the downstairs window every morning at six-thirty, just to snatch a glimpse of him as he walked over towards the house.

Sometimes she thought of taking tea up to them but then Dan would guess and that could never happen. He would see straight through her desperate eyes when she put the mugs down near him. He would judge her for the silly old fool she was and laugh at her for thinking she stood a chance with anyone like him. So she stayed downstairs and hid, peeping out when she dared.

After all, what chance did she have with that brazen hussy Libka up there? The girl's room had its own en suite but that didn't stop her wandering around with just a towel around her body and another on her hair after a shower – as well as the *de rigueur* outdoor shoes needed to trample over the miles of dustsheet on every surface. Did she really have to come downstairs dressed like that? Did she really have to torment Charlotte with just how perfectly white her skin was, and how tightly it clung to her toned arms and long legs? There was no unintended movement when she reached into a cupboard or bent down to the fridge, not an ounce of unwanted fat to judder or shake. Only her breasts, large for her slender frame, showed a mind of their own beneath the wrapped towel.

Every time Charlotte looked at Libka dressed like this she wanted to kill her. It wasn't personal. But she knew what Dan would be thinking when he saw her. She knew exactly how his mind would react when he spied the half-naked twenty-year-old parading around upstairs. He would look at her small bottom, perhaps, and imagine his hands clasped around it. Or he would see her long, slim neck and picture his mouth fixing on with animal hunger. Or he would watch the hypnotic tremors of her breasts and dream of his erect penis pushed aggressively between them like he'd seen in films and pictures on the internet. Charlotte knew all this. And she hated them both all the more for it.

'Do you like the way he looks at you?' she asked Libka one day.

'Who?'

'Dan. The builder. The young one.'

'I haven't notice he looking.'

Liar.

'You must have seen him, he hangs around when he hears you up and about.'

'No? Really? I don't think so. I haven't seen.'

Charlotte didn't believe her for a minute. How could Libka not see the effect she had on the builder? What was her game? Charlotte knew

the Pole didn't have a boyfriend. She was obviously hoping to get her claws into dishy Dan. Why didn't she just come out and admit it?

A new image flashed into Charlotte's mind.

'I bet they're already doing it,' she thought. 'The bitch. And on my time as well. While I think they're working hard up there he's banging more than timber.' She realised she was shaking with rage. Across the kitchen table, Libka had noticed as well.

'Are you OK, Charlotte?'

What? 'Oh, I'm fine, just . . .' – *just what?*

Charlotte looked at the girl's dark eyes and imagined how she must appear to her through them. I'm over the hill at 36. I'm overweight and I'm alone. And don't I look it.

She took a large breath of air and marched out of the room. If she'd stayed a second longer she would have cried. And what would Dan have thought of her then?

Charlotte spent the entire day in her makeshift bedroom. She texted her mother that she was ill and couldn't have dinner with the boys as usual, and hid beneath the safety of her dusty Egyptian cotton sheets. She read, she wrote in her diary and she thought. Two floors above she heard every hammer blow, every drill punch, every crash of girder on brick. She pictured Dan doing it all single-handedly, in just his white vest. And she found herself enjoying the image.

That evening, when the house was finally quiet, Charlotte recalled the noise and let her hand wander, for the first time in months, to that place between her legs. Why hadn't she done it sooner? No one had touched her since Franco. She hadn't even touched herself. But that night she did, although it was Dan's hand she imagined sliding two fingers inside her. It was his mouth she imagined biting hard on her responsive nipples. When sleep welcomed her, she imagined it was in his arms.

Falling asleep before nine o'clock meant that by five she was awake and alert. The memory of how she'd knocked herself out flickered

across her mind. A new urge occurred to her. She decided to check up on work in progress.

Silk pyjamas and Wellington boots wasn't a look Charlotte would ever leave the house in, but as she crept up the stairs to the first floor it seemed the most appropriate. The desperation of the previous day seemed to be wiped from her mind – *did I just need a good wank? Am I that simple?* – and the soft fabric against her skin reminded her that she was actually still capable of sensation. *I should wear these more often.*

The wellies, of course, were just practical on the filthy dustsheets.

She reached the top of the stairs and looked up. Once upon a time there had been a small square hole in the ceiling. Now a skeleton staircase descended from a full-sized doorway. Charlotte could see daylight filtering through the skylights in the roof and decided to go up.

The cool air at the top of the house surprised her. It felt more like a cellar. And the smell was so musty, so damp, which was confusing considering all the dust in the air. Heavy bags of cement powder were stacked in the middle of the room, like sandbags defending against a flood. Against one wall dozens of planks of wood lay ordered. Near another wall were three stools and two upturned boxes acting as tables. Cables and tools were positioned neatly around the room.

It was the first time Charlotte had dared step foot up here since the work had begun and she had to admit it was nothing like she'd expected. Somehow the men kept it so tidy. It was a few moments before she realised that she wasn't having to stoop to look round. They'd done it. They'd actually raised the roof. She scanned around with fresh eyes. Yes – the room was coming on. She could actually see the architect's plans – *her plans* – springing to life.

For the first time in weeks Charlotte felt an unfamiliar buzz of satisfaction.

She went to climb back down the stairs but stopped. Hanging from a column on the opposite side of the room was a dirty-looking cloth. She recognised it. A vest. One of Dan's 'white' vests. What was it doing

there? The image of him taking his top off while she was downstairs shot through her mind.

How did he leave the house without it, she wondered as she walked over. *Don't tell me I missed him topless? Did he walk down my stairs, out of my front door, in just his trousers?*

Charlotte picked the vest up from its hook and brought it to her face. It wasn't planned. She just instinctively needed to breathe in the man who had given her so much pleasure last night – even if he didn't know it. She closed her eyes and inhaled. There he was. His scent filled the room. It was like he was there with her. She could almost hear the floorboards creak as he entered the room behind her. But that was impossible. It was so early. He wouldn't be at the house for ages.

So whose were the footsteps?

'You like him, yes?'

Charlotte span round. Libka was standing behind her, the smallest of T-shirts stretched down over her beautiful body. For a second Charlotte wanted to scream at her, tell her to get the hell out of her house if she was going to go around spying all the time. But she didn't. There was something about the way the girl stood there, smiling. Something about the way she was pulling her faded Madonna T-shirt so tightly that her braless breasts were magnified against the greying fabric. Something about the way she was standing with one foot awkwardly in front of the other, trying to hide the obvious fact that panties were not part of her bedtime attire.

Charlotte didn't know what to do, so she did nothing. The vest was still pressed against her face and Dan's musty smell as powerful as ever as she studied the au pair.

'I heard someone up here,' Libka said.

'Don't tell me. You hoped it was Dan and you thought you'd try to catch him alone.' Visions of how the vest had come to be removed flooded Charlotte's mind. Of course. Why didn't she think of it before? That minx had taken it off him. They'd fucked like animals under her own roof. She was probably up here to take the vest for herself.

Libka looked confused.

'No,' she said slowly. 'I hoped it would be you.' Her eyes stared unblinkingly at her employer. 'It was you I wanted to find alone.'

Charlotte felt her mind go blank. When it burst back into life a second later it was packed with questions. *What did she say? What did she mean? What? What?*

'What?' she said.

Libka stepped forward and as she did so she released her grip on the bottom of her T-shirt. Her breasts rose instantly and bobbed with each footstep. Charlotte couldn't take her eyes off them, mesmerised. Their motion was nature at its purest. Even when Libka stopped walking, inches from Charlotte, her breasts still moved. Just the girl's breathing was enough to visit tiny tremors upon those wonderful, full tits.

Charlotte didn't plan to reach a hand out and let it rest on the T-shirt. She didn't intend to let her fingers spread eagerly around the heavy, round breast. She didn't expect to find herself gasping at the sensation of its weight in her hand. She didn't fight the urge to squeeze. She couldn't.

Libka moved closer and flung her arm around Charlotte's neck. Charlotte didn't resist as her face was pulled down to meet the Pole's. She didn't try to stop Libka's mouth attaching itself to hers, or her tongue forcing its way inside. She gave in to everything.

And gave the same back.

Charlotte had never been kissed like that before. Libka's mouth was softer than Franco's, her lips fuller. But her tongue was as insistent as any man's. It swirled around Charlotte's mouth, probing her, tasting her every millimetre, wanting to join with her. Charlotte felt the arm around her neck pulling her further into Libka's mouth and she didn't resist. She couldn't. She was lost.

Suddenly Libka pulled away. In one action she lifted the T-shirt over her head, sending her breasts into a carnival of movement. Charlotte thought she would faint at the sight of them crashing silently against

each other, then repelled by their own momentum. For a split second she was watching perpetual motion. A living Newton's Cradle. Instinctively she reached out to catch them, to contain them, to draw them to her mouth. But Libka pulled back.

'Not yet,' she said, and stepped behind Charlotte. The older woman stiffened. Not nerves; *expectation*. She hadn't seen this coming. She hadn't imagined for one instant that her au pair had designs not on the builder, but on her. Silly old her. At that moment Charlotte was no longer the frumpy housewife. She was a woman. She was sexy. She had a lover millions would kill for.

And Charlotte's lover was busy. Libka put her hands on Charlotte's shoulders and eased her backwards until she was against the room's supporting column. Then she arranged the compliant woman's arms around the post and pulled her wrists together.

'What are you doing?' Charlotte asked as she felt Dan's vest torn from her grip.

There was silence as Libka unwound a long electrical cable and looped it twice around Charlotte's wrists. She pulled hard and Charlotte yelped as her hands slapped together behind her back.

What was going on? She was tied to a post in her own house. This au pair, this stranger, had tricked her. Charlotte tugged at the cable but it held firm. She felt it cut slightly into her skin. It was very tight. Too tight to be enjoyable. She began to panic. If Libka walked away now Dan and his older mates would find her like this. And who knew what they would do. Any erotic thoughts of that man's body vanished. Charlotte was a victim. She was helpless. She was scared.

Suddenly Libka appeared back in front of her. One glance at that magnificent body and Charlotte's pain disappeared. She watched, confused, as the Pole picked up a short stepladder from the other side of the room, and dragged it over. Libka laid it on the floor in front of Charlotte, then pushed it with her foot until it hit Charlotte's boots.

'Take them off and step in,' she ordered.

Charlotte had been so entranced by Libka's movements that she

hadn't taken in what was going on. She was suddenly being asked to remove her Wellingtons and step inside the rungs of a ladder on the floor. *Why?* She lifted one foot up and Libka pushed the ladder underneath. As she lifted the other leg, the girl grabbed hold of the ankle and pulled it out wide. When Charlotte stood down again her legs were wide apart, like da Vinci's image of Jesus. The small gaps between the ladder rungs made it hard to move her feet again. Just to make sure, Libka had found more cable and was lacing it around Charlotte's ankles.

Charlotte was sixteen years older than this girl. She had a family, a career as a lawyer that she could go back to whenever she wanted. She owned a four-bedroom house – soon to be five bedrooms.

And she had allowed this girl to tie her ankles three feet apart. What the hell was going on?

Suddenly Libka stopped working and stepped in front of her boss.

'I dream of this,' she said quietly, and kissed Charlotte again. Charlotte felt her own mouth respond. She felt her tongue writhe against Libka's, she felt herself lean into the girl's mouth and sink her teeth into her bottom lip. If only she could free her hands.

'Untie me,' she said breathlessly.

But did she mean it?

Libka leaned into Charlotte's neck and nuzzled with her nose, then her teeth, nipping quickly at the skin, then kissing each wound, letting her tongue soothe the pain, before moving slightly and biting again. Each time Charlotte winced but she couldn't deny it: she was loving the pain. Who would have thought it?

As Libka kissed, she let her hands reach across Charlotte's body, sliding easily over the green silk pyjamas. Her touch was firm and busy. She didn't rest for a second, always smoothing across the material, covering every inch of her lover's body with inquisitive hands. She felt the roundness of Charlotte's bottom as it leaned back on the wooden column. She felt the dip of her waist and the swell of her beautiful, womanly hips. And she felt the pinprick nipple that stood proud against the sheer fabric.

Just as Charlotte fantasised that Libka would bite her small breasts, the au pair reached to the floor and picked something up. Then she stepped out of Charlotte's view. When she reappeared she was wearing Dan's old white vest. Charlotte grinned. *All my Christmases coming at once.* However good Dan looked in this tiny garment, Libka looked better.

They kissed again, but this time Libka pressed her body against Charlotte's and pushed up and down. She didn't use her hands, just her thighs to rub between the tied woman's open legs, just her taut stomach and mobile breasts to roll against Charlotte's silk top. Libka began to purr. Charlotte couldn't say anything. She was entrapped not just physically but emotionally. She wanted to scream but no sound would come out.

Libka dropped slowly to her knees and stopped. She was squatting, her face inches from Charlotte's groin. She didn't look up. She stared straight ahead then pushed out her tongue and let herself fall against the silk trousers.

Now Charlotte found her voice.

'Oh, God!'

It was amazing. So much anticipation, so much frustration tied up into one tiny area. And Libka had unwrapped it with her first touch.

Charlotte pushed her pussy forwards. She was restricted by her ankles and her wrists but she had to do this. She had to let Libka know that she wanted that tongue inside her. She wanted the young woman to feel her love for her, taste her hotness for her. She wanted Libka's face in her pussy now.

But Libka had other ideas. Yes, she pressed her tongue firmly against Charlotte's eager mound. Yes, she felt the woman's clitoris push back, her soft lips part, and the silk lose any trace of dryness as it was eased inside by Libka's probing tongue. But then she pulled herself up and for the second time that morning lifted her one item of clothing over her head.

'Libka, please,' Charlotte begged. 'Fuck me. I'll do anything. Just don't stop.'

Libka said nothing. She just took the vest between her hands and carefully twisted it. It was damp with her sweat and comfortably held its new shape. Then with no warning she flicked the cloth violently at Charlotte. The thick whip lashed exactly where she'd aimed. Perfectly against Charlotte's hungry, hungry cunt.

'Ouch!' Charlotte said, but she didn't mean it.

As the heavy vest swung against her it injected a shot of adrenalin and madness deep into her body. The whip stroke hurt like hell but the pleasure was greater. No one had dared hit her pussy before.

And no one ever made her feel like this.

Libka whipped again and this time the vest flailed further under, hooking the bottom of Charlotte's cheeks before drawing quickly back across her clit.

Again it lashed, again Charlotte squealed. She wanted to shut her eyes, but she couldn't take them off Libka's body. She didn't want to miss a second of this feast, as this pagan goddess prepared her sacrifice at the stake.

Charlotte ignored the burning in her wrists, the harsh splinters of the wooden stepladder cutting into her ankles. She didn't feel the stinging of the vest against her exposed inner thighs. All she knew was the pleasure building in her pussy, swelling with each heavy blow, pushing her closer to the edge. Could she come like this?

She was going to try.

But then Libka stopped.

'No! Please!'

Libka ignored Charlotte's desperate cries. She threaded the vest between her own legs then reached round Charlotte and pulled it between hers as well. Both women were joined at the hip by the small piece of cloth, pulled taut by a hand behind each of their backs.

Libka leaned into Charlotte's chest and both women kissed again,

neither of them able to use their hands. The sense of helplessness just isolated the pleasure in their mouths. But not just there.

For the first time Charlotte knew what was happening. And for the first time she had some control. Even as she kissed and felt Libka's hot tongue dance with hers, she writhed down on the taut cloth between her legs and jumped as she felt its thickness push up against her fat clit, cut into her open lips, pull against her skin and the silk at the same time. She could feel Libka doing the same, each woman's cunt desperate to feed off as much of the vest as possible. Still they kissed, and still they inched up and down, backwards and forwards, bound together at their pussies by the workman's vest, joined at the mouth by their hungry tongues.

Charlotte felt the orgasm grow and wished she could hold it back. She wanted to feel Libka's breasts for longer but there was nothing she could do. Part of her wished Libka would suddenly stop again, do something different, regain control. But Charlotte could hear the girl's noises, she could sense the climax was coming for her as well.

When it arrived Libka screamed like an animal in a trap. As she came she pulled hard on the vest with her hand, so hard that she dropped it with the other. But it was enough. Charlotte let the surge of elation spread out from her pussy, like ripples from a stone dropped in a lake.

It was later, minutes later, that she dared to open her eyes. Only then was she aware of Libka's warm arms cuddling tightly around her. Only then did the piercing pain in her ankles and wrists threaten to make her cry.

And only then did she notice the unmistakable figure of Dan the chippy standing in the doorway.

Charlotte smiled. She was going to enjoy this conversion after all.

Sixty Nine

The invitations had been distributed, sixty-eight in all, in the form of a gold card featuring the numerals '69' circled by Ouroboros, the tail-eating snake. No other information was necessary – no date, time or venue specified – since the invitation could only relate to one momentous event and such specifics were superfluous. Nor did the invitation request an *RSVP*, since a rejection was inconceivable.

The Countess Vanessa herself would be the sixty-ninth attendant at the Ball whose purpose was to mark her attaining an equivalent number of years. The date would also memorialise the two decades since the loss of her beloved husband, Occasus da Silva, the Count of a small corner of Old Europe whose enormous chateau and estate she now headed. The Countess had spent the years since her husband's death largely in the pursuit of corporeal pleasure and experiment that, in its public expression, had taken the form of expanding the Count's substantial legacy through establishing an exclusive *haute couture* emporium that was the very *ponctuation* of the *beau monde*.

The sixty-eight guests arrived from all parts of the globe to be accommodated in the rambling chateau in the days prior to the Ball. The

Countess had chosen her guests carefully, ensuring they would all know what was expected of them. The day of the Ball was spent in elaborate preparations of cuisine and décor: while the finest wines and condiments were delivered, sixty-nine of the chateau's countless rooms were each being draped by the Countess's throng of assistants in a distinct shade, so that, as one moved from room to room, one experienced a gradual transition from a pale pink through to the deepest purple. As the hour of the feast approached the guests were issued with a velvet floor-length domino cloak and mask corresponding to the shade of drapery in one of the chateau's rooms, and instructed to wear this clothing only to the Ball.

✳ ✳ ✳

Just before six o'clock, the guests arrived in the vast banquet hall to stand behind their assigned chairs at an enormous oak refectory table. Each neighbour was unknown to the other and in any case was disguised by their hooded cloaks and masks, beneath which they were all naked. Behind the head of the candle-lit table hung the impressive heraldry of the Estate featuring a 'globus cruciger' in which, blasphemously, the orb of a voluptuous, upturned derrière was crowned with a crucifix formed from a thighbone crossed by an erect penis. In the huge hearth at the opposite end of the hall, two giant boars stuffed with game fowl were roasting on a spit, their snouts inserted deep into the other's rectum.

Upon the sixth stroke of the clock the Countess Vanessa swept in with her retinue of attendants. She was masked, although her appearance was so striking that it left no doubt as to her identity: her hair was coloured and fashioned to rise up into a single flame from ice-blonde roots to crimson, spiked tips. She wore a yellow satin bodice with scarlet gossamer-silk gloves and behind her ran a floor-length, foaming organza and tulle train, in an identical flame design to her hair. Most notable, however, was that below the waist she wore only a pair of mid-calf, puce musketeer boots and that her *bonne bouche poilu* had been dyed to match that of her head. Her gait as she entered the hall was proud and regal as she surveyed the assembly, jutting her head to each side like some magnificent fire-hybrid of cockatoo and rooster.

The Countess reached her chair at the head of the table and stood at it. Behind her, high on the wall, was a life-sized painting of the deceased Count showing him as his proud distaff relative 'Scaramouche' in the style of the topical portraiture of the 1940s. An extraordinarily handsome beau of unmistakeable aristocratic bearing, the painting depicted him masked and wearing a scarlet bandanna, gold earrings, a voluminous laced shirt, black tights and brandishing a rapier overhead. With his arrow-straight spine and his head tilted back, he was the very image of haughty superiority, staring down his nose but with a play of humour around the eyes and mouth that was irresistible, the whole effect suggesting his great mentor and running mate of the post-war Riviera set, the movie star Errol Flynn.

The guests were all familiar with the legendary meeting of the Count and Countess at a grand hunt some fifty years before. He was thirty years old, a slightly world-weary aristocratic dandy, and she was an eighteen-year-old raw-boned trapeze artist (or 'aerialist' as she preferred) with copper hair. From an old circus family, Vanessa found no difficulty in impressing Count Occasus with her intellect, taste and poise. The legend was that within a mere five minutes of their introduction after table, the Count had entreated the young woman to walk with him in the gardens and there, at the heart of an Elizabethan maze, they had urgently and ravishingly enjoined themselves in sexual congress that had the inevitability of two planets on collision course in space.

As her husband's image stood over them then, the Countess's welcoming speech to her guests was brief and consisted mainly of instructions: no one was to speak during the meal, although the guests might feel moved to emit carnal expressions of engagement. These might be necessitated (the Countess paused dramatically) by the unusual seating she had devised: upon pulling their high-backed, oak chairs from under the table her guests would discover that its seat was a chrome-plated metal inlay moulded up in the centre to a thin, oiled, chrome-plated protuberance several inches in height. 'My esteemed guests,' the Countess declaimed, 'you are instructed to insert this protrusion into an orifice as you seat yourselves at table.'

As the guests pulled out their chairs and lowered themselves, hoisting their cloaks over their hips and pressing down onto their exotic seats, a wave of sighs and gasps was audible; the Countess preened and glowed with satisfaction as she herself mounted and sat upon her own chrome-dildo seat. Now, she clapped her hands and the roast boars were split open by a portly, naked grill-master as the steaming contents of wild game – rabbit, grouse, pheasant and snipe from the Estate's morning hunt – spilled from their bellies as they turned on the spit. A myriad of servants distributed platefuls of this dish to the impaled diners while yet others circled to fill their crystal goblets from flagons of a vintage ruby red wine.

The guests, by now squirming from the effects of their prosthetic seats, awaited the Countess's signal to begin the feast. Turning to them with a dramatic sweep of the arm she lifted her goblet and pronounced, 'And now we must be filled at the lesser end!' Raising a leg of flesh to her mouth she bit lustily into it and, in the absence of any cutlery, her sixty-eight dinner companions followed her cue, eating with their hands and swigging lustily at their goblets as they pushed their arses and cunts deeper down into their chairs. With their cloaks lifted over their hips, each could peer sideways and downwards into the groins of their neighbours as they rutted on their seats, occasionally reaching between their legs to smear the chrome shafts with the animal grease on their fingers.

Some time into this peculiar repast, it became apparent that the effects of the wine and meal were more than gastronomic. A glowing sensation emitted from the craws of the diners as they digested the herbal aphrodisiacs in which the food had been marinated and the wine fermented. As the infusions dispersed a floating sensation arose, relaxing the innards of the diners and opening their innermost flood-gates, which – together with their rutting and the scent of pheromones in the room – drove the guests' sexual excitement to the limits of restraint.

✳ ✳ ✳

By eight o'clock, when the gathering was in danger of reaching a plateau of sexual frenzy, the Countess clapped her hands and a dessert of figs preserved in cognac was distributed by the attendants, who blew out the candles as they circled. The guests, adjusting their eyes to the

twilight entering from the floor-length windows along the wall of the banquet hall, squinted into the gloom as a curious, ungainly creature entered through a window, shuffling between the shadows to climb with lumbering animal grace onto the great table.

The Countess's guests were suspended between curiosity and confusion. Music began: a seasick tarantella made the shadowy, two-backed beast lurch around, knocking plates of food and crystal goblets from the table to smash and splash upon the oaken floorboards. The Countess herself lit a single candle at the head of the table so that the diners could perceive the hybrid apparition in its full, horrifying beauty. A tall corpulent male, wearing a bull-like mask, carried a small woman clinging upside down to him, her thighs hooked over his shoulders either side of his neck, so that, with her arms wrapped round his waist, her body was locked to his and their bellies and chests rubbed together. The woman's hindquarters were thus positioned directly under the Minotaur's hirsute mask from which a supernaturally long tongue emerged from the mouth to flick and slather the length of her sexual ravine as she in turn arched her neck down to ingest the tip of his engorged penis into her mouth.

They commenced to stagger and dance together, locked in this curious embrace, circling slowly while the diners found their drug-induced sexual arousal heightening as their hands reached to finger their sexual parts and those of their neighbours. More erotic still were those who, in an ecstasy of heightened sensory experience, simply rubbed their legs against their neighbours, spreading their knees ever wider and lifting their toes from the floor as their sexes bloomed above the table rim into a ring of swollen, lubricious flesh thrusting into the air in front of their bellies.

As the tarantella ground to a tremulous fading note, the table-dancers reached a crescendo of swirling, sweeping more plates from the table before crashing to the floor in a gasping heap. But now, since the time was just on nine o'clock, the Countess arose, the candles were relit and a small gong was struck for attention.

The Countess barked at her guests: 'There are sixty-nine draped rooms in the chateau; please locate the one whose shade matches your

apparel. Remain there and await me. Each of you will be joined by a beautiful, keen lover equipped as Hermaphroditus to bid your every will. You are free to disport in your own manner but hold this in your thoughts: as I advance through the rooms, your ultimate release must coincide with my perusal and enjoinment with those actions that climax your excitement. Put simply, your orgasm must be postponed until I arrive in your presence to sanction and to trigger it.'

Many of the assembly looked somewhat sheepish at this pronouncement since the table legs, indeed the table-top itself, were already dripping with come, and the floor around was generally soaked and stained with sexual juices mixed with spilled wine and animal fat.

✳ ✳ ✳

Now, the guests were released to run through the rooms, matching their vestments to the shades of the drapery. Once ensconced, they relaxed on their divans and rested from the exertions of the banquet in front of roaring open fires. Those in the pinkest rooms were in the highest state of anticipation and readiness, calling their attendant-lovers forward in preparation for the Countess's arrival.

The coal fires in each room expended sufficient heat so that the guests' cloaks were by now abandoned, although their masks remained. Thus, the gender of each guest was now apparent although the Countess's invitation had been made by dint of their versatility. As the orgy commenced, the Countess began her peregrination.

In the first room, decorated the lightest shade of pink, a beautiful saucer-eyed young woman kneeled over a mature, grey-haired man. Her legs were splayed so far across the floor at either side of the man's head and her slim buttocks pushed down so hard onto his face that he had thrust up his entire distended tongue into her hole, like some tumid growth from the very earth beneath. This woman was pulsating and the man was probing with his tongue at one end while thrusting his cock into her mouth at the other so that they were sliding around and lifting off the floor in the heat of their lustful wrestling, scratching and clawing at the flanks of each other as they galvanised the muscles in their thighs, inching towards climax.

Thus, their coupling had reached a brink as the Countess arrived surrounded by her attendants, who were now also masked and naked. A few of these carried silver platters piled with all shapes and sizes of prosthetics equipped with straps and grips in a heap of bewildering possibility. First, the Countess snatched the man's cock from the young woman's mouth and then, with an expert, silken touch, jiggered it to a frenzy before replacing it like a cork into a hole. And then, bestriding the young woman's raised arse, without turning her head, she proffered her hand and requested a dildo from a minion, like a surgeon murmuring for his knife. The Countess licked and sucked the dildo to lubricate it with her saliva before slowly and evenly pushing it into the woman's anus, just over the place where the man's tongue vanished into her body. Lowering herself to sit astride the woman's back, the Countess rode the excited couple like a bucking animal until they each shot their come into the other's mouths, yelping and shivering with bestial release.

The Countess was wrought-up by this display and not at all displeased. A ripple ran through the rooms as she strode on to continue her tour through the chateau, from salmon to oyster pink, the rooms growing deeper-hued as if the cortege were itself penetrating a glorious, devouring sexual orifice. In each room the Countess viewed a series of *soixante-neufs* that stuck together so firmly they could barely move, resembling the fluttering sex between exotic jungle arachnids. Here, the Countess would watch for a few moments before clapping her hands to permit their bodies to tip into an explosive orgasm, as if detonating it.

The rooms had reached a shade of shocking pink when the Countess paused before two masked young men with lithe, muscular bodies and shocks of overgrown curls. They were stood in the heels-over-head position, with the smaller one of the two hanging down, his feet locked behind his bearer's neck. They were slowly sucking each other's penises, savouring the taste of cock as if enjoying a revivifying confection and slurping with unhurried gusto. Bacchic men-boys, their appearance suggested some antique Roman orgy and each had inserted several fingers in the other's arse, probing in time with the rhythmic sucking. The Countess, stepping forward, was pleased by this display and ran her hands all over them, rubbing the young men's oily bodies.

As she took the standing man's balls in hand she ran her tongue around his lips that curved around the root of the suspended man's prick.

The Countess ordered them to dismantle and arrange themselves on the floor in a sideways *soixante-neuf* before lowering herself to lie between them. First she took the penis in front of her face into her mouth. Then she crooked her leg in the air so that the same keen young man could reach between her legs to lick at her wet, swollen vulva like a cat. Lastly, she arched her back so that her anus could be penetrated by the second young man lying behind her. The Countess had always gloried in being fucked up her arse while being licked; something she was able to convey as she sucked avidly on the cock in her mouth.

Having relished the wonderful triad of sensations this tryst afforded, the Countess removed the cock from her mouth with one hand while pulling the second one out of her arse with the other. Grasping the two engorged pricks, she used a steady, rhythmic wanking to build the young men to spunk on her, the one behind all over her flanks and the one in front on her breasts as the men rolled away, groaning in ecstasy. Immediately, the Countess's assistants moved forward to wipe her shining body with silken cloths, although she insisted on pushing a small pearl of sperm into her distended arsehole with a crooked finger.

The Countess's convoy continued: in an orchid-coloured room, the retinue discovered two full-bodied buxom women, one crouched over the other with her tongue buried into her partner's cunt. Again the Countess arranged herself between the lovers, fingering and licking their openings like lotus buds, tonguing the concupiscent sap into her mouth until the women squirted all over her breasts and down between her legs so that the juice mingled with her own luxuriant wetness.

Thus was the evening of the Countess's sixty-ninth birthday spent, as she advanced through unbridled, imaginative couplings upon the theme of her year. Passing through the reddening rooms she and her retinue would stand about peering at the crazed couplings, the fucking and sucking; the biting, pinching and probing. And sometimes, according to her arousal, which was welcome and desired by all, the Countess would lend her hands or tongue, her anus or her cunt to the mix with which she was presented.

By the time the rooms were draped in darkening, luscious maroons and purples, the sexual engagements were increasingly agonised from prolonging their release to await the Countess's presence. As she passed through, the orgiasts shrieked and groaned as they shot into each other's mouths so that it was as if the Countess's procession were being followed by a seismic wave of squirting come, hovering at her back before crashing behind her as she strutted through the chateau.

✷ ✷ ✷

By midnight, the Countess Vanessa had passed through the sixty-eighth room and a gong was struck to call her satiated guests to assemble at the sixty-ninth: a darkened atrium of a small theatre with overlooking galleries. Climbing to their seats, the Countess's guests leaned over the balustrades to peer down from all four sides into the dimmed lyceum below.

Suddenly hushed, the assistants left the Countess alone in a pale pool of light. Her appointed lover stood in the shadows and the audience gasped: the apparition seemed to be Count Occasus da Silva himself, the masked, gallant young blade dressed in coxcomb finery as 'Scaramouche', stepped down from the painting in the banquet hall. As a small band off to one side struck up a funereal sarabande the Countess was spellbound by the vision of her husband as he was when they fell in love, and he stepped out of the shadows to stand before her. Slipping into the slow rhythm of the music the lovers circled each other around the floor, weaving and dipping in time, seeming for all the world like mating big cats, occasionally baring their teeth to hiss at each other.

After some minutes of this weird, achingly deliberate masked pas de deux, the Count and Countess met in the middle of the floor. With one swift movement, the Countess snatched the rapier from its sheath at the Count's side, spun it through the air, took a step backwards to catch the sword in her right hand, and pressed its tip to his throat. Still they circled in their weird sarabande, the Count seemingly fixed by his neck to the end of the sword as his arms lifted overhead, rippling and rolling like seaweed under water. With a flourish and without breaking step, the Countess flashed the rapier through the laces at the front of the Count's shirt, cutting it away to reveal his lean, muscular build.

Lowering the sword slowly, she deftly lunged to incise a circle from the front of his tights, exposing his cock and balls to the air.

The years peeling away, Vanessa cast the rapier aside and moved closer in to her beloved Occasus, the sweat on his chest wiping damply onto her arms and torso. She was flushed and aroused so that her back arched and her movement became lewd as she straddled his thigh, rubbing her naked groin up and down against him. She cupped the loosed balls in her hand and juggled them in her palm before fondling the Count's penis with slow, lascivious strokes until he was as stiff as marble. As the music suddenly ceased its dirge-like refrain, the only movement discernible in the gloom was the ominous lowering of a pair of trapeze bars from the ceiling at opposite ends of the room.

The band struck up again but this time with a lively bolero. The Count and Countess, facing each other across the room, seated themselves on their trapezes and were hoisted up into the air. As they swung, first apart and then towards each other, the guests, now level in height in the surrounding gallery, followed the couple's pendulum-like motion. The Countess executed a drop-and-turn so that, with her knees hooked over the bar, she swung with her head hanging down, facing into the arc towards the Count who by now was swinging from his bar by the hands. As they swung wider, their arcs inched closer together until at the apex of her sweep the Countess leaned out to slip from her trapeze into mid-air. As she fell upside down towards the floor, the Count, hanging from his swinging trapeze, reached her at the last moment and the Countess fastened to him, wrapping her legs and arms around him, clinging to him upside down so that they swung together suspended in the sixty-nine position.

As they dangled together in this way, sweeping the air in a wide arc, with the Count's hands tightly gripping the trapeze, they took each other's sex-parts into their mouths. The Countess felt the blood trickling down through her body to her head as she hung upside-down, intensifying the sensation in her cunt as the Count tongued her hole and bit at her clitoris while they swung back and forth across the room. She could feel his cock swelling as she sucked him in, expelling the air

in her mouth down through her nose so as to create an inescapable vacuum around the Count's shaft and helmet.

Now, the music switched time to become a fandango, lurching and aligning its rhythm with the swing of the trapeze. The audience in the galleries were restless and aroused again after their exertions earlier and some were openly wanking themselves or each other as they watched the Count and Countess swing before them locked in their incredible embrace. The Countess felt her arousal radiating to all parts of her body as she swung upside down and her orgasm built from a point far deep within her.

Indeed, as the Countess swung, inverted and clamped to the Count while he licked and sucked her engorged slit, she felt a momentous surge from the pit of her stomach that made her entire body shake with waves of excitement. In her first convulsion of orgasm, she felt the Count shooting his seed inside her mouth and she came more times in quick succession, finally reaching an explosive spending that made it impossible for her to hold on any longer, and as she slipped the band halted and the revellers gasped and then she fell abruptly like a sack of fragile coral, to shatter in a broken heap on the floor far below.

In the appalled hush, the Countess Vanessa uttered her last words to her beloved husband: 'My darling . . . at last . . . I am coming . . .'

The Libertine

W hat's in a name? Well, in the case of John Wilmot, Second Earl of Rochester, otherwise known as 'The Libertine', it's an awful lot. In the seventeenth century, Rochester had the dishonour of falling out with the King on a regular basis – often sent to the Tower – as well as being his favourite court entertainer. He died aged 33 of that scourge of the excessive life – syphilis. But what a lot he packed into those 33 years.

Born on 1 April 1647, Rochester was courtier, rake, satirist and libertine. As a friend of Charles II he got away with murder – quite literally, when one drunken escapade ended with a companion dead on a spike. He also evaded capture after twice kidnapping Elizabeth Mallet – who eventually agreed to marry the insufferable rogue.

During one of his episodes on the run from the law, Rochester set up a practice curing infertility in women. Rumour has it his bespoke method was not without success – although the many newly cuckolded fathers were none the wiser.

Fascinated by the theatre, Rochester wrote many scenes for various mistresses. But it was his ribald poetry for which we love him now. It's also the reason why Johnny Depp agreed to play Rochester in the 2004

film *The Libertine* and why Aphra Behn created the wayward character Willmore in her Restoration comedy, *The Rover*.

Judge for yourself. We've selected a few lines for your naughty delectation below. Be honest now. You'd like to be kidnapped by him, wouldn't you?

Love Miss A.P. x

A Ramble in St James's Park

Much wine had passed, with grave discourse
Of who fucks who, and who does worse
(Such as you usually do hear
From those that diet at the Bear),
When I, who still take care to see
Drunkenness relieved by lechery,
Went out into St James's Park
To cool my head and fire my heart.
But though St James has th' honor on 't,
'Tis consecrate to prick and cunt.
There, by a most incestuous birth,
Strange woods spring from the teeming earth;
For they relate how heretofore,
When ancient Pict began to whore,
Deluded of his assignation
(Jilting, it seems, was then in fashion),
Poor pensive lover, in this place
Would frig upon his mother's face;
Whence rows of mandrakes tall did rise
Whose lewd tops fucked the very skies.
Each imitative branch does twine

In some loved fold of Aretine,
And nightly now beneath their shade
Are buggeries, rapes, and incests made.
Unto this all-sin-sheltering grove
Whores of the bulk and the alcove,
Great ladies, chambermaids, and drudges,
The ragpicker, and heiress trudges.
Carmen, divines, great lords, and tailors,
Prentices, poets, pimps, and jailers,
Footmen, fine fops do here arrive,
And here promiscuously they swive.

Along these hallowed walks it was
That I beheld Corinna pass.
Whoever had been by to see
The proud disdain she cast on me
Through charming eyes, he would have swore
She dropped from heaven that very hour,
Forsaking the divine abode
In scorn of some despairing god.
But mark what creatures women are:
How infinitely vile, when fair!

Three knights o' th' elbow and the slur
With wriggling tails made up to her.

The first was of your Whitehall blades,
Near kin t' th' Mother of the Maids;
Graced by whose favor he was able
To bring a friend t' th' Waiters' table,
Where he had heard Sir Edward Sutton
Say how the King loved Banstead mutton;
Since when he'd ne'er be brought to eat
By 's good will any other meat.
In this, as well as all the rest,
He ventures to do like the best,
But wanting common sense, th' ingredient

In choosing well not least expedient,
Converts abortive imitation
To universal affectation.
Thus he not only eats and talks
But feels and smells, sits down and walks,
Nay looks, and lives, and loves by rote,
In an old tawdry birthday coat.

The second was a Grays Inn wit,
A great inhabiter of the pit,
Where critic-like he sits and squints,
Steals pocket handkerchiefs, and hints
From 's neighbor, and the comedy,
To court, and pay, his landlady.

The third, a lady's eldest son
Within few years of twenty-one
Who hopes from his propitious fate,
Against he comes to his estate,
By these two worthies to be made
A most accomplished tearing blade.

One, in a strain 'twixt tune and nonsense,
Cries, 'Madam, I have loved you long since.
Permit me your fair hand to kiss';
When at her mouth her cunt cries, 'Yes!'
In short, without much more ado,
Joyful and pleased, away she flew,
And with these three confounded asses
From park to hackney coach she passes.

So a proud bitch does lead about
Of humble curs the amorous rout,
Who most obsequiously do hunt
The savory scent of salt-swoln cunt.
Some power more patient now relate
The sense of this surprising fate.

Gods! that a thing admired by me
Should fall to so much infamy.
Had she picked out, to rub her arse on,
Some stiff-pricked clown or well-hung parson,
Each job of whose spermatic sluice
Had filled her cunt with wholesome juice,
I the proceeding should have praised
In hope sh' had quenched a fire I raised.
Such natural freedoms are but just:
There's something generous in mere lust.
But to turn a damned abandoned jade
When neither head nor tail persuade;
To be a whore in understanding,
A passive pot for fools to spend in!
The devil played booty, sure, with thee
To bring a blot on infamy.

But why am I, of all mankind,
To so severe a fate designed?
Ungrateful! Why this treachery
To humble fond, believing me,
Who gave you privilege above
The nice allowances of love?
Did ever I refuse to bear
The meanest part your lust could spare?
When your lewd cunt came spewing home
Drenched with the seed of half the town,
My dram of sperm was supped up after
For the digestive surfeit water.
Full gorged at another time
With a vast meal of slime
Which your devouring cunt had drawn
From porters' backs and footmen's brawn,
I was content to serve you up
My ballock-full for your grace cup,
Nor ever thought it an abuse
While you had pleasure for excuse —

You that could make my heart away
For noise and color, and betray
The secrets of my tender hours
To such knight-errant paramours,
When, leaning on your faithless breast,
Wrapped in security and rest,
Soft kindness all my powers did move,
And reason lay dissolved in love!

May stinking vapors choke your womb
Such as the men you dote upon
May your depraved appetite,
That could in whiffling fools delight,
Beget such frenzies in your mind
You may go mad for the north wind,
And fixing all your hopes upon't
To have him bluster in your cunt,
Turn up your longing arse t' th' air
And perish in a wild despair!
But cowards shall forget to rant,
Schoolboys to frig, old whores to pant;
The Jesuits' fraternity
Shall leave the use of buggery;
Crab-louse, inspired with grace divine,
From earthly cod to heaven shall climb;
Physicians shall believe in Jesus,
And disobedience cease to please us,
Ere I desist with all my power
To plague this woman and undo her.
But my revenge will best be timed
When she is married that is limed.
In that most lamentable state
I'll make her feel my scorn and hate:
Pelt her with scandals, truth or lies,
And her poor cur with jealousies,
Till I have torn him from her breech,
While she whines like a dog-drawn bitch;

Loathed and despised, kicked out o' th' Town
Into some dirty hole alone,
To chew the cud of misery
And know she owes it all to me.

And may no woman better thrive
That dares prophane the cunt I swive!

How to ...
Host Your Own S&M Party

I hear that some of you, having read the 'how to' section in our pink side, yawned and said, 'And?!' Well, my dark little horses, you should perhaps eschew your 'daily latte' for a 'double espresso' – with a 'shot', as it were.

It might not be something that you want to do every day – or night – but I for one sometimes get the urge. Doesn't everyone?

Maybe there'll be two of you, maybe a threesome, maybe moresome. The lights could be on . . . or do you want it pitch-black? Maybe you'll have the most decadent toys or maybe you'll improvise. Whatever the scenario, one thing is sure: clever girls always want to know how to do it better.

You have come to the right place.

Welcome to Miss A.P.'s dungeon.

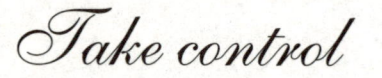

Take control

So, you are in a dominant mood. What do you want from your sub? Is he your plaything or your pet? Your partner or your possession? Perhaps he is to be your experiment to perfect as you will?

You could lead him around your house on a leash; he could work for you while a gag-ball stops him answering back. Or perhaps you want him chained to a table, licking your floor, licking your feet . . . licking everywhere you wish? You might prefer to keep him perfectly still while you study his skin as the hot wax drips on his nipples or solidifies on his cock; or watch the burn as ice takes its fiery grip.

Show some restraint?

A little restraint can do wonders. A lot of restraint can achieve much more. Handcuffs are a wonderful way to assert who's boss. They come in all shapes and sizes and can be used for myriad delights. (Imagine that satisfying click as you adjust to wrist size.) What could be better if you want your playmates to feel cold steel cut into their wrists. And once in place there's no turning back. Only one thing can save your prisoner, and that's the key. But where did you put it? He'll have to look very hard.

If it's image you're interested in but pain isn't for you, there are softer options. Or you could simply use a silk scarf to bind – tight.

Handcuffs are wonderfully adaptable. Tie hands behind the back, in front or round a lamppost. Wherever you need to keep your prisoner, they can oblige.

Ah, but I can see that you have quite elevated tastes. Wish to try something more esoteric? Try the thumb-lock? Tiny holes that shrink further when opposable digits are inserted – small, but oh so captivating.

I remember with particular fondness a tryst in which I found myself pleasurably tangled in a web of restraint. My lover had had the courtesy to blindfold me, heightening the experience. My wrists, pulled

back above my head, with leather leashes, comfortably lined with suede. My ankles, however, were not treated with such mercy and as I wriggled and squirmed my objection to my (albeit favourable) situation, I deduced that what at first seemed a firm grip was actually a fine sandpaper lining which caused the most delicious burning sensation the more I moved. I then presume that my ankle restraints also had a buckle attachment because my master had secured my feet behind my knees with yet another leather band. But the really clever part was the constricting mechanism which got tighter the more I pulled. The human knot that I presented must have been a delectable sight.

Next time I feel I might return the favour with rubber . . . or simply rope. Or maybe rope upon rubber.

I have a close acquaintance who loves to wear her opera gloves – with a difference. They are made of seductively soft leather, in black of course, that pull on up above the elbow. Their secret is that they are joined at the fingertips. From their sideseam hangs a length of leather by which they can be secured to . . . well, anything. Furthermore, a series of hooks up the side of the gloves make them the perfect way to restrain the arms behind the back.

Do you like the sound of these? You do? Then you'll love full-arm binders. And don't forget your silk stockings. Very effective.

Now gloves and cuffs are perfect for the naked body, but sometimes, I imagine, you don't want to see anything apart from the look in their eyes as they struggle. You will find, dear pupil, that there's something so satisfyingly claustrophobic about a perfectly fitting straitjacket.

Then again, you might be in the mood to glimpse a little flesh after all. It is our prerogative to change on a whim, of course. Tiny bolero jackets that expose your victim's breasts are a delightful innovation.

The one thing all of these restrictive habits have in common, marvellously, is a firm grip between the legs. Do you want your prisoner to show his or her backside? Or not? Your choice . . .

But what if this doesn't really fit your bill? What if the fit is not really

tight enough at all? What if you want your partner to be really snug? You need a sleepsack. I heard it once described as 'Iron Maiden meets a sleeping bag' – a strange description of course, yet curiously apt.

If you prefer to mix and match with your straitjacket, why not try a leather leg binder?

Suspension

You've secured your playmate, he won't cause you any more problems, but how do you make sure he's really going to benefit from your generous correction? You might go for crucifixion, of course, but if you're out of nails there's only one option: suspend him from the ceiling via a suspension bar and wrist fasteners. You can improvise with broom handles and ropes, but they're so useful for other fun so I suggest a bespoke steel bar and buckled attachments. Nothing says vulnerable like a man on a hook. He'll beg to be let down and you'll put your heel on his chest and tell him to shut up. If you push hard enough he'll spin round on his chains.

Solitary confinement

Even the best lovers need to rest and recuperate sometimes but how do you stop your slave running away as soon as your back is turned? It's a problem that vexes us all.

A dungeon collar around the neck – spikes pointing inwards or out – is a good enough starting point. But if the wall you're fastening to is a little suspect then what about a ball and chain? Can your prisoner really lift that weight to get up the stairs? Or what about the good old-fashioned doggie spreader? Get your pet on his knees, clamp shut this giant curved bar – and laugh in his face as his wrists become locked to his ankles.

This dungeon has, as you would expect of me, plenty of room to manoeuvre, therefore I have this metal cage. The gaps are wide enough

to encourage the victim to reach out – and, of course, allow me to reach in – but narrow enough to prevent actual escape. Replacing a good slave can be an expensive business.

Sensory deprivation

In the end, it's all about the senses. How does he smell, how does she feel, how does he taste, how do they look? Deprive them of one of their senses and watch control become yours. And which one's best? For me, the answer is simple: I love to restrain but my skin prickles when I deprive my slave of their vision. When they can't see, they can only imagine. And there's nothing more powerful than an imagination under pressure.

Start with a blindfold. Sometimes an item of silk clothing tied firmly around the head will be enough. Sometimes you'll want to go further, maybe a velvet mask with no eyes cut out. Still want more and you're in bondage territory, with nowhere else to go but the full mask. They call it a gimp mask in films, and they always make them out of latex. But you can improvise. A loose hessian sack tied just too tightly around your slave's neck will work as well as rubber clamped all over his face. He won't see you, he won't know what you're about to touch him with. He won't see the paddle strike his wicked arse. He won't know the wax is poised an inch above his sturdy, expectant cock.

The full-head seclusion cage is not to everyone's tastes but some slaves deserve nothing less. If your playmate suffers from claustrophobia – perfect. If he doesn't – then he soon will.

Japanese rope bondage

So much of what I've shared so far can be tried by beginners. Now I come to an area where the more you know, the better it works. Forget practice makes perfect – practice makes pervert.

Japanese rope bondage takes submission to a new level. It is artistic

and precise. But there is one important difference. The slave can find it very enjoyable. Ask yourself this question: do you want your slave to be happy?

Of course, these techniques are traditionally used on women. Lucky us.

Shinju, meaning 'the pearls', is a method of restraining your subject's breasts – and heightening the sense in them at the same time. A rope is tied around the torso, just under your sub's titties, and tied at the back. Then another, then another, and another still is added. Tie the ends together so the knot is near the spine – then add another rope above the breasts.

Now take your final rope and loop it under the strands and pull – there should be a 'V' shape leading over the shoulders. Now the fun begins. Pull the V and watch the lower ropes rise over the breasts. When you've tied the knots the spine will be stimulated. And before you know it her breasts will be alert to the slightest sensation. If a breath, a feather can work such miracles . . . imagine what a smart smack could do!

Another technique is the Sukaranbo, which means 'the cherry'. This is to feed a rope carefully around one leg between your sub's labia and over her clitoris. Tie the whole thing again at the back. Maybe you want another knot near her little hole as well? Then tie another around the other leg and watch the knots form the cherry. Yes, she'll have permanent contact on her clit, but watch as she gets a sensation from her rubbed thighs that she's never felt before.

Oh, and her bottom will feel like it's never been touched before. Now, I suggest, is the time to let her know what a smack really feels like.

For the full-body effect you can use a Karada – a non-suspension harness. Bind your sub in it or humiliate her by making her wear it to parties.

Canes and whips

Sometimes depriving the senses is the only way to do things. But other times you want your sub to sense every little thing. You want them to see the whip raised above your head. You want them to hear it cut the air behind their head. And most of all you want them to feel.

There's no excuse for not spanking because you don't need any props. Your bare hand will make a wonderful impression. On his backside, on her breasts, on his face. But when you do have time, why not experiment with something a little more exciting?

The wooden ruler will remind him of the times he came in his pants when the French mistress kept him back after school. He'll call you 'Ma'am' and pretend he can't conjugate his verbs, but he just wants another smack with your thirty centimetres.

If maximum coverage is your aim, why not use a wooden paddle? The handle might be made of willow or gold, but as long as the flat part can sting the back of both legs at once you'll be doing it right.

Personally, I like the crop. Very specific, very quick – and very, very painful. Watch the fear in her eyes as you bend it back in your hands and let fly. Every stroke will mark. But perhaps build up to that with something less harsh. A whip lashed with the right action can raise a sweat in any sub. But that's not all. Use the hair – tie it around his cock and pull viciously away so you can almost smell the burn. Tie it around his neck and make him beg for breath. Flick it between her legs and let her eat it with her pussy then flail her with her own heavy juices.

You'll find her begging to take the handle as well. You'll have to be strong – don't give in to the call of her cunt. Not till you're ready.

Remember who is in charge.

Occasional extras

There are some things that even I don't get out every night. These are for special occasions. When he has been a very, very naughty boy.

Only you will know when the time is right.

Don't be afraid to reveal your dark side

Someone once said about sex: 'If it hurts then you're doing it wrong.' How dull must life have been! In this little lesson, I've only just scratched the surface. You might want to scratch a whole lot more. Take control. Improvise. And show your sub who's boss.

They'll thank you for it later.

Marquis De Sade

T he Marquis gets a mention along with our other favourite scribes in our Essensual Reading list, but if anyone has contributed more to the sub-dom area of literature then we've yet to read them. After all, he literally put the 'S' into S&M (Leopold von Sacher-Masoch contributed the 'M').

We've got to be honest. Some of the things he does, some of the things he says, are a little – well, not for all girls' tastes, let's put it like that. But Donatien Alphonse François de Sade was more than a sexual imaginist, he was a philosopher. Simone de Beauvoir said he invented modern existentialism 150 years before her boyfriend Jean-Paul Sartre. You could even say his declaration that sexuality is life's greatest motive pipped Sigmund Freud to the post. There are critics, of course, and feminist Andrea Dworkin for a while has been the loudest. Her own novel, *Ice and Fire*, however, has been accused of having similarities to De Sade's *Juliette*.

Where do we stand? He's the Master.

Do you want him to be yours?

Love Miss A.P. x

Extract from 'Justine (or Good Conduct Well Chastised)':

'Our number is always maintained constant; affairs are so managed that we are always 16, eight in either chamber, and, as you observe, always in the uniform of our particular class; before the day is over you will be given the habit appropriate to the one you are entering; during the day we wear a light costume of the colour which belongs to us; in the evening, we wear gowns of the same colour and dress our hair with all possible elegance. The superintendent of the chamber has complete authority over us, disobedience to her is a crime; her duty is to inspect us before we go to the orgies and if things are not in the desired state she is punished as well as we. The errors we may commit are of several kinds. Each has its particular punishment, and the rules, together with the list of what is to be expected when they are broken, are displayed in each chamber; the Officer of the Day, the person who comes, as I explained a moment ago, to give us orders, to designate the girls for the supper, to visit our living quarters, and to hear the superintendents' complaints, this monk, I say, is the one who, each evening, metes out punishment to whoever has merited it: here are the crimes together with the punishments exacted for them.

'Failure to rise in the morning at the prescribed hour, 30 strokes with the whip (for it is almost always with whipping we are punished;

it were perfectly to be expected that an episode in these libertines' pleasures would have become their preferred mode of correction). The presentation during the pleasurable act, either through misunderstanding or for whatsoever may be the reason, of one part of the body instead of some other which was desired, 50 strokes; improper dress or an unsuitable coiffure, 20 strokes; failure to have given prior notice of incapacitation due to menstruation, 60 strokes; upon the day the surgeon confirms the existence of a pregnancy, 100 strokes are administered; negligence, incompetence, or refusal in connection with luxurious proposals, 200 strokes. And how often their infernal wickedness finds us wanting on that head, without our having made the least mistake! How frequently it happens that one of them will suddenly demand what he very well knows we have just accorded another and cannot immediately do again! One undergoes the punishment nonetheless; our remonstrances, our pleadings are never heeded; one must either comply or suffer the consequences. Imperfect behaviour in the chamber, or disobedience shown the superintendent, 60 strokes; the appearance of tears, chagrin, sorrow, remorse, even the look of the slightest return to Religion, 200 strokes. If a monk selects you as his partner when he wishes to taste the last crisis of pleasure and if he is unable to achieve it, whether the fault be his, which is most common, or whether it be yours, upon the spot, 300 strokes; the least hint of revulsion at the monks' propositions, of whatever nature these propositions may be, 200 strokes; an attempted or concerted escape or revolt, nine days' confinement in a dungeon, entirely naked, and 300 lashes each day; caballing, the instigation of plots, the sowing of unrest, etc, immediately upon discovery, 300 strokes; projected suicide, refusal to eat the stipulated food or the proper quantity, 200 strokes; disrespect shown toward the monks, 180 strokes.

'Those only are crimes; beyond what is mentioned there, we can do whatever we please, sleep together, quarrel, fight, carry drunkenness, riot and gourmandising to their furthest extremes, swear, blaspheme: none of that makes the faintest difference, we may commit those faults and never a word will be said to us; we are rated for none but those I have just mentioned. But if they wish, the superintendents can spare us many of these unpleasantnesses; however, this protection,

unfortunately, can be purchased only by complacencies frequently more disagreeable than the sufferings for which they are substitutes; these women, in both chambers, have the same taste, and it is only by according them one's favours that one enters into their good graces. Spurn one of them, and she needs no additional motive to exaggerate her report of your misdeeds, the monks the superintendents serve double their powers, and far from reprimanding them for their injustice, unceasingly encourage it in them; they are themselves bound by all those regulations and are the more severely chastised if they are suspected of leniency: not that the libertines need all that in order to vent their fury upon us, but they welcome excuses; the look of legitimacy that may be given to a piece of viciousness renders it more agreeable in their eyes, adds to its piquancy, its charm. Upon arriving here each of us is provided with a little store of linen; we are given everything by the half-dozen, and our supplies are renewed every year, but we are obliged to surrender what we bring here with us; we are not permitted to keep the least thing. The complaints of the four friars I spoke of are heard just as are the superintendents'; their mere delation is sufficient to procure our punishment; but they at least ask nothing from us and there is less to be feared from that quarter than from the superintendents who, when vengeance informs their manoeuvres, are very demanding and very dangerous. Our food is excellent and always copious; were it not that their lust derives benefits thence, this article might not be so satisfactory, but as their filthy debauches profit thereby, they spare themselves no pains to stuff us with food: those who have a bent for flogging seek to fatten us, and those, as Jerome phrased it yesterday, who like to see the hen lay, are assured by means of abundant feeding, of a greater yield of eggs. Consequently, we eat four times a day; at breakfast, between nine and ten o'clock we are regularly given *volaille au riz*, fresh fruit or compotes, tea, coffee or chocolate; at one o'clock, dinner is served; each table of eight is served alike; a very good soup, four entrees, a roast of some kind, four second courses, dessert in every season. At five-thirty an afternoon lunch of pastries and fruit arrives. There can be no doubt of the evening meal's excellence if it is taken with the monks; when we do not join them at table, as often happens, since but four of us from each chamber are allowed to go, we are given three roast plates and four entremets; each of us has a daily

ration of one bottle of white wine, one of red, and an half-bottle of brandy; they who do not drink that much are at liberty to distribute their quota to the others; among us are some great gourmands who drink astonishing amounts, who get regularly drunk, all of which they do without fear of reprimand; and there are, as well, some for whom these four meals still do not suffice; they have but to ring, and what they ask for will be brought them at once.

'The superintendents require that the food be consumed, and if someone persists in not wishing to eat, for whatever reason, upon the third infraction that person will be severely punished; the monks' supper is composed of three roast dishes, six entrees followed by a cold plate and eight entremets, fruit, three kinds of wine, coffee and liqueurs: sometimes all eight of us are at table with them, sometimes they oblige four of us to wait upon them, and these four dine afterward; it also happens from time to time that they take only four girls for supper; they are, ordinarily, an entire class; when our number is eight, there are always two from each class. I need hardly tell you that no one ever visits us; under no circumstances is any outsider ever admitted into this pavilion. If we fall ill, we are entrusted to the surgeon friar only, and if we die, we leave this world without any religious ministrations; our bodies are flung into one of the spaces between the circumvallations, and that's an end to it; but, and the cruelty is signal, if the sick one's condition becomes too grave or if there is fear of contagion, they do not wait until we are dead to dispose of us; though still alive, we are carried out and dropped in the place I mentioned; During the 18 years I have been here I have seen more than ten instances of this unexampled ferocity; concerning which they declare it is better to lose one than endanger 16; the loss of a girl, they continue, is of very modest import, and it may be so easily repaired there is scant cause to regret it. Let us move on to the arrangements concerning the monks' pleasures and to all of what pertains to the subject.

'We rise at exactly nine every morning, and in every season; we retire at a later or an earlier hour, depending upon the monks' supper. Immediately we are up, the Officer of the Day comes on his rounds; he seats himself in a large armchair and each of us is obliged to advance, stand before him with our skirts raised upon the side he prefers; he

touches, he kisses, he examines, and when everyone has carried out this duty, he identifies those who are to participate at the evening's exercises: he prescribes the state in which they must be, he listens to the superintendent's report, and the punishments are imposed. Rarely does the officer leave without a luxurious scene in which all eight usually find roles. The superintendent directs these libidinous activities, and the most entire submission on our part reigns during them. Before breakfast it often occurs that one of the Reverend Fathers has one of us called from bed; the jailer friar brings a card bearing the name of the person desired, the Officer of the Day sees to it she is sent, not even he has the right to withhold her, she leaves and returns when dismissed. This first ceremony concluded, we breakfast; from this moment till evening we have no more to do; but at seven o'clock in summer, at six in winter, they come for those who have been designated; the jailer friar himself escorts them, and after the supper they who have not been retained for the night come back to the seraglio. Often, all return; other girls have been selected for the night, and they are advised several hours in advance in what costume they must make their appearance; sometimes only the Girls of the Watch sleep out of the chamber.'

'Girls of the Watch?' I interrupted. 'What function this?' 'I will tell you,' my historian replied. 'Upon the first day of every month each monk adopts a girl who must serve a term as his servant and as the target of his shameful desires; only the superintendents are exempted, for they have the task of governing their chambers. The monks can neither exchange girls during the month, nor make them serve two months in succession; there is nothing more cruel, more taxing than this drudgery, and I have no idea how you will bear up under it. When five o'clock strikes, the Girl of the Watch promptly descends to the monk she serves and does not leave his side until the next day, at the hour he sets off for the monastery. She rejoins him when he comes back; she employs these few hours to eat and rest, for she must remain awake all night throughout the whole of the term she spends with her master; I repeat to you, the wretch remains constantly on hand to serve as the object of every caprice which may enter the libertine's head; cuffs, slaps, beatings, whippings, hard language, amusements, she has got to endure all of it; she must remain standing all night long in her patron's

bedroom, at any instant ready to offer herself to the passions which may stir that tyrant; but the cruellest, the most ignominious aspect of this servitude is the terrible obligation she is under to provide her mouth or her breast for the relief of the one and the other of the monster's needs: he never uses any other vase: she has got to be the willing recipient of everything and the least hesitation or recalcitrance is straightway punished by the most savage reprisals. During all the scenes of lust these are the girls who guarantee pleasure's success, who guide and manage the monks' joys, who tidy up whoever has become covered with filth: for example, a monk dirties himself while enjoying a woman: it is his aide's duty to repair the disorder; he wishes to be excited? The task of rousing him falls to the wretch who accompanies him everywhere, dresses him, undresses him, is ever at his elbow, who is always wrong, always at fault, always beaten; at the suppers her place is behind her master's chair or, like a dog, at his feet under the table, or upon her knees, between his thighs, exciting him with her mouth; sometimes she serves as his cushion, his seat, his torch; at other times all four of them will be grouped around the table in the most lecherous, but, at the same time, the most fatiguing attitudes.

'If they lose their balance, they risk either falling upon the thorns placed nearby, or breaking a limb, or being killed, such cases have been known; and meanwhile the villains make merry, enact debauches, peacefully get drunk upon meats, wines, lust, and upon cruelty.'

'O Heaven!' said I to my companion, trembling with horror, 'is it possible to be transported to such excesses! What infernal place is this!'

Behind the Mask

'I hope you know what you're doing.'

Her companion nodded wordlessly, visible only by the streetlamp outside the cab. As the car pulled away from the traffic lights they were plunged back into darkness. And silence.

Another set of lights, another burst of illumination. Another attempt at conversation.

'Help me with this,' she said, and offered a small, silhouetted object. In the half-light it looked black but he knew it was dark green. He'd chosen it with her, after all.

'Your mask should match your dress,' he had said. And it did. Both were the richest shade he'd ever seen. 'Myrtle', the shop assistant had described it as, although it looked 'Racing Green' to him – far more adventurous. Whatever it was called, it looked beautiful. It was hidden beneath her floor-length coat right now. But he knew it was there. And he knew what was underneath it.

Layers excited him. Peeling the layers. Stripping them away, trying to get to the prize beneath. Being kept from seeing everything. Wanting to and not wanting to at the same time.

Which is why he had wanted to see her in the mask.

He took it from her and examined its intricate design. They'd toyed with others in the shop. The Venetian style had obscured too much of her face. The narrow eye-band concealed too little. Cats, birds, animals – too bizarre. Too distracting. He needed her to be the centre of attention. Not her mask. It should add to her beauty. Not replace it, not hide it.

This 'demon' style was perfect. Half a dozen curlicues, like licks of flame, lashed out from the edges of the mask. He remembered seeing her try it on that first time: a ring of fire around her dark-brown eyes. Dangerous, exotic, intimidating.

He pulled the mask to his own face and let the underwired velvet smoothness rub against his cheek. The next time he felt it against him, she would be wearing it. A shiver ran through his body. The expectation . . .

He edged over and lifted the mask's elastic fastener above her head. Rich, straight hair, directionally cut across her shoulders rising left to right. So dark it was almost black. He could smell the cinnamon of her shampoo. He wanted to bury his head against her neck now, nuzzle into her hair and lose himself in the cab, there and then.

But that wasn't the plan.

'Careful,' she said softly as his left wrist knocked carelessly against the side of her head. She heard his mumbled apology and concentrated on keeping her head as still as possible to aid his positioning of the mask. She knew he was nervous. She quite loved him for it. This was his night. He needed to be in control. But she knew he wasn't. He was on the edge. So excited. Barely holding it together.

✳ ✳ ✳

Richard and Suzanne. Lovers of almost a year. Her, 23, in her first job from university. Him, more than a decade older but in many ways so much her junior. She had studied in London, she was adventurous, she pursued her passions, followed her instincts and relished every moment. For Suzanne, life was for living. Life was about her pleasure.

And then she had met Richard.

Handsome, physically prepossessing, funny – *and shy*. Twelve people had been sitting around that boardroom table. She had only been there to make up the numbers. Nothing important ever got decided at those things and it was a struggle to keep her chin from falling drowsily onto her chest. But then she had heard a new voice and something made her look up from the doodles on her minutes sheet. His glasses she spotted first. Unusual, interesting. Then the twinkle in the eyes behind them. Then his forearms, 'ripped' and tanned in an unseasonal short-sleeved shirt. He looked somehow out of place in the office environment although he seemed unaware how.

Just as he seemed oblivious to the fact that his life would never be the same again.

A few months later Richard walked out on his girlfriend of nine years. Nobody had seen that one coming. His feelings for her hadn't changed in the near decade they'd been together. He still loved her – enough to just hand over the keys to his flat and say, 'Keep it, all of it,' even as she spat shocked abuse in his face. Enough to be struck numb by guilt every moment that he wasn't with Suzanne.

Nine years of bliss – that's how he would have described his old life. They never argued, they had shared interests, their sex life would have been the envy of most of their friends. There had been nothing wrong with it. He had everything. He enjoyed each day.

And then he saw a fire in Suzanne's eyes that had cast a shadow on his life and ignited something in him. Her eyes lit up his world in a new way. Illuminated the truth.

Yes, his life had been perfect. For someone else. Why had he never noticed? It had been like walking around in an off-the-peg Armani suit. Yes, it was comfortable, yes, it felt luxurious and yes, he looked great. But it wasn't made for him. It would never feel as good as something designed just for him.

And that's how Suzanne had made him feel.

Being with her was like burning and drowning and falling from an

aeroplane all at once. Feelings of suffocation, exhaustion, exhilaration –
extreme forms of love and lust he never knew existed.

Until his dying day he would deny he left his old girlfriend for
another woman. *Because* of another woman, definitely. But *for* her? No.
Suzanne had demanded nothing of him. The day he walked out on his
old life he had no guarantees that she would take him. But it didn't
matter. One night with Suzanne had opened his eyes. To possibilities.
To potential. Risks were there to be taken, not avoided. Clocks offered
guidelines, not laws. Work was lucky to have him; not vice versa.

But she had taken him. They became a couple. The most passionate,
sparkling pair of lovers history had ever produced. That was how he felt.
And then the pressure had started. The pressure of distancing himself
from his old comfort zone. Of making the most of his new shot at life.
Most of all – of keeping Suzanne's interest in him.

He was older, he was sure she wanted him to be the experienced
man of the world. He needed to deliver new sensations. Prove he was
worth her time.

❋ ❋ ❋

Which is why he had suggested the DecaDance Masked Ball.

Of course she would love it. An evening of glamour, wild
entertainments and the provocative hint of unnamed naughtiness.
The event's website was almost coy in its disclosures – but there were
clues in the 'rules'. 1) No cameras. 2) No mask: no entry. And 3) 'No'
means 'no'.

By coincidence, 'no' is exactly what Suzanne had said when he'd first
suggested it. 'It will be full of sad old men,' she said.

'No, there's an equal mix of men and women,' Richard recited from
his web research.

'There must be a catch. It's probably like those strip clubs in Soho –
they get you inside, charge you two hundred pounds for a soft drink
and don't put any strippers on.'

'Trust me,' Richard had begged. 'It's on the level. I've looked into it.'

And so she'd agreed. Only now, as she felt Richard tie her mask, did she reflect on what an error it had been. She knew he was really trying to impress her. And that was nice. But he didn't have to – well, not this hard, anyway. Their own sex life was explosive enough. It knew no bounds. Positions, places, styles, risk factor – every box was ticked. She had never known such fulfilment with one person. And he was so strong – when he'd turned her upside down that first time, just as they'd stepped out of the bath together, and lowered his face between her legs she'd smiled as she thought, 'Now *this* a 69. That lying down stuff, that's not a "6" and it's definitely not a "9".'

Yes, he was enough for her. But as himself. Sometimes he seemed to try too hard to excite her. It was like he was trying to distance himself so much from his old life. But who could blame him? Who hasn't reinvented themselves at least once? A new job, a new lover – a potential clean slate. Suzanne had done it herself. She'd been 'Sooz' or 'Susie' all her life. Then she'd started work and decided, 'I'm going to be Suzanne.' For weeks any friends or family phoning had struggled to get past the switchboard. 'The receptionist said no one of that name worked here,' they all complained.

She'd even taken the trouble to master a new signature. A grown-up one, more distinguished, more suitable for adult company.

So she knew what Richard was going through. Desperately trying to reposition himself in the world. He wasn't the pipe-and-slippers guy any more. He was adventurous. He went to masked balls. And he would participate fully in whatever went on there.

They'd made the agreement – 'Anything goes tonight' – but she had resigned herself to it being an evening of watching him sleep with other women. She wouldn't mind, she promised herself. She wouldn't ruin his pleasure. He was trying to impress her. And after all the sacrifices he'd made, he deserved it.

But this would be a one-off. Definitely. She just prayed they could survive it.

She heard the cab driver announce they'd arrived, and peered out the window. Funny how quiet Mayfair can be on a weekend, she

mused. And odd that a national embassy would hire itself out for something like this. She smiled. Obviously someone hadn't admitted all the details.

Richard appeared outside her door and opened it to help her down. She could see the excitement in his face and that lifted her spirits. And he really did look cute in his own 'Zorro'-type mask. Quite subdued next to hers. She looked like an envoy from Hades – he was closer to Robin the Boy Wonder. But it suited him. Highlighted the strength of his face. He was working the look, although she knew he wouldn't understand how.

A crispness in the air made her glad for the overcoat. But even if it had been midday in Jamaica she would still have worn it. It was part of the costume. She wasn't on her stage yet. The unveiling would come later. In front of the right audience.

As their cab pulled away, another two took its place. Similarly disguised couples disembarked, each of them observing the unwritten need for silent decorum as they approached the foreboding steps of the Georgian-style embassy building. Unsuspecting onlookers would imagine they were all attending a Viennese ball. Expensive but dry.

Suzanne felt Richard's hand squeeze hers. 'Are you sure about this?' she asked. 'We can still go somewhere private and unwrap each other. It might be nice after all this effort.'

How she willed him to say 'yes'.

'Darling, you promised,' he said earnestly, just keeping on top of his nerves. 'It will be an experience for us. We agreed.'

'OK.' Suzanne squeezed him back and flashed a reassuring wide smile. This is his night, she reminded herself once more. It will be fine. It will be just like a normal summer ball.

And then they stepped through the austere building's front door.

It wasn't immediately obvious to either of them that the *de rigueur* black-tie suits of the security men and women checking their tickets and bags were actually painted onto their finely toned bodies. The only items

of clothing the guards were actually wearing were imperious golden-eagle beak masks. Nude and yet effortlessly conveying the impression that they were in charge. It was an impressive skill, Suzanne thought.

And then for the disrobing. Queuing to hand over a street coat in exchange for a raffle ticket and a scowl in a club takes the shine off any night out. The organisers of the DecaDance obviously agreed. Once past security, each new arrival was greeted by a beaming faun bearing a flute of chilled champagne and directed towards a changing suite. Suzanne felt herself staring. The fauns weren't exactly clothed, just somehow covered in downy hair all over their lower bodies. And if she didn't know they were wearing masks she could believe they were genuine satyrs' faces looking back at her, with real horns. *It's like we've wandered into Narnia.*

Suzanne felt a small hand slip into hers as one of the imps – female but boyish – led her into the changing area. It was the size of her entire flat. On a weekday it probably welcomed visiting dignitaries. Tonight it played host to a carousel of Bacchanalian costume changes.

She looked around the subtly lit room as the faun unbuttoned her coat. There was so much to take in. And not just visually. The silence of the street was a distant memory. Audible excitement filled the air – the rhythms of loud music pounded through the giant doors from the main ballroom.

A couple nearby were being helped out of their travel clothes by Pan himself. Perfectly respectable one moment – encased head to foot in Edwardian-style finesse with era-perfect full-face masks. Only when they passed did Suzanne notice the one discrepancy. Each outfit was fully backless. Calves, thighs, back, shoulders, neck, waist, bottom – all perfectly displayed thanks to transparent clasps at strategic load-bearing points. Beyond them, three older ladies were putting the finishing touches to their own décolletage, prominently exploited beneath different-coloured horse-mask manes and battle plumage. The women moved as one, via practised dressage routines, bushy tails swishing from their rears.

'Do you think those tails go where I think they go?' Richard asked.

Suzanne nodded distractedly.

'I don't think we're in Kansas any more,' he added.

'I feel positively overdressed,' Suzanne replied.

'I think you look perfect.'

She jolted. The words hadn't come from Richard – he looked as shocked as she was. Between them, the female faun was folding Suzanne's heavy wool coat over her arm and gazing appreciatively at the green-clad woman before her.

'Your dress is as beautiful as I thought it was going to be,' the faun added. 'Do you mind?'

And without waiting for a reply, she reached a small hand around the back of Suzanne's waist and ran it up the fine boned line of her corseted upper body. Suzanne was shocked. But not as much as Richard, by the look of his face.

This wasn't the unveiling of his lover he had planned. He had looked forward so much to unfastening her coat and exposing the hourglass formation of her whaleboned dress, the unnatural smallness of her waist and the majestic way her breasts fanned so imperiously over the top of the bustier. That first glimpse had been tormenting him all night. That's why they had dressed in separate rooms. The revelation, when it happened, was going to set the tone for their evening. He had mapped it all out in his mind. That first glance of the myrtle fabric hugging her lithe thighs then blooming crazily to the floor, split at the front to just below her belt line like a debauched bride. That whole vista of enticement should have been his.

He never expected to have a furry-legged waitress obstructing his view – and getting closer to her than he was.

The faun's hand reached as high as Suzanne's arm and then slowly pulled round to the front. Richard could see everything: the hand had run out of dress. There was nowhere to go now but flesh.

Was it caution or teasing? The little hand hovered at the cusp of the pushed-up white breast – one second, two seconds, three – then lowered imperceptibly. Richard couldn't tell: had contact been made?

One look at Suzanne's face told him it had.

One of the reasons for choosing the 'demon' mask was because of its generous eye holes – the full extent of Suzanne's hypnotic dark eyes and naturally long eyelashes needed to be framed by the mask, not obscured by it. Through those very holes now, Richard could see his girlfriend had closed her eyes. He knew that look. When expectation was about to overwhelm her she submitted to darkness. Let the pleasure come and let her body discover it, not her eyes.

Richard looked quickly around at the other guests. No one else's faun was being so inappropriate. What was wrong with this one? And was it him or was the room getting unbearably warm?

A single party-goer, dressed in a James Bond penguin suit and similar Zorro mask to Richard's own, stopped on his way from the room. His gaze lingered as the faun's hand worked its way across one breast, across the plunging valley, then onto the trembling mound of the next. 'Way to go, girl,' he said. 'Get this party started.'

Suzanne's eyes remained shut but Richard had seen enough. He thrust his empty champagne flute into the astonished spectator's hand and stepped pointedly between the faun and Suzanne, knocking her hands clear from the breasts that were his.

'Come on, honey,' he said. 'We can't hang around in the cloakroom all night.'

Suzanne's eyes flashed open and took a second to adjust to the new development. But she nodded and let Richard lead her from the room. She didn't turn back. She didn't need to. The feel of the faun's touch was still burned on her skin.

Just as she knew the faun's eyes would be burned on her back.

✳ ✳ ✳

The grand hall was like something out of a dream. Or a nightmare – with so many weapons and S&M outfits on show, Suzanne found it hard to tell. People in all shapes and sizes, wearing all manner of costumes – some revealing, some enveloping, some flattering, some not

intended to be – mingled, chatted and drank. She hadn't been expecting this. It was a normal party. Sort of.

She felt Richard's hand tighten on hers as he struggled to take in the wealth of sensory information. Over there a couple chatted to two girls – linked to each other by a short chain that appeared to be attached to their clitorises. Nearer, a chap had stopped to speak to a seated couple. Was it an accident that his groin was level with their faces? His handsome lion mask concealed whether he was shocked to find his penis being stroked by a riding crop in the woman's hand while her partner continued the conversation. Suzanne squeezed Richard's hand. He turned and kissed her hard on the mouth. From the closeness of his body she could tell that wasn't all that was hard.

'Are you enjoying yourself?' she asked.

'Yes,' he said, smiling at the thought of the feast of opportunities before them. 'Are you?'

'Yes.'

'Really?'

'Really, yes.'

And she was. This wasn't a room filled with lonely old men. Not that she could tell, anyway. Numbers were fairly even, although couples weren't necessarily the majority. Lots of single people had apparently arrived in pairs. And as far as she could tell, people were a lot more attractive than she'd expected. Perhaps that was the point of a masked ball? But it was more than that. There was a sexiness to everyone. No one had planned their outfit that day. Work had gone into them, serious hours. And that was sexy. Men and women Suzanne wouldn't have looked twice at on the street now had an allure that radiated from somewhere beyond the physical. There was power in the room. There was confidence, equality, comfort. Everyone fitted in, no matter what they looked like.

But some fitted in more than others. The moment they had stepped into the grand hall, both Richard and Suzanne had felt strobing eyes cast all over them, like the glare of a thousand flashlights swung in their

direction. It was palpable. No one tried to hide it. In the outside world they were both traditionally attractive. Tonight Suzanne was elevated to the role of goddess. Richard saw it immediately. That's what made him hard. Who could miss a man with such a treasure on his arm?

They moved beyond the crowded entrance area and found seats at one of the empty round tables at the back of the hall. All the while Suzanne could feel eyes burning into her from behind myriad mask designs – and Richard's eyes burning everywhere else. The sheer volume of nakedness, of titillation and 'newness' was driving him crazy. She could tell. *He's a kid in a sweetshop. It's everything he never did in his twenties all at once.*

'Why don't you mingle while I watch the show?' she said to him. *Get it over with.*

'Are you sure?' he checked. *Am I really allowed to do this?*

'Of course. Have fun.' She pulled him to her and they kissed again. 'Don't worry about me.' *As if you will for a minute.*

Thinking about what Richard was doing or where he was going or who he was seeing or speaking to – or touching – would have disturbed Suzanne's night . . . but only if she thought about it. So she didn't. There was a defence mechanism in her head. A switch that once flicked just said, *Let's worry about me.* There was so much else to look at, after all. A series of cabaret artistes performed on the main stage while others mingled among the tables. Costume-wise there was little between performers and guests, and the lights had dimmed so much in the main hall that Suzanne struggled to tell them apart. Food was served for those who wanted it. And champagne flowed freely, delivered by ever-obliging fauns. But Suzanne was aware that this audience was interested in neither. There was something else going on. Since the lights had dimmed people had begun leaving their tables. Couples had become threesomes or moresomes. The main act had yet to start, Suzanne realised. She wondered what it was.

Well, I won't find it sitting here.

She decided to explore. Before she could even rise from her seat a

couple appeared at her side. Him late forties, her in her twenties. Him displaying his midriff and a wealth of flesh – her on a leash with apposite feline mask and breasts fully exposed beneath a clear vinyl baby-doll dress.

'Do you mind if we join you?' the man said.

'I was just going to take in the sights actually,' Suzanne replied, half standing up.

She paused. *What the hell.*

'But why not?' she added, sitting back down at the table.

Seconds later she was sharing Dom Perignon with Hank and Persia. They had been on the scene separately for ages and come together two years ago. She liked to roll over and play pussycat. He liked to stroke. They fitted well together. Oh, and they liked doing both with strangers. The last detail wasn't spoken but it didn't need to be. The way Persia had climbed on the table before the hellos were even over and lowered herself onto Suzanne's lap rather than take her own chair had made it plain.

This was done like it was the most normal thing in the world. For Hank and Persia, it clearly was. But all the while they spoke, Suzanne became more aware of the level of contact between the girl on her lap and her own body. The high front slit in Suzanne's dress meant her stocking tops – and so-white thighs – were in direct touch with Persia's vinyl outfit. It felt odd. Odd in a good way. But not as good as the areas where the baby-doll design fluffed up and let Persia's nakedness through. As she and Hank spoke, Suzanne was becoming more and more transfixed by the sensation of Persia's bare legs – and shaved pussy – straddled warmly across her own lap.

Still maintaining eye contact with Hank, she started to stroke Persia's long blonde hair. Gently, she smoothed it down from her crown, round the back of her head, along her shoulders and down. Then again. Gently and rhythmically. Still she spoke to Hank, but all the while aware of the purring noises coming from the exotic creature on her lap.

'I think she likes you,' Hank said, nodding at the girl at the end of his

leash. Persia rested her hands on Suzanne's shoulders and leaned her head down into Suzanne's chest. Purring loudly now, she rubbed her head firmly against the tightly bound breasts then pulled back so just her hair flicked quickly across the skin. Suzanne closed her eyes. For those moments she could feel each individual strand as it teased along her skin. She was being kissed by a thousand tiny mouths. Stroked by a thousand minute hands.

The next thing she felt wasn't Persia at all. Hank was standing behind her. He began massaging her neck. His hands were so hot. So light. *Is he even touching me?*

Eyes still closed, Suzanne let her head fall where it needed to. Tipped fully back, staring up at her talented masseur, seemed most natural. Her demon mask hid the redness of her cheeks. She was sure she must be blushing. She could feel the burning in her face. The furnace of pleasure, the lack of control within her own body. She was in the middle of the most sensuous, sensual moment of her life.

Nobody said anything. Even the cabaret music and the background noises seemed to still. Suzanne could hear her own heartbeat racing.

Each sweep of Persia's hair pulled Suzanne's attention back to the growing demands of her body. Her breasts, so powerfully constrained, were seared by each blonde flick. Her nipples, buried for so long beneath the solid bodicework, were alive with frustration. She needed to release them. She needed to give in, to feel Persia's hands, her mouth around them. Then Hank moved his hands and Suzanne's mind blanked once again.

The silence enveloped her. So relaxed, so content, so fulfilled by the older man's fiery fingertips. Real, visceral heat built up through her skin, burning her. *But how is this possible? He's barely touching me?*

And then another shake of Persia's head and the swelling frustration in her body was back – quadrupled, octupled. Just so much more powerful than it had been before.

Suzanne knew what was going on. She'd played similar games herself. Fire and ice. The application of one exacerbating to the nth

degree the contrasting effects of the other. But there was no ice here. And no fire, not really, although it would not have shocked her to see a flaming torch in Hank's hands. No, there was no ice and no fire but the result was going to be the same. She could feel it. In fact, it was going to be a whole lot better.

Now what?

A new sensation. Pain around her neck. *Concentrate, Sooz, focus. Ignore the throbbing building up inside you, think: what is it?*

From the shift of weight on her lap she knew what it was. Persia's leash, released by Hank's busy hands, was looped around Suzanne's neck. She could feel the leather cutting into her skin, pulling loose strands of hair. It hurt. She knew that on any other occasion she would be screaming with agony. But this was different. The pain was different. Harsh and brutal, but disguised as something else.

Persia leaned back, arms at full stretch, two hands pulling on the lead for balance. Still straddling Suzanne's legs but standing now, she ground down on the warm thighs, prickly suspenders biting into her most sensitive places. Then she stood and arched her back away, then pulled herself down once more, all the while swinging her head in wide, violent half-circles, whipping the round whiteness of Suzanne's exposed breasts. Left and right. Left and right. Metronomic regularity. Whipping with a thousand tiny lashes.

Suzanne felt it build. She let it. She had no choice. Her pussy was screaming. She needed to get a hand down there, to ignite the explosion that she knew was coming. Just one second, just one finger. But she couldn't move. Persia's weight, the whipping, the pain of leather burning into her skin all stopped her reaching out. She bucked in her seat. *Touch me! Touch me!*

And then it came. Hank's magical fingers could delay it no longer. A burst of electricity and Suzanne's whole body jolted into the air. Wave after wave flooded through her and out. Her head writhed from side to side and if she screamed she didn't hear it. Deafening pleasure, crushing pleasure, painful pleasure.

Suzanne dared to open her eyes. She was amazed her mask was still on. She was barely on the seat. Her magnificent cleavage rose and fell with each breath. Her entire body was trembling. Perched on the edge of the table, Persia was licking her fingers like the cat who really had got the cream. Hank stood next to her, stroking her hair. Beads of sweat ran down her neck and into the vinyl dress. Hank was palpably breathless. They looked how Suzanne felt. But how? *What just happened to me? What do these two get out of it?*

As she pulled herself upright, Hank leaned forward and kissed Suzanne's hand. Persia bared her teeth coquettishly and smiled. And then they walked away.

What was that all about? Suzanne's mind was spinning. She was so confused. Confused and suddenly aware of a piercing soreness in her neck. *Ouch!* Her salty fingers reached the open wound and quickly withdrew. *What the hell have they done to me?*

But there was another sensation that was stronger. Even more dominant than the savage sharpness in her neck.

Without looking around her, Suzanne plunged her right hand down between her legs and let her middle fingers sink into the silky wetness of her black panties. *Oh my God.* She didn't understand it. She'd just experienced the biggest orgasm of her life but her pussy felt like it hadn't been touched in weeks. *I need a fuck.* And she slipped two fingers inside her cunt.

'May I?'

She knew that voice. The boyish faun from the cloakroom was kneeling next to her, her hand already poised to take over from Suzanne's own.

'Do it. Please!'

The faun didn't even try to tease. Four fingers eased into the welcoming hole then pumped hard. The faun's thumb hooked over the top of the hairless mound, smothering Suzanne's clit, working it with every thrust of her hand.

This time Suzanne didn't close her eyes. Whatever new magic was performed on her she wanted to see. Which is how she saw the other faun approach and look at his friend and then up at her. He stepped in front of Suzanne, paused briefly then tore savagely at the bodice of her dress. She gasped. She heard the rip. And then she felt two strong hands cupping her tits and she thought she was going to die with pleasure.

His hands were big but her breasts were bigger. He buried his hands in her firmness and twisted, pulling the skin, clawing at the nipple. And she loved it.

'Don't stop!' she demanded, but she knew he wouldn't. He wasn't one of those. He wasn't like Persia or Hank. He needed something from her. She could see his naked hard-on, sprayed to look fur-covered, inches from her own face. And she knew what it was he needed.

Suzanne hooked an arm wildly around the man's leg and pulled him closer. In the same movement she reached out with her other hand and grasped his cock. *God, this feels good*, she thought, and pulled it urgently into her mouth. The more he squeezed her nipples, the more she pulled his body into her, the more she bucked towards the faun between her legs.

Suddenly she stood up and pushed them both away. 'Come here,' she instructed, and threw herself back onto the table, pulling the girl with her. Suzanne flung herself down on her back and span the young faun above her. Each woman's face was inches from the other's cunt. Suzanne sank her nails into the young girl's back and buried her face in her wetness. She wanted to be smothered. She felt the girl do the same to her. And then she felt something else.

The other faun, the Pan, was pushing his cock into her. Crossed signals rippled up Suzanne's body. Two contrasting and complementary shots of pleasure. She pulled the faun's cunt down harder, working every part with the whole of her face. She was losing it. Her entire body shook as the man's thighs slammed into the table edge with every thrust. Oh, she was losing it. She was being sucked, she was being fucked. She was losing everything. She hugged the faun's back like a boa constrictor claiming its prey. She desperately wanted to keep control. She wanted the faun's tongue to stay on her clit for ever. She

wanted to feel the man's cock pounding into her all night.

She wanted . . .

She wanted . . .

She wanted to come.

'Yes!' she screamed and every sound in the room rushed back into her ears at once. She was in the middle of a storm, her senses were overloading. She was out of control. She was . . . she was so tired.

The two fauns helped Suzanne to her feet and both kissed her tenderly on the lips. The girl brushed her hair and blew cold air onto the angry welt on her neck. The man kissed both breasts passionately then very gently eased them back into the dress's corset top. No words passed between them. None were needed. What was needed was champagne and that soon arrived via another faun. *What would I do without them?* Suzanne thought.

And then she remembered Richard. A few minutes later he appeared next to her, carrying both their coats. He looked flushed, pleased with himself. Suzanne was glad. But something was wrong.

'Honey, you haven't moved.' Richard sounded disappointed. *I knew it was a mistake to come. If I tell her how much fun I've had will she leave me?*

'I'm OK,' Suzanne said. 'I didn't feel like moving. I have everything I need here. But maybe we could go now.'

Richard nodded and managed a smile. *Talk about making someone feel guilty. I can't believe she's just sat here for the last two hours. What the fuck have I done? I've ruined everything.* He held her coat out and was still worrying about losing her as she stepped back into it. Tucking her hands behind her head, Suzanne expertly flicked her hair out from inside the coat. Richard had seen her do that so often he almost missed it. It was only a brief glimpse. Or perhaps he'd imagined it. He must have done, it was impossible. And yet . . .

Was he mistaken, or did Suzanne have a ring of blood around the back of her neck?

Essensual Reading

B ooks – and really we mean fiction – are very important in our lives and they fall into two categories. We call it the Two Ms – that's Memories and Menus.

Some stories we read are so familiar to us that it's like reading a page from our diary. Those are the memories.

And then there are the others, the ones where characters do things that we haven't got round to, or haven't thought of doing – or maybe haven't yet dared to do! These are our wish-list books. Each page offers a menu of illicit sexual adventure that we might want to try.

And there are so many wonderful menus out there for us all to consider and explore. They take us to the darkest corners of carnal experimentation and back again, stopping off at every point en route. We've chosen a few for you here. Take your pick, but choose wisely. After all, are you sure you're eating in the right restaurant?

Love Miss A.P. x

He wrote about philosophy, morals and social wellbeing. But we know Donatien Alphonse François de Sade because he disguised it all in some of the naughtiest prose ever written. The Marquis' wildly graphic and incredibly dark books – *Justine*, *Juliette* and *120 Days of Sodom* being the most widely available – were so bulging with depictions of adventurous group submission that his name itself became synonymous in the sexual lexicon with brutal gratification, and Napoleon himself ordered the author to be arrested in 1801. Do we care that a lot of the best 'sadism' was written in prison or an asylum? Lock us up now . . .

If your lover is a fan of romantic poetry, we recommend the depraved quatrains of the irrepressible John Wilmot, Earl of Rochester as the perfect starting place. In fact he's so wonderfully wicked we have dedicated a section to him on page 57. But there are other risqué rhymers who tickle – until we can barely breathe – our fancy. What about the sonnets of Pietro Aretino? He may have lived in the late 1520s, he may have written in Italian, but we think he knows what his audience wants: strong women being royally rogered – then turning the tables. Did Shakespeare boast that his sonnets were awash with 'people both fucking and fucked-out / Cocks and cunts innumerable'?

Aretino's female characters knew what they wanted from a lover and so did the *Wife of Bath*, Geoffrey Chaucer's multi-married love-maker in the early 1400s. We wouldn't cite her tale as erotic in the tingly sense, but don't you get goose bumps thinking of a woman as empowered as her in life and love? We do!

Empowered women take a step further in Leopold von Sacher-Masoch's *Venus in Furs*. Such a heady mix of supra-sensuality and weak men even in 1870, it makes us positively weak at the knees. Wanda doesn't just make Severin submit to her – she enlists a trio of scary African women to aid her work. Every home should have them to keep those tricky men in check.

Maybe you prefer to play the submissive part yourself? Don't be as silly as Livia in Camillo Boito's *Senso* (1882) who gives away her place in society and all her wealth to prostrate herself in front of a wickedly undeserving Remigio – but do try to have all her fun. Her diary mesmerisingly describes every erotic encounter and thought with the

ungrateful beau – none more thrilling than as she watches his death by firing squad.

The Way of a Man with a Maid is a bit of a mouthful but a good eyeful too. Written anonymously in 1924, it tells of the forcible seduction of young servant Alice by the man of the house, Jack. Always one to care for his bashful beauty's feelings, Jack even constructs a bespoke torture room for Alice, called the Snuggery, where she can enjoy her episodes of bondage, feathers and even lesbianism without worrying about ruining the lay of the house. What would the neighbours say?

Which brings us to *The Story of O* (1954). It's the one book every visitor to the dark side of sex has heard of – the *Emmanuel* of literature. Such willingness to suffer, such desire to take punishment to prove the extent of love – you'll want to feel the chains of sexual and psychological torture by the end of Pauline Reage's seminal tale. We did – and we never looked back.

Now, we like the sound of the man called 'The Collector'. He had a taste for erotic writing – nothing flowery; simply graphic and arousing – just like us. Publishers in the 1940s didn't cater for his needs, so he commissioned his own. And that's how we have the deliciously decadent work of Anais Nin (a bit 'nice' for us – see Essensual Reading in the Pink Section) and Henry Valentine Miller. Miller was not necessarily the romantic his middle name suggested – but he knew how to turn a girl on. His books were so charged with accounts of his real-life sexual sating that they were banned in his native America – eventually challenging the country's obscenity laws. Financial help from Parisian lover Nin saw the controversial publication of Miller's steamy *Tropic of Cancer*, with *Tropic of Capricorn* following five years later in 1939. We defy you to not love these books. The sexual revolution of the 1960s would never have happened without them.

Vampires make famously tricky lovers but who better than an expert on the undead to compose particularly tasty S&M fairytales? *Interview with a Vampire* author Anne Rice wrote several erotic novels as Anne Rampling, but saved her really kinky ideas for her A N Roquelaure pseudonym. Imagine if Sleeping Beauty weren't awakened by a chaste kiss from Prince Charming, but a full-on penetrative onslaught? Rice

did – naughty girl – in *The Claiming of Sleeping Beauty* in 1983, but she didn't stop there. Beauty is transported to the Prince's kingdom where she is trained in the art and the pain and the pleasure of sexual submission. There's many a happy ending but does Beauty live happily ever after?

What was it Bridget Jones's mother said about the Japanese? 'Very cruel race'. And that's why being called 'the most celebrated writer of popular S&M novels in Japan' is a big deal where we're concerned – let's face it, that's one country that knows its way around the subject. Oniroku Dan's *Flower and Snake* was the first of his 200 genre novels and not only brought sadomasochistic fun and games to book lovers, but was transformed into a highly successful – if slightly tame – film in 1974. His movie success didn't stop there, with many adaptations from the Nikkatsu studio in their much-loved *Roman Porno* series. Read him and weep.

Plenty of potential tears in *The Story of the Eye* where the unnamed narrator and his teenage lover Simone venture into the blackest arts of lovemaking, incorporating exhibitionism, off-the-wall sexual insertions and the use of broken glass. For some the orgiastic scenes featuring mentally ill teen Marcelle were too much from Georges Bataille. But I think you can guess our opinion of this 1928 masterpiece . . .

And then there's *Lolita* – you know you shouldn't find it erotic but you do. The passion, the control, the domination of the innocent Delores. Incredible. Is Vladimir Nabokov's 1955 novel the best book ever written? We think so. And what a bonus that it's so thoroughly, taboo-bustingly rude.

Don't like men writing for women? We understand that. Sometimes there are words that only a woman can write. When we're in the mood for something darker than Colette, our favourite slice of Sapphic love is *Olivia*, Dorothy Bussy's wayward tale of a pupil's sexual awakening at the hands – and more – of her exotic headmistress. Bussy was Lytton Strachey's sister and the book was published anonymously by Virginia Woolf's Hogarth Press. Perhaps more charming than dangerous, for its time it was a risky endeavour. And we do love a risky endeavour.

If you thought the best dirty deeds were done decades ago, then you haven't read *The Ages of Lulu*. Almudena Grandes Hernández wrote this graphic tale of a young girl's lust for darker carnal pleasures as recently as 1989 and it has already been filmed (showing a mere flavour of the naughtiness on the page). Like so much of our favourite writing, the line between morality and perversion isn't so much blurred as broken.

The one thing all these writers have in common is experience. Maybe they made the odd thing up, possibly embellished here and there, some of them even borrowed a couple of details told to them by a friend. But in the best erotica from the dark side you can see the memories behind the scenes. These things happened. You can smell the anxiety, hear the groans, taste the pleasure. And nowhere more so than in our favourite compiler of 'real women's' stories, Nancy Friday's collection of letters, case studies and reminiscences from women scaling the heights of their sexual ambitions. *My Secret Garden, Forbidden Flowers, Women on Top* – hundreds and hundreds of mini sexual adventures. Bite-sized, even, you might say.

✳ ✳ ✳

There's so much to read. Of course, no decadent bookshelf should be without *Secrets, Confessions, V* and *I* – something for all tastes there from the authors of this very book. In 2000 Lisa B Falour wrote a book called *I was for Sale: Confessions of a Bondage Model* and, to be honest, we didn't expect to like it but can't help poring over our favourite passages again and again. Same too for the travelogues of Xaviera Hollander (Holland's 'Happy Hooker') and the lip-smacking wonders of Penny Birch. If you can find your way past their garish packaging – what are the publishers thinking? – then you'll enjoy in that special way the adventures of these two modern women. Finally the 'true or not true' Victorian memoirs of 'Walter' in *My Secret Life*. He's a man, he isn't very good at sex – but he loves it so much. We want to despise him but we can't. His appetite is just so . . . huge.

Which reminds us: remember what we said at the beginning? Reading is just the menu. Now you have to order the meal – and eat.

Happy dining. X

L'Appartement

Ma Chère Claudine

Yes, it's me! Georgette, or 'Hugo', I should say, as that is who I am known as around here. My darling girl, did you think that you would never hear from me again? By now you probably know all about my midnight escape from St Colette's Correctional Convent, but had you guessed that I had made it to Paris? Yes, all the way to the *cité de l'amour*, just like I always said I would.

After that last episode with Madame Gringot, the new music teacher and the three girls from the fifth form, I knew I couldn't stay at St Colette's a moment longer, so I snuck away and stole some clothes from Alexandre – you know, the young kitchen boy we lusted after (and some of us did more!) – and dressed as a boy. Of course, those old nuns didn't bat an eyelid as 'Alexandre' strode right past them and out of the kitchen door – ninnies!

So then I hitchhiked all the way to Paris, and now I have my own little *appartement* in a big, old town house. I decided to keep the clothes,

so 'Hugo' I now am. Only the old girls in Pigalle have ever rumbled me . . . but even then they've offered me 'one on the house'!

There are so many people here, all going about their business, and I have to admit to you, Claudine, it is a little lonely for a *garçonne* from the provinces like me. Just in this building alone there seems to be so much romance: the man in the apartment next to me sings beautiful songs to his wife every morning and makes love to her all night, and there's a young man on the top floor who is obsessed with a different woman or man every day – he tells me about them all.

I think he would like to fall in love with 'Hugo' too, but you know me, Claudine – what would I want with some swooning mooncalf? What's fun about that? No, Claudine, I have to let you into a secret. I am in love. I really am. And I do not even know her name. Well, I know her surname because it is written on her door, but I cannot whisper that beneath her window every night, as I did for you, my sweet, back when you were the sauciest girl in the third form.

You're probably thinking that this doesn't sound much like the Georgette you know so well – the Georgette who climbed into Mme Rose's chamber and seduced her so she'd let you pass your oral *examens*, or the Georgette who made love to every girl in the fourth year for a dare – *hélas*, I have a good reason, *mon ami*.

This beauty – and oh, her skin, Claudine, you would die for it! – has a husband, confound him! A real Bluebeard of a man too, though *entre nous* I suspect she must rather like that. I think they have a little agreement.

But I am getting ahead of myself here, *mais non*? How do I know so much when I have never even spoken to her nor been invited into their *appartement*? Well, Claudine, it just so happens that my window looks right across the courtyard and into their home – that is how I first saw her, when she was scrubbing the floor. To my eyes it was sacrilege – I want to kiss her beautiful knees, not see them made red and rough by kneeling – but as I said, when I watched a little more I learned something about this couple.

They play a little game, all the time. He is the master and she is his

slave – this sounds like fun, *non*? I'm sure you can guess just what I would make you do if I were your master and you were my slave, dirty little Claudine, but this man, how can I say this? He does not have much of an imagination. Yes, he does tie her up, but then he makes her bake cakes or stay at home all day being bored like a housewife.

Of course, that means I can watch her all day from my window, and I do. I can really feast my eyes. And dream a dream or two about what I'd do if I were her master instead of him. And do you know what, Claudine? I think I have a plan.

But I am so cruel that I won't tell you what it is until you write back to me!

Xxx

Georgette

Paris, February 12

Bisoux, my naughty Claudine, I knew you would beg me to tell you! Are you sitting comfortably? I will tell you the whole story. As I walked back from posting your letter I bought a rose – just the one, and I wrote a little letter to say: 'Think of me when you imagine you are all alone – I will be watching.'

Then I wrapped it around the rose and posted it through her door – I knew her stupid husband would be out at work. I hurried back to my *appartement* so I could be at the window and see her reaction when she read it.

First she sniffed the rose – really buried her nose in it and inhaled – then she unrolled my note and I could see she was shocked! Claudine, I knew she would be a little scared at first, but she surprised me. She came straight to the balcony that faces my window and looked right at me – and such a look! It went right to the bottom of my soul –

Claudine, I fear your Georgette may have met her match! She left my head whirling. But . . . she could not know it was me who sent the rose. I thought I would be given away immediately, but my identity is safe. For now.

I couldn't think of anything but her – I couldn't sleep. That night I wrote another note, and another, and another . . .

Claudine, I have bombarded her with billets-doux for almost two weeks now, and when our eyes meet I am sure that she feels she has grown to love just like I, even if she has no idea of who I really am. But still there is this idiot husband who comes home every evening and demands his dinner and . . . well, Claudine – let's just say that you and I both know that I would make a much better job of things.

Schoolgirl letters are not going to turn this into the *affaire* I crave, though. I think it is time to introduce 'Hugo', don't you? A decent enough match for that brute of a husband, I am sure of it. It's about time he got just what he deserves. I have to go now and deliver another note.

Xxx

Paris, February 14

A quick scribble, *chère* Claudine, to tell you that you should send no more letters to this address because I am leaving tonight. I will write to you as soon as I can, and I am sure we – yes, *we* – will still be in Paris somewhere, and then you can come and visit us – yes, *us*.

Have you guessed yet? Well, perhaps you will have worked out what is going to happen, Claudine, but I bet you'll never guess just how Georgette is going to save her princess from the ogre. You noticed the date I wrote this, though, I'm sure. Of course, my favourite saint – Valentine. A perfect opportunity to deliver the most beautiful things that I have hoarded for my secret love. Just now I have wrapped and perfumed so delicately, into perfect pink boxes, the most beautiful

lingerie you have ever seen, my dearest. The next time my hands touch the softest silk imaginable . . . it will be on her!

Claudine, expect to see me sooner than you might have anticipated. If all goes well we will come to you in our old meeting place and perhaps she and I will spring you from your prison too!

Xxx

G

The Director's Cut

What *is it with Americans and timekeeping?* She had been standing in the lobby of the Charlotte Street Hotel for twenty minutes. On any other engagement she would have left by now. But getting Jack King to his own premiere had been an assignment she had been hand-picked for. The US film company knew he was an awkward SOB, that's why they'd hired her: Claire Jackson, queen of behind-the-scenes efficiency, PA to the stars and the indiscreet – often the very same people. Claire had a reputation for organisation that somehow managed to feed the masses' demand for media access and fuel the egos of the stars she was paid to promote.

But this Jack King was seriously getting on her tits. Three days of sulks, tantrums, sheer jaw-dropping rudeness. And now this wilful defiance. She was going to kill him.

'I'm going up,' she told the desk clerk, who knew better than try to stop her. Claire caught a glimpse of herself frowning in the lift mirrors and smiled. *Don't let the jerk get to you.* She forced a smile at her own reflection and enjoyed what she saw. Late thirties, red-haired, shapely, good skin. The mirror confirmed it all. If anything it seemed more flattering than usual elevator fare – obviously down to the subdued lighting in the little cubicle. Claire instinctively checked the ceiling. Either there were no cameras in there or they'd been fitted with infrared filters to pick up nocturnal action. *Discreet. Something worth remembering.*

Fourth floor, penthouse suite. So predictable. So ridiculous. Jack King was 23. Before making his name in that embarrassing US reality show he had been a surf bum. As far as Claire was concerned, he was still a surf bum. Just somehow fluking his way to directing the hottest Indie flick of the year couldn't change that. Not for an old hand like Claire Jackson. She'd seen them all. Nicholson, De Niro, Marty, Woody, Sly, Stiller – seen them, looked after them, sent them home with a clean bill of health. At least as far as the media knew. Which, as far as her industry was concerned, was the same thing.

Claire never waited to be let in. Knock and enter. That was the only way to do it. A copy of King's room card had been part of her contract. *He probably doesn't know that.*

The thick Charlotte Street carpet insulated any noise from the door although Jack King wouldn't have noticed if it had smashed off its hinges. He was standing by the window with his back to the door. His laptop blazed on a table in front of him. He was wearing those trendy giant headphones, a brown beany hat – and the biggest hard-on Claire had ever seen.

It wasn't the first time she'd walked in on a client wanking – or worse. But this idiot was doing it in front of the balcony – and by the look of that green light above his screen, the Mac's inbuilt camera was beaming his every jerk into the virtual ether.

Prick.

'You ever hear of something called the paparazzi, Junior? Zoom lenses mean anything to you?' Without breaking her stride Claire reached the window and yanked the curtain pulley hard. The swish of fabric made the young director look up. But only for a second. Just long enough to scowl. And his hand never stopped sliding up and down his impressive tool. 'Or internet hackers?' Claire's hand slammed the lid of the laptop flat.

Now he was paying attention.

'What the fuck?' He span angrily towards her and ripped the headphones from his ears. But still his hand glided up and down. Was it

Claire's imagination or was the rhythm getting faster?

'Get dressed.'

'Fuck yourself.'

Claire didn't even hear him. She was at his wardrobe door in the next room, pulling out clothes. *Something to make an impression. Not exactly a great choice. What about this?* As she pulled the wet-look black shirt from the rail her eye caught the mirror on the door. Through the doorway behind her she could see Jack still masturbating wildly. That thing must take a lot of effort. Claire checked herself. *Don't get distracted. Focus on the job in hand.*

Oh, look at that job in hand.

She threw the clothes on the bed and marched into the living room of the suite. Jack King's hand was blurring to nothing. His eyes were closed. They had eight minutes to leave the room. She needed him dressed.

'Come on, Junior, let's move.'

Nothing. He was just ignoring her.

'Well, if you insist on playing games,' Claire said, and wrapped her hand around the surprised man's thick shaft.

Oh, momma.

But she said, 'Time for a nappy change, Junior.' Claire tightened her grip and felt her thumb and forefingers squeeze just below the head. 'Walk and talk.' *Keep the conversation light. You're a professional.* Desperately trying not to notice the pulsing beneath her grip, she began to march towards the bedroom. If he didn't follow her now she would rip his cock clean off.

But he followed. How could he not? With each stride Claire took she sent a spasm of sensation along the man's stretched penis. She didn't care that her angle was too low to be comfortable for him. She tried not to notice the powerful resistance from a cock that wanted to stand proud. She ignored the smooth pressure of the incredible glans swollen beneath her tight fist. She just kept walking and didn't let up for a

second. If anything she was twisting harder as she hurried across the floor. He was literally being dragged by his cock.

They reached the bedroom door and just as suddenly as she'd grabbed him, Claire released her grasp. She didn't stop walking into the room so she never saw the released cock spring upwards with relief. She didn't see Jack King spread his arms to stop himself falling backwards out of the door. But she did see the arc of liquid as it rained down onto the bed – and all over the black shirt.

What a waste.

But she said, 'Seven minutes, Jack.'

'You're fucking mad.'

'I will be if you don't get dressed.'

She threw over a new shirt – red, nowhere near as nice as the black one, but not covered in spunk either.

Claire was impressed when a fully dressed Jack King presented himself at the room door 300 seconds later. She was less impressed when she realised he was wearing the black shirt. Now with a fetching slash of white across its back.

'You've got to be joking.'

'You wanted me to wear it.' The sulking teenage persona was back. Five minutes from jerking to jerk-off. *Pathetic.*

'Fine,' Claire sighed. 'At least put this on.' She threw him a white jacket. 'Gaultier?' she sneered. 'Is he still going?'

'Are we?' Jack said.

✳ ✳ ✳

They didn't speak in the limo on the way to Leicester Square. He hid beneath that ridiculous hat and even dafter headphones, staring out the black tinted windows like a child enduring a marathon motorway journey. She ran over the itinerary for the evening and made seventeen calls during the twelve-minute journey. She tried to ignore the

inappropriate memories that kept coming into her mind. Her hand couldn't still feel his cock's animal pulsing, could it? Like it had a heartbeat of its own. She hadn't washed, hadn't even rinsed her left hand since. *Is that wrong?*

In the darkness of the car Jack King didn't see Claire quietly rest her face on her hand to test whether any trace of his aroma still lingered.

※　※　※

Claire had previously organised film premieres for Hugh Grant, Spielberg, *Spider-Man*. She'd been there for the full three hours of Tom Cruise's 'love me' walkabout. She'd held the umbrella over Daniel Craig. You name it. For this one, though, she'd taken a back seat. Her job was literally baby-sitting 'The Talent' until the star's regular management team arrived later that night.

So far, so good. The crowds were impressive. The boy wonder was present and conscious. And she'd personally vetted the press passes. There wouldn't be one photographer who wasn't on message. She looked at the sulking director. *Thank God. I'll need all the help I can get.*

The crowds at Leicester Square are marshalled with military precision. That's the theory. In effect, barriers are erected and fans duly queue behind them. If they ventured towards Piccadilly a little bit, they might occasionally catch a glimpse of something really worth snapping on their iPhones. A team of PR girls with security in tow flag down the cars at the foot of Wardour Street, vet the PR guests then trickle-release the celebrities for the awaiting packs. It would never do to have everyone arrive at once. These things require more choreography than a J-Lo video.

Claire's car was waved straight through the secured barrier and she carefully wound down the electric window on Jack's side. Much to his annoyance. The sudden scatter-gun onslaught of flashbulbs caught Claire out – she would never get used to that. Jack King stayed rooted in his seat. But at least he was taking his headphones off.

'Remember: punters, pictures, competition winners. Think you can do that?'

No answer. Claire knew that meant *yes.*

'Well, are you getting out?'

He turned towards her. 'Door?'

Actual hatred flared up inside her. Client or not, he could screw himself. She caught her temper. *I've already seen him try.* Besides, she didn't want to give him the satisfaction of seeing her riled.

The flunkey greeting the car had opened her door first. Claire dashed round the other side and flung Jack's door wide.

'If you didn't wank so much you could open doors yourself,' she hissed.

He ignored her like he always did. Just looked straight through her, at the screaming fans. And then he smiled.

Thank Christ for that. Work the crowds. Do your fucking job.

Claire heaved a sigh of relief and slammed the limo door shut. *Just a few more hours.* Her clipboard told everyone that she was Important. The buzz in the air established Jack's importance was on a whole other level. The fans loved him and he loved them. He was posing for photos, signing things, talking to some kid's mum. He was the living embodiment of the American Dream. He was everybody's favourite surf dude. The kid with talent who got lucky. He was just like them. A regular guy. Every mother's dream son.

An asshole. And just when Claire was close to forgetting, he reminded her again and again.

Part of her job was to guide Jack around the fenced area and ensure the paparazzi got their pictures. She put a hand on his elbow to steer him onwards.

'You don't normally hold me there,' he said loudly. 'Have you washed your hands yet?'

Bastard.

'Come on, Jack,' Claire laughed effortfully. 'You know you love posing for men with cameras.'

He swore under his breath at her but the smile never even flickered.

Five minutes of solo shots then the final hurdle. Claire made sure the cameras were still trained on the star of the show when she brought over a waiting girl and her mother – radio competition winners. She'd never seen two more excited people. Or such strange-looking ones. But she didn't let it show.

'Jack – this is Kirsty and Jean.'

If the overwhelmed women noticed the shock on Jack's face they didn't let on. They were so excited to meet him in the flesh he was almost lifted off his feet.

'Woah, ladies,' he charmed them. 'Plenty to go round.' Claire watched as he posed for myriad snaps in front of the world's press, including two taken on their own phones. *Why do people do that?*

Claire looked on, almost impressed by the level of professionalism at work. See – he could do it if he wanted to. But it was time to go into the auditorium. The rest of the VIP guests had already swanned past and most of them would be taking their seats. Claire couldn't wait. The form was always the same: meet and greet the great and the good on the way in; wait for the lights to dim, opening credits to come up, then the stars just up and leave. And the moment Jack left was the moment her contract ended. She looked at her watch. *Another half-hour and this will be over.*

'Time to move, Jack,' she called out and beckoned him towards the main entrance. As soon as he was out of earshot of the press Jack snarled, 'What the fuck are you doing, sticking me with those freaks?' Behind him the crestfallen faces of Kirsty and Jean rewrote the definition of disappointed.

'He's talking about the cameramen,' Claire said quickly.

'Yeah, whatever,' Jack said and barged past her.

When Claire caught up with Jack he was entering the gents' toilets. That didn't stop her.

'You're a piece of work, you know that?' she called out as he took his

place at a urinal. He didn't even flinch. 'Would it have killed you to bite your tongue for another five minutes? If they tell their story to the press you're screwed.'

Still nothing. No response from him at all. Claire continued.

'Rude to me, that's fine. I get paid big time to look after jerks like you – I eat you pricks for breakfast. I've got a teenage son – this is a piece of cake for me. But do you know what the really funny thing is? You're the one paying me. How stupid does that make you? You can't stand the sight of me and yet you're the moron paying me to make your life hell. And you probably don't even know it. Pathetic.'

She watched as Jack went over to the sink. Still he didn't say anything. *What's the point?*

Claire walked angrily towards the door. 'Let me tell you how it is. You're going to get in your seat, you're going to be polite to the hoi polloi and as soon as the lights go down we get up, we leave and I never have to fucking set eyes on you again.'

✳ ✳ ✳

She was waiting with the rest of the media team when he emerged into the foyer and immediately set off towards the screening room. 'Have the cars ready in ten minutes,' Claire called back as she walked.

'Don't worry on my account,' Jack's voice called out.

Shit. What now?

'You don't want a car now?' Claire asked exasperatedly.

'Sure I want a car. I just don't want it till after the movie's finished.'

'You cannot be serious. You're not going to watch the film. Nobody watches the film. You must have seen it a dozen times.'

'Not in London I haven't.'

Claire stared at his young blue eyes. What the hell was going on behind them? Was he playing games again? It was because she'd told him she was leaving in ten minutes. The bastard was letting her know

who was boss again. But at least he was looking at her now. Usually he stared through her as though she wasn't there.

'Fine,' she said. 'Well, let's get a move on. Don't want to miss those lovely adverts, do we?'

Their seats were good – de luxe bucket numbers, nearly twice as wide as usual and with plenty of leg space. Claire didn't need much, and neither did Jack. After all that surfing he didn't have an inch of fat on him and looked lost in the chair as he shook hands with everyone within reach. There was a spontaneous round of applause as the lights dimmed and his name appeared on the screen. There was a real energy in the room, a real sense of seeing something good for the first time. Claire would be so fucking annoyed if she enjoyed the film. But there was no point worrying. She knew Jack would drag her out as soon as he thought she was having fun.

Ten minutes in she found herself gripped. The film was art house, it was commercial, it was strong – everyone in the room was enrapt. Even Jack. She stole a glance at him. His handsome tanned profile was a study of concentration. He was perfectly still. Only his hand moved, quietly tapping on the chair arm between them.

A few minutes later Claire found herself totally lost in the plot. She'd let herself relax. Her brain, normally so efficient, so self-sufficient and in control, had slipped out of professional mode. She was enjoying herself. Relishing the images and words displayed in front of her. Totally entranced by the wash of visual beauty before her, adrift in the movie's fantasy world.

She didn't consciously lean forward in her seat. She didn't notice herself grip both chair arms with fear for the characters. It even took a few moments to realise that the inside of her forearm was being stroked. So gently, barely contacting her skin, but perfectly rhythmically, definitely intentionally. She was being stroked by Jack King.

And she was loving it.

What's he doing? Why is he touching me? And why is it so nice?

Claire focused. She could tell he was just using the back of his hand,

just the edge of his fingernails, in fact. It was so delicate. She felt goose bumps rise up her right arm and spread all over her body. A Mexican wave of sensation rippling across her. Her shoulders, her neck, the back of her head, her left arm, her back, her left leg, her right leg and – no, that was impossible. *You can't get goose bumps there!* So what was that tingling sensation between her legs?

The film continued. Claire kept her gaze fixedly forward. Onscreen the plot thickened. In the back row of the royal box it went off the scale.

Claire felt the chairs shudder as Jack shifted his weight. His hand didn't falter. If anything the strokes got longer. Down to her wrist, dwelling on the smooth, sensitive hollow in the centre, then back up, but this time past her elbow, up along the outside of her arm, up to the top of her shoulder. Then down.

Images of Jack's incredible cock flashed into her mind. Was that what all this was about? For three days she'd been wanting to punch the little toad and now she was opening up her soul to him. Was it because she'd seen – felt – that huge thing? Had that turned her?

Claire was confused. Not enough to stop her body responding to the elongated sweeps of Jack's fingers. *No*, she thought, *it's not just about his penis. I shouted him down in the toilets. I told him some home truths.* She had been right: Jack had looked at her differently after that. Maybe he respected her now? Maybe he realised he had been a prat? She didn't really mind. Not now, not while his hands were – touching her breasts!

'Oh.'

Her sigh was pure instinctive response. She was wearing a smart Oscar de la Renta shirt suit. Short sleeves, efficient office-type, red silk – but tight. It pulled snugly around her overflowing half-cup bra. It was a style she loved. Total support underneath, but a reckless bounce to her breasts when she walked. What's more, at least 50 per cent of each breast was loose against the shirt. More often than not that included a nipple.

Tonight it was both.

She felt Jack's nail trail down from her shoulder, down against the

soft fullness of the side of her breast, following the curve down further, making it shudder with his touch, till it met the resistance of the bra. Then nothing. Claire felt herself panic. Jack lifted his hand – and placed it back at the wrist, then started the same long line to her chest again.

The characters on the screen were talking Latin. It was set in Ancient Rome or was it China or Fulham? Claire didn't know, she didn't care, she didn't remember. The only thing she knew for certain was her body was alive with Jack's touch.

She flinched as the graceful hand cut along her neck, like a surgeon's knife, and she knew that her nipple was erect. She could feel it pushing against her silk shirt. Each breath lifted it and moved it and rubbed it. She knew Jack's fingers would find it this time. She willed him to rip her shirt open and squeeze.

But she knew he wouldn't.

He was playing her like a concert pianist over his Steinway grand, not some barroom honky-tonk upright. Fingers instinctively positioning themselves before striking. Caressing the keyboard before selecting their notes. Perfect weight, perfect pressure.

But how she wanted him to press harder. Her breathing was getting harder and faster. Her breasts were quivering even before each stroke reached them. When his fingers arrived Claire froze. A sharp intake of breath each time. She needed to focus entirely on the sensation. She didn't want her breathing to get in the way.

Still though, she stared towards the screen. Without looking, she knew Jack was glued forwards as well. He didn't need to see where he was going. His fingers were his eyes and they saw everything.

I wish he would suck my tits, Claire thought. *If he doesn't, I'm going to find someone who will.*

She thought again of his hidden cock. Was it hard again? Had she turned him on? Or did he only get off on the internet? In those stupid chatrooms with hookers pretending to be schoolgirls?

She didn't dare look but she could imagine the line of his trouser

ruined by the thick bulge of his penis. *It must be uncomfortable. He's going to have to release it soon.*

A second later she didn't care about him. Jack's hand had reached her waist again, but instead of lifting and returning to her wrist, it had continued. Down along her lap, across her thigh. Down around the top of her leg, past the hem of her tight black skirt. Down to the skin above the top of her stockings.

Then back. She felt his wrist meet resistance from the bottom of the skirt, but he kept pulling. So gentle, no danger of damaging the fabric. All the while his fingers trailed delicately along her prickly flesh. The skirt was pulled back as far as it would go but he kept moving his hand. As the side of Jack's palm drew slowly over the top of her clitoris, Claire thought she was going to explode.

She couldn't help moving in her seat. Her legs almost fell open. She wanted to remove all obstacles from his path.

But Jack didn't need her help. He didn't lick his fingers and slide them expertly inside her wet pussy. He didn't drop to his knees and suck upon her proud clitoris. He just slowly withdrew his hand back to her wrist and started another lingering lap of the right side of her body.

'I need you to finish this,' Claire gasped. Jack said nothing. *That figures. He hasn't changed that much, then.* He ran his hand more firmly over her breast this time, almost lifting it out of the bra. He made a point of circling her erect nipple and pinched it on his way past. His nail dug deeper into Claire's clothes.

When he reached her lap his fingers pressed more firmly still. For a second his entire hand slipped underneath the exposed stocking tops, and he dug his nails into the top of her leg. Then he withdrew, slowly again, so the palm of his hand pulled flatly up towards Claire's tummy, pressing as it moved, planting pressure all over the mouth of her vagina, really forcing down on Claire's insistent clitoris. And then he stopped moving altogether. His hand just rested there. But so firmly Claire felt like she was being fucked and licked at the same time.

What was he doing to her?

She instinctively tilted her hips and encouraged his palm to resist against her grinding pelvis. For a moment she thought he was going to lift again, but he didn't. He pressed more firmly and let her wriggle underneath. Jack's eyes never left the screen but underneath his hand Claire's clit ground in small but firm circular movements.

Round and round she pushed, throwing her hips up into his reach. She was so close. But what if he moved? Claire threw a hand over Jack's and pressed again. She couldn't help it. She needed to know he wasn't going to stop her. She needed to take that final step. She needed to –

Claire's fingers gripped over Jack's hand and squeezed. She didn't feel him wince. She didn't notice how he tried to shake her off. She had no idea she was so close to breaking his knuckles. The explosion in her pussy had taken out all other senses. She was empty. A husk.

She was absolutely fucking shot.

A few minutes passed. Maybe more. The throbbing in her pussy was dying down. Sensation was returning to the rest of Claire's body. She felt Jack lean into her.

'Come with me.'

He didn't wait for a reply. She followed clumsily. Had the people near them seen what had gone on? It was dark, the film had been utterly engrossing before she was distracted. Maybe they'd got away with it.

She watched as Jack left the auditorium and reached the toilet door. He paused in the doorway, silhouetted by the harsh neon bulbs inside. *So this is his plan.*

'I need to get something,' she whispered. 'Go and wait for me.'

Five minutes later the toilet door opened again. Jack was obviously waiting in one of the cubicles.

'About time,' he shouted. 'Don't leave me hanging here.'

Jack flung the door open and posed there triumphantly with a hand furiously working his impressive hard-on. But Claire didn't see it. She

was on her way out of Leicester Square. The only people who saw Jack King wanking himself were Kirsty and Jean, mother and daughter competition winners. They saw it and they photographed it.

As she hailed a cab, Claire wondered how far it would go. She had seen him being led by his cock – literally – that day already. But she knew he had been physically repulsed by the two fans. Would his lust get the better of him? Would they let him? Or would they just sell their pictures to the *National Enquirer*?

She didn't care. She was leaving. The picture was over. So was her contract. If she was lucky, she might just get work again.

But it had been worth it. In more ways than one . . .

Julia at the Glory Hole

Julia didn't normally need to use a telephone box but on this occasion her mobile-phone battery was flat. The box was up a side street in Soho and, predictably, was plastered with cards advertising the telephone numbers and wares of sex workers: transsexuals and dominatrices in the main. But as she fumbled in her bag for her phone book (she diligently still recorded numbers by pen even though they were stored in her phone), her eye alighted on an unusual advert right in the centre of the eye-snagging patchwork of explicit cards.

The image was a photograph of a simple circle of red velvet tucked and studded around a hole in a door or board. The legend was muted in a small, discreet typeface: 'You are invited to visit the Glory Hole', underlined by a telephone number.

Julia quickly made her call to cancel a follow-up date with a rather earnest and intense man she had met the previous weekend through the prestigious dating agency to which she belonged. Now she returned to her office and set to the long list of tasks she'd assigned for that

afternoon. Yet she found her attention wandering and when she closed her eyes the image of the velvet-surrounded hole in the phone card was embedded in her retina. She had heard of glory holes before, of swinging orgies in which a man pokes his cock through a hole in a partitioned wall to be serviced (anonymously) by someone on the other side. But she hadn't realised that such an exchange could quite simply be purchased, rather than acquired by having to negotiate oneself into a swinging club or party (which in any case would usually require an accompanying partner, which she currently didn't have).

In fact, it had been quite some time – several years – since Julia had last been in a relationship and almost a year now since she'd had sex. Having been through a brief period of fairly perfunctory sex with a man whom she thought of mostly as a friend (she hadn't fancied him), since then work was the only thing that occupied her. Except on occasion she would find herself, midway through preparing food, urgently employing a vegetable (a carrot or a courgette), as a prosthetic sex toy. She would squat, knees apart in the middle of the kitchen, skirt lifted and her panties pulled aside in order to frig at her clit and cunt hole with the vegetable in order to produce a quick, clinical climax before straightening and continuing with the cooking.

Julia diligently completed her office tasks for the day as the image of the Glory Hole receded behind more mundane concerns. However, the next day at lunchtime, when Julia set out to the café she found her feet gravitating away from her usual route in the direction of the telephone box. Her pulse quickened and she felt like, well, like a predator; it was a feeling that was very different from trying to pull someone in a nightclub. It felt more primordial, since she was aware that her hunt would be for an encounter solely with an anatomical appendage rather than with a person – she felt herself unhinging as she imagined an anonymously passive and beautiful stiff cock poked through the Glory Hole.

The card advertising the Glory Hole remained in the phone box and Julia snatched it down and put it in her bag whilst pretending to dial, speak and hang up. Returning to her desk, she spent a fitful afternoon during which she looked at the card at regular intervals as if for deeper

meaning. As she did so, she felt her labia swelling stickily inside her knickers. At one point, a senior male employee stood beside her as she sat squirming slightly, trying not to think about unzipping him right there, extracting his hardening cock and slipping it slowly into her mouth.

When work was done (in a trice so that she would no longer procrastinate), Julia called the number on the card from her desk. A mature female voice brusquely announced that she had reached 'The Glory Hole', and queried when would be a convenient time to visit? This demand was so sudden and confrontational that Julia stammered that she would go there at whatever time was available. The woman gave an address (quite close to the office) and the time, 6.30 p.m. – just one hour away.

Leaving work, Julia walked towards the address. She had decided that she would not attend the appointment but curiosity demanded that she at least view the exterior of the building. It was a fairly smart-looking town house, not at all like the sleazy walk-up clip joints in the surrounding streets. There was a single buzzer with the letters 'G.H.' printed rather ornately beneath. Somehow, Julia found this external discretion and smartness encouraging and she began to waver as, for the umpteenth time that day, she felt her clitoris stiffen and her legs tremble slightly with spasms of deep lust. Briskly walking past the house, Julia dived into the pub on the corner and ordered a large gin and tonic while she collected herself.

The whole experience was undoubtedly exciting but also terrifying. Her appointment was now only twenty minutes away and seemed utterly absurd and impossible. However, the bus-ride home and the proposition of another lonely night of reading, cooking and correspondence filled her with dismay. She thought about the Glory Hole and the sheer unimaginable nature of the encounter, its combination of lewd, stark explicitness and dark mystery. As she felt herself becoming aroused again she quickly downed her drink and, in one decisive move, left the pub, marched to the house and pressed the buzzer. The door clicked and, bracing herself, she walked in.

Julia found herself in a smart reception area rather tastefully

decorated with Edwardian fittings, as if designed for an expensive private health consultancy. A woman, whose voice confirmed her as being the same person Julia had spoken to on the telephone, addressed her in tones that were reassuringly efficient. The fee seemed quite steep but Julia paid it mechanically before being led along a corridor to stand outside an oak door, where the woman left her. Catching her breath and drawing on the momentum that had propelled her thus far, Julia entered the room.

At first she felt that the small room was entirely empty as her eyes adjusted to the dim lighting. There were no furnishings although the walls were tastefully painted a deep plum colour. But looking around to the left of her she saw, silhouetted against the far window, an erect penis protruding from what she realised was a partitioned wall. Julia moved closer and observed that the penis emerged from a hole in the half-light, stiff and unmoving like a beautifully carved piece of burnished and polished wood. The rim of the hole in the wall was cushioned with a circle of studded red velvet and the penetration of this thin partitioned wall by the cock, right up to its hilt, seemed absolute and excruciating.

Julia circled the room for some time, eyeing the ceremoniously rigid and immobile cock. Approaching slowly to bend over it, she licked her finger and softly ran it around the curved ridge of the cock's helmet until it jolted – just once – and she jumped back. Hitching up her business-suit skirt Julia kneeled in front of the cock and placed her hands flat against the surrounding wall. Releasing her hair from its ponytail she brushed the cock softly with her soft brown tresses, marvelling as it leaped about in front of her face. Eventually, after much deliberation, she softly kissed the tip of the cock and then with agonising slowness sucked it into her mouth. She felt it sit heavy on her tongue, still pulsing but with less urgency.

Drawing saliva into her mouth, she slowly moved her lips up and down the smooth shaft of the cock, occasionally pressing with her flattened tongue towards the roof of her mouth in order to increase the suction. And then she entirely opened her mouth's cavity to simply run her lips up and down the shaft, up and over the bulbous tip and then

down as far as possible until she could reach no further, where she held. She felt a mounting, wild excitement stirring within her as she sucked and kissed the beautiful taut flesh of the penis protruding from the wall.

Releasing the cock from her mouth, Julia kneeled back and contemplated it again for a full minute or more. It remained constant in the erect position, almost touching the wall with its tip. Julia could feel the juice sliding from her moist cunt and, pulling her skirt higher, found that her knickers were soaked and tangled in the crevice of her sex. Using both hands, she pulled her panties up by their sides and gasped as the elastic caught against her clitoris. Feeling the friction and pressure as the wet cotton pulled tight, Julia's hips began involuntarily thrusting until, crouching low, she splayed her knees until she was almost rubbing the carpet with her cunt. She then leaned forward to extend her tongue to lick the rim of the statuesque cock so that, as her arse lifted, her cunt became exposed and her hot, wet lips swelled out into the room's cool surrounding air.

With one abrupt movement she stood up. Simultaneously she reached to pull down and step out of her panties. Bending forward at the hip, she leaned over towards the wall and took the cock back into her mouth. Julia shifted to stand with her legs apart so that she might use her wetted forefinger to brush at her clitoris. She wanted to fuck but had always been passive within that desire and was now at something of a loss. Finding her resolve and initiative, she hitched her skirt right above her hips and turned around. Bent double and backed on to the wall, she reached behind to take the stiff cock in hand, then eased it slowly inside her as far as it would go.

For a while Julia remained bent over and exulted in feeling the warmth of excitement running through her. At first the cock pulsed against the walls of her cunt but then, of a sudden, it returned to its constant stiffness. And then she stood back up, erect, backed hard up against the wall, her arse sufficiently pert and the cock lengthy enough so that the bell-end and a good half of its shaft remained inside her. The cock protruded from the wall at such a height and her skirt was slit so high at the back that she could pretty much lower it down around her thighs again. They stood there locked together like canines for

seemingly an age until, eventually, the door knocked and Madame's voice announced that today's session was finished.

Removing herself and dressing quickly, Julia hurried from the house. She returned home and spent the most fervid evening of her life drinking G&Ts, reclining on the sofa and wanking herself to a climax, licking her fingers from time to time, pushing her vibrator deep inside her until she was utterly spent.

✳ ✳ ✳

The next day, back at work, Julia applied herself with more diligence than usual to her tasks as if to expel the very taste and feel of the cock – 'her' cock, as she'd started to think of it – from the core of her being. But then, work over, she found herself repeating the ritual of dialling the number, diving in the pub and visiting the house to anonymously suck and fuck again at her beautiful cock.

Thus did life proceed, with Julia's visits becoming more regular and more urgent. In all this time, the cock had remained dutifully, satisfactorily stiff at all times. She could sense its peaks of throbbing excitement but never once had the cock splashed its spunk against or inside her. Julia began slowly to desire this but, try as she might (by sucking or fucking more urgently), the cock would not release its elixir.

By now, Julia was visiting the Glory Hole most days, either at lunchtime or after work. After one particularly exciting, yet entirely static session (backed up against the wall again), Julia resolved that she would have to have the penis come inside her. She decided she would make it throb and squirt inside her even as she stood entirely still.

Her plan was simple: she would strengthen the muscles in her cunt so that she could clutch so hard at the cock as to make it spurt at will. She would feel it throb and leap while ejaculating, and then she would walk from the room with stinking sex juices dripping down her legs and return to work to demurely sign for the innumerable leather-clad couriers' deliveries. With this plan in mind, Julia foreswore visiting the Glory Hole again until she felt confident of realising her resolution.

One day – a Saturday – Julia found herself in a sex shop run 'by and

for women'. Waiting patiently until the shop was empty, she approached the counter assistant, a rather voluptuously intimidating young woman with dyed hair and face jewellery. Blurting, Julia asked whether or not there might be a way to increase her 'physical hold' on a man, in order to cause him to ejaculate. The assistant (sporting a badge saying 'Loretta') made a number of recommendations for vibrators (all of which, apparently, would exercise the most intimate corners of Julia's anatomy), but finally insisted that a pair of small brass balls, about two centimetres in diameter ('Geisha Balls'), would – truly – be the precise instruments to achieve her purpose. Julia purchased the balls and returned home.

That night, after an elaborate meal cooked whilst downing the best part of a very good, expensive Merlot, Julia retired to her room and inserted the two balls – with the aid of a little lubrication – into her vagina. They slid in one above the other, resting at the extremities of her vaginal passage. She lay there immobile for a few minutes, feeling the coldness of the brass before the spasms started to overtake her body and she began to squeeze and clutch internally at the metal balls. Restraining herself with some difficulty, she resolved to lay still and rigid and to let her muscles operate independently. After a good half-hour of clutching and releasing the hard metal balls with the muscles of her soaking-wet cunt, finally she could resist no more and – swivelling wildly around her bed as her fingers rubbed frantically at her clitoris – she released a cry as her entire sex shattered in climax.

Julia continued this 'exercise programme' for nearly a month, rigorously and alone, bringing her own particular talent for self-discipline to bear on the task. After only a short period of time she could feel the muscles in her sex strengthening and toning themselves around the metal balls to the point where she had maximum control of her physical release. Returning to the sex shop, Julia bought a pair of brass balls that were merely half the size of the original ones and began the whole process over again, but with increased accuracy of sensation.

By this time, Julia was barely capable of restraining herself from visiting the Glory Hole again, although she knew that mere repetitions of the original routine would lead to diminishing returns. She wanted

more: specifically, she wanted the cock to come, to throw its spunk deep up inside her. Midway through her exercise programme and late at night, wild with lustful thoughts, she had telephoned the Madame of the Glory Hole and asked whether or not it might simply be a discreet matter of increased payment in order to arrange for the penis to ejaculate from the hole in the wall. As expected, the reply was brusquely, coldly negative.

After all, Julia speculated, throughout all the hours that she worked in her office, the marvellous, silky, stretched-hard cock was busily being sucked and fucked while it miraculously resisted release in order to dutifully maintain its erect condition. Julia set to wondering and fantasising. Was the cock she'd encountered, in point of fact, a different series of appendages? No. Aside from its consistent size and shape, she'd noticed a small freckle right at the tip of that fleshly lip that curled over the grimacing smile of the bell-end, which looked so much like the upper lip of an obscure species of browsing animal: a tapir perhaps? She'd also visited at various times of the day and it would always be that one particular freckle-marked, beautifully attendant cock.

✳ ✳ ✳

The time had come, after a month, for Julia to pay for a visit to the Glory Hole. One particular morning, the anticipation was so unbearable that Julia called to make an appointment that day. The only time available was during her lunch break and she considered waiting another day or two, but felt she really couldn't delay any longer and so booked the appointment.

Julia stood at the oak door to the almost-empty room. Entering, she chose to stand against the wall opposite the erect cock, staring at it. She had negotiated a 'double session' with the Madame – forty minutes – so there was time for rumination. The cock was as fixed as ever, polished and beautiful, with its taut smooth skin tightly sheathed over its engorged muscle. Julia had removed her panties at work before the lunch break. She had gasped her way through telephone calls and several banal tasks, including the visit of a helmeted courier who had loitered a while for her signature – it had taken all her strength not to grasp him by the buttocks and unzip his leather pants to yank out his

cock and suck it into her mouth.

But now was her time. She would spend it with consideration. She wouldn't use her mouth and she wouldn't simply back on to the cock-statue. Instead, having removed her skirt, she stood over the Glory Hole and pushed the side of her face up against the wall. Lifting her left leg she reached down with her hand to grasp the cock and swiftly pushed it deep inside her. Spread-eagled in an X-shape, pushed up hard against the wall with the cock sucked deep inside her cunt, she stood there, quite still.

Julia's vagina muscles, her newly strong and toned sex, performed one long, tightening suction on the rigid penis and held it there at her inmost depth whilst five or more minutes passed. And then, moving in isolation from the rest of her sweating, tumultuous body, Julia's sex muscles began to ripple and then to clutch and squeeze as tightly at her beloved cock as she could make them. She could feel the cock leap and throb inside her.

Julia became aware – alarmingly and for the first time – that a real person, some man struggling with his commotion, was behind the partitioned wall. Spread up against the wall, Julia discovered that if she increased the rapidity with which she flexed her tough, ultra-fit cunt muscles around the cock, then a low groaning sound would emerge from the other side. She would grip hard and the cock-man would groan; squeeze/groan, over and again. Splayed up to the wall and working her beautiful new cunt muscles as hard as possible, Julia estimated that only a few minutes of paid time were left.

Pausing, her cunt cradled the lovely cock inside her in a relaxed way, for fully one minute. And then, without moving another muscle in her entire body, she flexed her cunt as quickly and hard as possible, enclosing the cock as tightly as if she had grasped it with all the strength in her fist, until, quite soon, she felt it shudder with a different sort of spasm. Beside herself with lustful desperation she began to move her hips, frantically pushing and rubbing her mons against the wall. She did this with increasing force and speed, until at the blinding moment of climax she felt her cunt rush and shudder along the length of the cock when it too suddenly erupted in a wild spasm and she felt herself split

open, seemingly to the waist, as the first spurt of lava-hot spunk shot into her. Upon that instance she jumped back away from the wall and, quickly landing on her knees, she captured the jets of spunk into her mouth, swilling it around her palate before drinking it.

As she did so, her sex involuntarily retracted and sucked in on itself, shivering uncontrollably deep inside and then bursting a shower of sweet, hot juice down her thighs to soak her ankles just before Julia collapsed, akimbo, to the floor.

❅ ❅ ❅

Having somehow managed to return to work and sit at her desk all afternoon, Julia was unable to actually do much, endlessly recalling the moment of the Glory Hole's cock spunking inside her cunt and then (thanks to her lithe dexterity) in her mouth. The sexual process was complete, she felt, with both anonymous agencies melded into that one particular satiation. Even as she sat in reverie at her desk she had, nonetheless, decided that she would return to grinding sexual frustration since she knew her satisfaction couldn't eternally be purchased.

After work Julia decided, out of curiosity (and the possibility of achieving some kind of closure), to take a table in the corner pub that afforded a vantage point onto the Glory Hole house. She sat there from 6 p.m. sipping G&Ts and (since she was in fact an unobtrusive yet enticingly sexual woman) vanquishing a series of half-drunk suitors as she became increasingly intoxicated herself. She observed a series of women, and indeed men, entering and leaving the house at intervals.

On the stroke of eleven o'clock – by which time Julia was more than half-cut – the Madame of the Glory Hole emerged, locked up, and walked off down the street in the opposite direction. Soon after, a short and nondescript man in an overcoat with his hat pulled down approached the house and looked about him furtively before using a key to let himself in. Julia had been about to leave the pub but now, puzzled, decided to wait and see if the man re-emerged, which he did after only a minute or two. Julia watched as he inserted a bunch of keys through the letterbox as he left, before registering in alarm that he was

heading towards the packed pub, where the only available seat was opposite her.

As the man entered the pub, he removed his hat and Julia was startled to realise that she knew him as a fellow office worker who had left the firm a few months back under the cloud of some rumours of embezzlement. The man, 'James' if she recalled rightly, likewise recognised her and, after buying his drink, came over and politely requested to take the seat opposite her. Julia noted from where she was seated that this man was exactly the right height – slightly on the short side – to be the man behind the Glory Hole. He was friendly and struck up easy conversation, but seemed distracted, even dazed. The conversation turned to the firm and the manner of his leaving, and he unabashedly confessed that he'd been lucky not to have been prosecuted.

'It's not like I needed the money so much as I was bored and wanted a thrill.' This was said in such a deadpan and rueful way that Julia felt prompted to take all her courage in hand and to enquire as to his current occupation?

'Oh, I'm in the corporate-entertainment business these days,' he said and again cast a distracted rueful smile to himself in such a self-intimately ironic manner that Julia knew for certain, instantly, that he was indeed her cock-man.

'Or I *was*. The thing is,' he continued, 'I've made another mistake in this job. Not embezzlement but, er . . . its opposite.' Such a gnomic statement seemed to invite further enquiry, but when she asked what he meant by that James just shrugged and said he'd been too generously entertaining with one customer, so that this very afternoon he'd been 'indisposed' and unable to 'perform' properly, and so had now lost his job. In fact, having been sacked on the spot, he had just now been back to his workplace while it was closed to collect a few belongings and to drop off the keys.

Julia could barely believe that she was sitting opposite the man she had been fucking and sucking for months now. She reflected, with some astonishment, that whilst she found James pleasant enough, she had never really noticed him when they had been colleagues and even

now, as she talked with him, she found something flat and dead about him that she could never find attractive. Just as she felt that the conversation might enter a revelatory stage, fuelled by her inebriation, the man glanced at his watch, suddenly stood up and exclaimed that he would have to go – after all, he'd be looking for new work tomorrow.

Preparing to leave and putting his coat on, James stood beside her as Julia sat at the table. She turned her head almost involuntarily to stare at his crotch little more than a foot away. Pretending to awkwardly reach below the table for her bag, the movement brought her head very close to his trouser-fly, from where she inhaled. There could be no doubting that the man's groin was heavily perfumed with the strong putrid whiff, the acrid, truffle-like stench of mixed sex fluids, of spunk and cunt-juice combined. Turning her head away she leaned forward and sniffed down at her own sex, still naked beneath her skirt, and noted for certain with a degree of intense satisfaction that the powerful aroma emanating from her was an exact match with that coming from James.

✳ ✳ ✳

Not long after this, Julia met someone and fell in love. However, she still hankered for the Glory Hole: above all, for its thrilling anonymity. One day she fitted floor-length curtains in the bedroom of her flat. When her lover came round that evening she led him wordlessly to stand behind the curtain. Gesticulating, she pointed him to a slit in the curtain, at his crotch height, and then she left the room. When she re-entered some minutes later, her pulse raced as she viewed the sight of a beautiful, rigid and shiny-smooth cock emerging from the slit in the curtain.